New York Times and *USA TODAY* Bestselling Author

MAISEY YATES

Rancher's Forgotten Rival
&
Claim Me, Cowboy

HARLEQUIN
DESIRE

HARLEQUIN®
DESIRE™

Recycling programs for this product may not exist in your area.

ISBN-13: 978-1-335-47374-5

Rancher's Forgotten Rival & Claim Me, Cowboy

Copyright © 2022 by Harlequin Books S.A.

Rancher's Forgotten Rival
Copyright © 2022 by Maisey Yates

Claim Me, Cowboy
Copyright © 2018 by Maisey Yates

This edition published by arrangement with Harlequin Books S.A.

For questions and comments about the quality of this book, please contact us at CustomerService@Harlequin.com.

Harlequin Enterprises ULC
22 Adelaide St. West, 41st Floor
Toronto, Ontario M5H 4E3, Canada
www.Harlequin.com

Printed and bound in Barcelona, Spain by CPI Black Print

CONTENTS

RANCHER'S
FORGOTTEN RIVAL

Legends of Lone Rock

The Sohappy family has its roots in Lone Rock. So deep that they precede the first European settler to come to North America. The ranch is part of their family heritage, passed on from generation to generation, from father to son.

The ranch has survived flood, famine and the perils of modern life.

In 1955, having no sons to pass the land to, Casper Sohappy passed the land on to his son-in-law. As family legend goes, the son-in-law did have roots, true and deep as the rest of the family. One night, he went out drinking at the local bar. The exact details of that night remain a mystery. But he woke up with a hangover, and a piece of paper indicating he'd lost the stretch of land between Sohappy Ranch and Evergreen Ranch, granting essential water rights to the Carson family.

Since then the Sohappy families and Carson families have feuded.

And when the son-in-law passed on, his son vowed the land would never pass into the hands of someone who didn't carry their family's blood again.

He also vowed to see the Carsons pay for what they'd done.

And the hatred between the families began to go deeper than roots ever could.

Chapter 1

Chance Carson couldn't complain about his life.

Well, he could. A man could always find a thing to complain about if he was of a mind. But Chance wasn't of that mind. Every day was a gift, in his opinion. The sun rose, the sun set, and he went to bed and woke up and did it all over again, and that was success no matter how it was measured.

Add in the fact that he got to work with his brothers, or take off and compete in the rodeo circuit as he saw fit, and he really did feel like he was living the dream.

And hell, he had to, right?

No one was guaranteed life.

Much less a dream. He knew well the tragedy of a life cut short. It was a different grief to the death of an older person. It changed you. That unfairness.

He'd tried to at least take some good from those changes.

"You look smug," his brother Boone said from his position on his horse.

Five of the brothers were out, riding the range and looking for stragglers.

They had the biggest spread in Lone Rock, Oregon. Evergreen Ranch.

It had been in the family for generations, but had essentially been bare dirt until their dad had made his fortune in the rodeo, and further still as the commissioner of the Pro Rodeo Association. Now it was a thriving cattle ranch with luxury homes adding a touch of civility to the wildness of the surroundings. Courtesy of his family's status and success as rodeo royalty. They competed together, and they worked together. They practically lived together, given that most of them had housing on the ranch.

Though the rodeo hadn't always been a source of family togetherness.

Their sister, Callie, had nearly broken with the family over some of it, making inroads for women who wanted to ride saddle bronc, and now there was a blooming movement happening within the Association.

Chance was all for it.

Well, not as much when it concerned his little sister.

But in general.

He liked a little feminism. Who didn't?

Right now, they were off for the season, and hanging around the ranch, which was a bit more togetherness than they often got.

Flint, Jace, Kit, Boone and himself, all together like when they were kids.

Almost.

Sophie was gone, and there was no getting her back, a pain that he'd had to figure out how to live with. Grief was funny that way. People talked about "getting over it" and he didn't see it that way. It was just learning to live with it, learning where to carry the pain so you could still walk around breathing through it.

Then there was Buck. But his absence was his choice.

Being a prodigal in the Carson family—which was full to the brim with disreputable riffraff—was really something. But Buck had managed it.

But he was focusing on what he had, not what he didn't.

Which was good, since tomorrow he had to head out for a few days, just to see to a meeting with a man about buying another head of cattle.

"I *am* smug. It's another beautiful day in the neighborhood."

"If Mister Rogers were a cowboy…he wouldn't be you," Flint said. "You're an asshole."

"I'm not," Chance said. "I am the cheerfulest motherfucker out there."

"That's not a word."

"Your mom's not a word," Chance said.

"Your mom is *our* mom," Flint pointed out.

"Oh well. It stands. Anyway, I'm just enjoying the day. I'm heading out tomorrow, so I won't be around."

"Right. More cows," Jace said, and if he was trying to look excited about it, he was failing.

"It is what we do," he said.

"Sure," he said.

"You going to have time to come over to the bar tonight?" Jace asked. "Cara has some new beer she's trying out. She was wondering if we could all come taste it."

"I wouldn't mind having a taste of Cara's beer," Kit said.

And that earned him a steely glare from Jace. Cara was Jace's best friend, and it was not *like that*. And hell and damn to any man who wanted to be like that with her.

Especially if he was one of Jace's brothers. Not, Chance imagined, because Jace was jealous, just because he knew how they all were. And that was shameless and not looking for a commitment.

"And where exactly are we putting the cattle?"

"You know where," Chance said.

"So, I was just wondering, because I was trying to figure out how long it would be before one of the Sohappy sisters was up in my face."

"Well, Boone," Chance said. "I think you know that Juniper and Shelby will be right at us like clockwork."

"It's like four feet of fence," Boone said.

"Doesn't matter. She thinks our great-great-granddad tricked hers into betting that land in a poker game while he was drunk and she lays into me about it every time we're near each other. And now it's been a fight for…oh, three generations, and our grandfather literally died mad about it." Not that their grandfather had been the most sterling guy, but it was the principle. "And I'm not moving the damn fence. And I'm not letting her badger me into signing something over to her just because of some tall tale that's been passed around the families."

"Well, yeah, because it's like four feet one way and like a mile the other," Kit pointed out. "Plus accusations of sabotage, cattle rustling and all manner of other bullshit."

"And I don't care if she has her panties in a twist about it, it's not my problem. If she wants to try and retroactively prove that her great-great-grandfather wasn't fit to sign over the land, that's on her, she's welcome to do it."

"She?" Boone asked. "I thought we were talking about both Sohappy sisters. Weird how it ended up being about the one."

And Chance wasn't at home to any of that. His brother

liked to tease him that there was more than just rage between himself and Juniper. But no. Sure, she was beautiful. Both of the Sohappy sisters were beautiful. But ironically named, as far as he was concerned, because he had never seen them do much of anything other than scowl. At least, his direction.

Women loved Chance. He was a charmer. He loved women, so long as it stayed casual, and physical only.

But Shelby and Juniper Sohappy did not love him. And Juniper in particular.

Hell, yeah, Juniper was beautiful.

Long black hair, eyes the color of bitter chocolate, golden-brown skin, high cheekbones...

Shame about her personality.

She'd been a spiteful little scorpion since they were in school. And he didn't call her that to be hollowly mean; she'd once put a scorpion in his backpack when she was ten and he was twelve.

She'd hated him from the time his family had moved to the ranch when he was ten, taking over for his grandfather after his passing.

She'd hated him just because he was a Carson.

And hell, if he'd sometimes responded in kind to her provocations, who could blame him? And if he'd once bid on her at a charity auction and used her to do menial ranch tasks and carry his books at school—which she'd walked out on in the middle of, thanks—again, who could blame him?

Well, she could. And did. But that was beside the point.

And the fact that he'd do it again, even with all the sparks and spite it earned him, well, that was a whole other issue.

He liked sparring with her as much as he wanted to tell her to leave him the hell alone and never come back.

It was like a disease.

Like wanting to pull a girl's pigtails in second grade.

Except his other feelings about her were not remotely childish. Not at all.

"It's pretty bitter," Boone said. "Don't you think we should just get some surveillance done and see if that solves the issue?"

"Our grandfathers didn't. Our fathers didn't."

"Yeah," Boone said. "Grandpa also took cold showers because he thought that instant hot water bullshit made a man soft. I'm not sure 'because it's always been this way' is a good reason to do anything."

"You know," Chance said, "I would like at least one of them to ask nicely."

"And I would love to be standing there when you told her that," Flint said.

"Whatever. Juniper Sohappy and her bad attitude isn't my problem. She knows exactly what she can do if she wants to escalate it. But she isn't interested in that. She's just interested in being in a family feud that seems to always center squarely on me."

Because she could yell at any of his brothers. And never seemed to.

Almost as if she liked yelling at him.

Maybe *yelling* was an overstatement. When they'd run into each other at the market, in the cold beer fridge, each of them picking up some brews, she'd hissed. Like a feral weasel.

Gotta burr in your britches, Juniper?

Just a burr under my saddle. For life. That's you, Carson.

Yeah, I got that.

Flint shrugged. "All right, you may not want Juniper

to be your problem, but I have a feeling she'll make it her goal to be."

Chance chuckled. "I'd like to see her try."

"Sure you would."

"You drinking later?" Boone asked.

"Nah. Gonna get an early night in so I can get on the road first thing."

They finished up their work, and his brothers trickled back home. And for some reason, Chance found himself riding toward the fence line, to the part of the property that bordered the Sohappy family's ranch.

It was just a shame, really.

A shame that he didn't see the rattlesnake. A shame that his horse chose to freak the hell out. A shame that his horse was a dirty deserter and ran off somewhere.

And it was a shame that when he fell, he hit his head directly on a rock.

It was raining. Of course it was raining.

Visibility was shit. Juniper had a feeling that she might end up taking calls tonight, whether she was supposed to or not. When the weather got like this, accidents happened. On these windy rural roads it was unavoidable. She wasn't supposed to be on shift tonight. She was supposed to be getting a good night's sleep. She'd gone for twelve hours in a row already.

Then there wasn't enough energy drinks in the world to keep her going at this point.

Maybe she was just being grim.

But it was that damn Chance Carson. The Carsons in general were a pain in the butt, but Chance specifically had gotten under her skin for years. She was two years behind him in school, but it had been enough for them to be in each other's paths quite a bit, and every time they'd ever crossed…

It had been bad.

Then there was the general Carson-ness of it all.

Her parents told her that she was overreacting to the whole border situation, but it mattered to *her*.

It mattered to her grandpa, who had hated the Carsons for as long as she'd been alive, and had told her stories of how they'd set out to undermine the Sohappy family from the beginning. And most of all how Chance's great-great-grandfather had gotten her great-great-grandfather drunk, and conned him into betting a portion of the ranch in a card game.

The legend went that he'd cheated. And he'd taken a valuable piece of the Sohappy ranch away, for nothing.

Your father doesn't love the land, not like you do. And I have no grandson. You're the firstborn of this generation. The ranch is going to go to you.

But Shelby is getting married. Shouldn't Chuck…

You know what happened. When a man was prized over blood. When the ranch passed from our direct line. It has to be you. You must care for it. Nurture it like it was your child.

So she'd taken it on. Rearranged her ambitions. It had been easy, actually. To put off pie-in-the-sky dreams like medical school and pretend they'd never really mattered.

The truth was, it had never been a particularly attainable dream.

So she'd thrown herself into Lone Rock. Into the ranch. Into life here. When she'd decided, at seventeen, that she'd stay, she'd rearranged every thought she'd had about the future.

She'd let her roots go deep.

She was one of the ranchers down at the Thirsty Mule, hanging with the guys and telling tall tales. She'd earned that place. She could castrate calves and move a herd with the best of them. And could drink most of their sorry asses under the table.

She worked hard, she played hard and she didn't accept double-standard bullshit.

What was good for the goose and all that.

She'd made a life she was proud of, and she'd taken on the EMT job to pay the bills and satisfy the medical itch she'd had when she was younger.

Now she'd educated herself on ways to expand the ranch into something more lucrative.

A horse breeding and boarding facility. And while she liked ranch work in general, horses were her passion.

And if she got the facility going and got people to pay for boarding, then she wouldn't have to work two jobs.

She was having to pay for ranching like it was her hobby, and the only thing that her family just had was this land.

Everything else was an expense. Everything else came out of all the hard work that she put in.

Her dad's soul just wasn't in the land the way it was hers. He cared, but he was devoted to his business, his career.

It was why Juniper had decided against pursuing medical school. Against leaving. Being a doctor was a calling, a vocation, and…

She wouldn't have been able to do both.

So she'd knuckled down and focused on what she could do. And now she was grateful she had. She'd figured out what to do with the ranch that excited her, made her happy.

And she was just fine. Just fine. And she didn't even want things to go differently.

Maybe don't think about that when you're angry and gritty and half-asleep.

Maybe. Yeah, maybe that was a good idea.

The dirt road that led up to her cabin was mud now, and she was feeling pretty annoyed. And when her headlights swept the area as she rounded the corner, she might have thought that her irritation and exhaustion played a role in what she saw.

It looked like a body. A body out there in the field.

Sprawled out flat. But it *couldn't* be. She slammed the brakes on in her truck and stared.

Yes. The rain was pouring down on what was very definitely a male form sprawled out there on the ground.

But why?

How?

She looked around for a second, evaluating the risk level of the situation, because if something had wounded or killed this man, she didn't want to be next.

She wasn't about to be the first fifteen minutes of a crime scene investigation show.

But she didn't see anything, and there were no points for sitting there wondering about it. Juniper got out of the truck and ran out to that spot in the field. And her heart hit her breastbone.

It was Chance.

Chance Carson.

She knelt down and felt for a pulse. She found one. Thank God. He drove her nuts, but she did not want him to die. At least, not on the border between Carson and Sohappy land. That would be unforgivably inconvenient.

She could call someone, but not here. There was no cell service right out in this spot in the ranch.

But she had her truck.

She rolled him onto his back and did a quick assessment for spinal injuries. None of that. But he was out cold. And what the hell was he doing out here anyway?

She couldn't tell what the hell had happened. But she had some medical equipment in her truck.

She ran back to the road, then pulled her truck out to the field, getting it as close as possible to him. He didn't rouse.

Shit.

She had a board in the back of her truck, and with great effort, she rolled him onto it, strapped him to it and used it to drag him over to the bed of the truck. He was strapped securely in like a mummy in a sarcophagus, so she propped the top up against the tailgate, then lifted up the end by his feet, and pushed him back into the bed of the truck.

"Sorry," she said, slamming the tailgate shut. Was she, though? She wasn't sure.

Well, she was sorry that he was hurt.

Her cabin was the closest place that she could get him dry, warm and examined. She was a medical professional, after all, and he certainly wasn't the first person with a head injury she'd ever dealt with.

The road to the cabin was bumpy, and she winced every time she hit a big pothole. She really didn't want to *kill* Chance Carson. He might think so, but not even she was that petty. At the end of the day, land was land, and it wasn't a human life.

It might feel like it was sometimes. It might feel like looking at this place was the same as opening a vein and letting all her hopes and dreams run red and free.

But it was land.

He was a human being.

Even if he was the human being who left her angrier, hotter, more stirred up and just plain trembly.

She hadn't realized quite how tense she was until her little cabin came into view, and then her shoulders relaxed immeasurably.

She just didn't like driving with him in the bed of the truck like that. It was unnerving.

She got as close to the front door as she could, and felt a little bit exhausted and sweaty staring at his inert form in the back of the truck, still on the board.

She could get him down there, to the front door, but it was just going to be a little bit of a trick. She eased her shoulders upward and rolled them, then grabbed the end of the board, doing her best to lower it gently down to the ground, getting him out much the same way as she had gotten him in. And then she… Well, she dragged him. Up the front steps, slowly, methodically, careful not to jostle him.

She got him into the front room of the house and looked around. Then she took all the cushions off the couch and laid them down on the floor. She unstrapped him from the gurney and rolled him onto the cushions.

He groaned.

Well, at least there was a sign of life.

His clothes were soaking wet, but she was not stripping him naked. No. She had lines, and they were definitely around stripping Chance Carson naked.

Her heart bumped up into her throat.

Well. Dreams weren't anything to get too worked up about. Granted, her grandmother would disagree.

But that didn't matter. Juniper didn't put any stock

in them. And the fact that she had dreamed a time or two about what it might be like to rip Chance Carson's clothes from his body at the end of an invigorating argument was… It was immaterial. She didn't think about it consciously. She didn't marinate on it or anything. It was her subconscious mixing up its passions. That was all.

She opened one of his eyes and shined a flashlight in it, then the other. "You are concussed," she said. "Sorry, my friend." She was going to have to observe him. Well, *someone* would.

She could take him down to the hospital…

Suddenly, a hard, masculine hand shot up and grabbed her around the wrist. "What's going on?"

His voice was rusty and hard. And she was…

On fire.

Her heart was racing, her skin suffused with heat. He had never…touched her before. In a panic, she pulled away and he released his hold, but the impression of his hand on her skin still remained.

"I…"

"Where am I?"

"You're at my house. I found you in a field. Can you tell me what happened?"

"I don't know what happened," he said.

"You don't know what happened?"

"That's what I said."

"Right. Okay. You don't know what happened."

"Yes," he said.

"That doesn't matter. It doesn't matter what happened. Can you see all right?" She put her finger off to his left, then his right, and watched as he tracked the movement. "That seems to be fine."

"Yeah," he agreed.

"No double vision?"

"No," he said.

"You definitely hit your head," she said.

"Right," he said.

"I'm just trying to figure out how serious it is."

"You a doctor?"

"No. I'm an EMT..." He knew that. Chance Carson knew that she was an EMT. Everybody did. "Do you know who I am?"

"No. Should I?"

Oh. Well. Holy crap. Chance Carson didn't know who she was.

"Juniper," she said slowly. "Juniper Sohappy."

"Name doesn't mean anything to me. Sorry."

"What's your name?"

His brow creased. "You know... I don't know."

He didn't know his name? Juniper couldn't wrap her head around that. He could be lying, of course. Though, to what end she didn't know, but how could you ever know with a Carson?

Wasn't her whole family history a testament to that?

If he was lying, she wasn't going to give him the satisfaction of tricking her. She...

She stopped herself just as she was about to open her mouth.

If he was lying, it might be funny to go along with it, see how long it took him to reveal himself.

And if he wasn't?

She thought back to the humiliation of when he'd had her working his land. Of every insult over the years, of everything.

She was going to keep an eye on him tonight, make sure he didn't lapse off and die of his head injury. And she was more than qualified to do it. She also knew if he really was suffering from some temporary memory loss from the fall he'd taken, it would resolve quickly enough and you weren't supposed to go heaping facts on people while their mind sorted things out.

What would it hurt if she taught him a little something in the meantime?

"You don't remember your name?" she pressed.

"No," he said, his eyes blank, and she looked hard to see if he was being genuine. "I don't remember anything."

Chapter 2

It was the damnedest thing, and he hadn't realized it until his pretty little rescuer had asked the question.

What's your name?

He didn't have a clue. Reflexively, he reached toward his back pocket, and felt that there was no wallet there. Which meant no ID.

Somehow he knew *that*.

"You can't remember," she pressed.

Her dark eyes were intense, and he couldn't quite get the read on them.

"No," he said.

But his head hurt like a son of a bitch. And apparently he knew enough to know that. But this wasn't normal, that he didn't like it.

"Chance," she said. "You don't know?"

"Chance," he said. "That's not a name."

"It is," she said. "Your name."

"Oh." He tried to see if it rang any bells, but it didn't. It didn't ring any at all.

Didn't bring to mind anything. There was just a big expanse of blankness.

"Well, you clearly know me. Who am I?"

"You… You work for me. You work here," she said.

He let that settle over him. "Okay."

"That doesn't ring any bells?"

"No," he said.

"You're… You're a cowboy," she said.

That felt right. It didn't ring bells, but it felt right.

And apparently he worked on her ranch.

And he didn't know who this woman was, but she was the most beautiful thing he'd ever seen. Well, he didn't know all the things he'd seen. But he knew that. Somehow. Instantly. Electrically.

But it was more than beauty. It was deep.

He could swear he did know her, and that she mattered. That she was singular, significant. That she was the woman who occupied his thoughts, his fantasies.

"A ranch hand," he said.

"Well. Yes. But you know, you had such a hard time lately and… Anyway."

"A hard time?"

"I'd rather not tax you, Chance."

"You'd rather not…"

"You had a head injury," she said slowly.

"Yeah," he said. He rubbed the back of his head and felt dried blood.

"I don't think you need stitches," she said. "But it's pretty bad."

"Well. I don't have any context for that. Or if I've ever been… Hurt very bad before? How does this stuff work?

Why can I remember… How to talk? But I can't remember who I am."

"Head injuries are complicated," she said. "That much I know. I can't say as I've ever run into anyone with amnesia…"

"It's not amnesia."

"I think it is."

And one thing he knew for certain right then and there was that he was not the kind of man who was used to being without his faculties. He wasn't the kind of man who wasn't used to being in control.

This was something he hadn't experienced before. And he didn't like it. Not in the least.

"I could drive you down to the hospital…"

"No," he said.

"No?"

"No. I don't want to move. I'm not… I'm not gonna die."

"No," she said. "And I have… Look, you definitely need someone to stay with you. You can't go back and sleep on your own."

Something fired in his blood, and he wondered then if… If there was something between him and Juniper.

Because it seemed fair to think there might be, considering the way she got a response out of him even when he was in this poor of shape.

"I'll sit up with you," she said.

"Would I be alone otherwise?"

"Look, what you get up to with people is none of my business, but you don't live with anyone."

"Okay," he said.

So they weren't together. Had they been? Had he touched her? Kissed her? Held her naked in his arms?

The thought sent a surge of heat through him.

But he supposed it was just that she was his… His boss. That was strange, he didn't feel like he was the sort of man who had a boss. But he wondered if maybe he just wasn't the best judge of that sort of thing.

Maybe no man felt like he should have a boss deep down, but most people did. Because they had to.

"You should probably try to stay awake," she said.

"I'm so tired," he said. And that immediately felt… It was a strange thing, that admission. It was honest, but there was something about the admission of what was akin to vulnerability that didn't sit right with him. So whatever kind of man he was, he didn't truck with that sort of thing.

"I'll fix you some food," she said.

"Well, I don't want you to do that," he said.

"I need you to work it so that you are in a sitting position as soon as possible," she said. "You've got a concussion, and I don't want you dying on me."

"Can I help with anything?"

"No. I'm going to make you fry bread, and you need to stay away."

"If I've had it before, I can't remember."

"You probably have," she said. "But likely my mother's. Which is better than mine."

"I bet not." He didn't know why he said that. He just bet that he would rather have something made by Juniper than by… Maybe anybody else.

"I have dough ready to go." She took a bowl from the fridge and uncovered it, then took a large jug of oil from a cabinet beneath her stove, got a large pan and put a generous measure of the oil in it.

She waited, bustling around the room doing what appeared to be busywork to keep from having to look at him. He didn't know why he knew that, only that he did.

Then she took a small wooden cylinder from a container on the counter and retrieved dough balls from the bowl, rolling each of them out quickly, before dropping them into the hot oil.

Her movements were practiced and eased, whatever she said about her mother doing a better job. And as the smell filled the room, his stomach started to growl.

She put a wooden spoon into the pan and did something he couldn't see, then a couple of minutes later removed the dough, which was now golden and glistening.

She placed the bread in a stack on a plate and put what looked like a heap of powdered sugar over the top.

"I'm not giving you alcohol," she said. "Not with a head injury."

"Well, I don't even know if I want alcohol." Except he found that he did. But he wondered if that was a good thing or not. Maybe he was one of those people who didn't drink in moderation. Maybe he had a problem. Maybe that was part of the troubles that she'd been talking about him having.

He didn't know, and he hadn't known for all of twenty minutes and it was starting to frustrate the hell out of him already.

There were too many unanswered questions in a moment. He had no idea what he was going to do if he eventually walked out of Juniper's cabin and found that he still didn't have any answers.

"Here," she said. "I'll give you a pop."

"A pop?"

She grinned. "A soda. My grandpa always called it that. So I do too. I don't actually know why. I think his wife was from the Midwest."

"You don't know for sure?"

"No, not about the crap on my dad's side. Because he had a few wives. On my mom's side, yes. My grandparents that are still here on the ranch have been together for sixty-five years."

"Hell," he said. "That's a long time."

"Yeah. I guess so. My mom's family has had this land for generations."

"Family ranch?"

"Yes. And it's very important to us." The sentence was heavy, and he couldn't quite say why.

"Do you work on the ranch, or just as an EMT?"

She laughed. "Just an EMT? I'll give you a pass because you just hit your head."

"That isn't what I meant. I meant... How do you find the time?"

"You make time to do what you need to. To do what you love. That's how it works. You do what needs to be done. At least, if you're worth anything."

"And you do what needs doing," he said. He had no trouble imagining it.

She brought a Coke and a plate of fry bread to where he was on the floor. "But you have to sit up," she said.

She reached out, and grabbed his hand, and helped him.

And maybe he should be embarrassed about that. But the only real thought he had was just how surprisingly soft her hands were, given that she was a woman who clearly worked hard. He had expected something different.

Surprising softness.

That was what he would remember.

Would he remember? Would he forget all this when everything else came back to him? He didn't know, and there was no way to know, so he just needed to quit thinking about it.

"How long have I worked here?"

Because what the hell else was there to do but ask questions about himself?

"A while," she said. "Eight months."

"Right. Where do I come from?"

She looked to the side. "Honestly, I don't really know. Sorry. You haven't shared a whole lot. I just know that you were going through a bit of a rough time. And we… Well, we've given you a lot to do, and focus on. Kind of a new start."

"That's nice of you."

"Yeah."

He didn't know why he needed a new start. And that was disconcerting as hell. Because that could mean a whole lot of things. He didn't know what kind of person he was. If he was a good one. If he was genuine in his appreciation for what this family had done for him, or if he was a con man. It was near impossible to know. And he didn't like that. Here she was, making him food—damned delicious food—and offering him beverages and to sit up with him all night, and he didn't even know what his intent was toward her. Or if he had any way of ever knowing.

"What about you?"

He wanted to know something. And if he couldn't know something concrete about himself, maybe he could learn something about the woman sitting across from him.

She looked confused, surprised. He wondered now if they'd ever talked before. If he'd ever asked her about herself. "Like I said, I'm an EMT."

"How did you get into that?"

A funny little smile crossed her face, the dimple to one side of her lip creasing her cheek. "My sister got hurt. When we were kids. We were playing out in the woods and she fell and she broke her leg. I wanted to be able to help her. I didn't know how, though. I didn't know how to help her, and that ate at me. I didn't know what to do to fix her. I asked my grandmother to teach me some things. Basic survival skills. She did, and I just got really into it. I thought maybe I'd…you know, go into medicine, be a doctor. But there's a need out here. I'm actually based out of the fire department. The rural fire department handles a lot of the medical emergencies. We're the first responders, until somebody can get here from the hospital. There isn't a hospital for forty miles."

"Wow," he said.

"Yeah. I don't know. I just like knowing how to fix things, more than I really wanted to help people, I guess." She laughed. "I mean, I like helping people, don't get me wrong. But my original motivation was… I wanted to be able to fix myself. Because, isolated like we are, we can't count on anyone else. It's like you and me right here. I can't call from my cabin. I don't have cell service. We would have to go down to the main house, and it's quite a drive. So… It just makes more sense for me to treat you here. And I know how."

"It's not serious?"

She laughed. "Well, I didn't think so until you didn't remember anything. I'm a little more concerned now. But as far as what I can tell? You're okay."

"What about the ranch?"

"It's been in my family for generations. It's… It's important to me. It isn't important to my dad, and it's the most important thing to my grandpa, and someone has to…carry the torch, I guess. That's me. My dad's a contractor. And the house that he's made for us there is amazing. And he makes enough money from it to support us.

But he isn't interested in growing the actual ranch. He has his passion. And... The ranch is what my grandfather loves. He had horses. But that's all gone away now because he can't take care of things the way that he used to."

Conviction and passion rang in her voice, something that spoke to even deeper truths than she was admitting. It made him want to dig deep.

And he had no reason to question himself. Because he knew nothing. Why shouldn't he know everything about her?

"Does your grandfather still live on the ranch?"

"Yes. He and my grandmother still live in the original house. Not the grandfather that's had a lot of wives."

"I understand that."

"But... You know, there's this big family feud," she said.

"Family feud."

"Yeah. With us and... The neighbors. They're... They're dishonest is what they are. Crooks. They've been disputing the border of the land forever. But it's ours. In fact, years ago, all this land was ours. But my great-great-grandfather fell on hard times and he had to sell off a portion of it. And it just hits me wrong the Carsons are trying to take more. More than what we even had to get rid of back all those years ago."

She looked at him expectantly, as if she was very curious what he would say about that.

"Well, sounds like some bullshit to me. Why are they trying to take your land?"

"They're greedy," she said. "They never think they have enough. And it started with the great-great-grandfathers. When...when theirs took mine out drinking and got him to sign over a portion of the land that... It's very important. It sparked a major feud. Anyway. It's just important. And it's frustrating when something that matters so much to you is being badly used by a bunch of idiots who don't even really have ranching in their blood."

"They don't?"

Her lip curled. "They're showmen. Rodeo cowboys. My ancestors didn't believe in owning land. But the rules changed, and now we have to live by those rules. To have more taken from you is…"

"It's unconscionable," he said.

Land mattered. That he knew. That he felt in his blood, in his bones. With certainty. He didn't know why or how he felt it so deeply, only that he did.

It was real. That sense of ownership. It was real and it mattered.

"I've always thought so."

She sat down with him, and took a piece of bread from the platter.

"This is my favorite," she said, taking a bite. "My sister likes it with cinnamon sugar."

"I doubt you can go wrong," he said.

"Not in my opinion," she said. "My grandparents met in Arizona. This is my grandmother's family recipe. She moved out here to be with him when she was only eighteen. And her parents were furious. I can't imagine. She got married at eighteen. It seems almost ridiculous."

"Does it?"

She scrunched her face. "Don't you think?"

"I don't know. I don't know how I feel about marriage," he said.

Right now, he could see the benefit of it. You could hole up in a cozy cabin with a woman, she could cook you food and sit on the floor and talk to you. He didn't know anything except this moment with Juniper, and it felt like something important. It felt like something real. And he could imagine spending every day after this here.

That was probably the amnesia. Maybe. Maybe he was a commitment-minded man.

Maybe he was married. Maybe he had left a wife and children somewhere.

The idea was disconcerting.

"Maybe I should drive you down to the main house…"

"No," he said.

Something about expanding the scope of his reality didn't feel… It didn't feel right just now.

"Why not?"

"Honestly… I don't know. But the thing is, I don't know anything. I don't know anything, and the idea of jumping into… A lot doesn't sit well with me."

"Okay," she said slowly. "Then I'll sit with you."

Chapter 3

Juniper felt like a jerk. Well, it fluctuated. But right now she did. It was why she'd offered to at least take him down to her parents' place. Where they could tell her she was being awful and maybe help take control of this situation.

But he'd said no, and she was happy to back out. She knew why she'd let her own meanness goad her into this.

She'd been thinking about the time he'd bought her services in that high school auction and had made her work on his ranch. Mucking stalls and all things she was accustomed to, but working his land was anathema to her and he knew it.

And now she was sitting here cooking her grandmother's recipes for him, and in general sharing things with him she knew she shouldn't.

But he was still Chance.

And he'd been…well, unapologetically a jerk to her for the past twenty years, so what was so wrong with getting a little back while taking care of him?

Bottom line, she'd saved him.

And she really didn't think it was the right thing to do to explain everything to him. At least, she felt like she knew that from somewhere. She had given him his name, and she had talked about the Carsons, and nothing seemed to jog his memory. That concerned her, but so did the wild look in his eye when she had said that they ought to take him back to the main house. The fact of the matter was, she didn't know what had happened to him. He didn't know what had happened to him.

That thought made a shiver of disquiet race through her. Maybe there was danger out there. It was likely he had fallen off his horse…

But for all she knew, there was something else to it.

Anyway, there was no harm keeping him for the night. Keeping him settled here.

She really didn't think he was in any physical danger from his injury. If she did, she would've run him down to the hospital right away. But it just didn't seem likely. She knew enough about head injuries to evaluate him, and the fact that he was up and talking was a good sign. His speech was clear and coherent, and it wasn't slurred. His eye movement tracked, and they looked clear—no visible bleeds or anything. He seemed completely with it. Except for the whole *not remembering who he was*.

"Thank you," he said, taking another piece of bread.

And her heart did something weird.

Chance Carson had never been nice to her a day in her life. And now he was being… Well, he was being very nice.

And he looked disheveled and handsome, and she did wonder again if she should help him strip out of his wet clothes…

Probably not. Probably that was a really bad idea.

She needed to stop thinking of him out of his clothes.

She looked at him, and her heart did something very strange. And it was the heart reaction that really bothered her. Because a regrettable physical reaction to Chance wasn't completely unheard of. He was a good-looking man, and the fact that she noticed was inevitable to an extent. But she had to remember that he was her enemy. Her enemy. The Carsons were her enemy.

Fortified with that, she took a breath. And then took another piece of bread.

"Did you always know you wanted to stay here?" he asked.

And she wondered why he was asking her so many questions.

Maybe it was because he was trying to orient himself in a certain space and time. She could understand that.

What she really didn't know was why she was answering them.

"I… Yeah, I guess so. I've always been very close to my grandparents. And the land means everything to them. It's really hard to make a good living ranching. Especially if you don't have a lot of capital to invest to begin with. I want to move into hire and horse breeding. That's really where there's a shot of making some money."

"And money is important to you?"

He asked the question earnestly enough, there was nothing behind it. How could there be? He was a man who didn't remember anything. Just a big, beautiful log. He reminded her of Brendan Fraser in *George of the Jungle* right now.

That movie had been responsible for a certain level of awakening in her youth.

But she had never figured she'd meet a man who didn't understand the way the world worked, who was gorgeous and full-grown on top of it.

"It's not money so much as… Succeeding. Making my grandfather proud. I… I sacrificed some of my dreams and learned to make this my dream and I need it to matter." And she didn't know why she told him that. Hell, she could've made everything up, and he never would've known the difference. Even if he remembered everything, he wouldn't know the difference. She had known who Chance Carson was all of her life, but they did not know each other.

Amnesia or not, he wouldn't be able to pick her life story out of a lineup. So why she was telling him now, over her grandmother's recipe, she didn't know.

"Because your dad wasn't able to do it with the ranch?"

"I don't know that he wasn't able to do it. He just didn't care. But it's ours. It's our heritage. It's…"

"And that's important to you," he said.

"Yes," she said. But what lay beneath the surface of that affirmation was the fact that her grandfather was important to her.

The most important person in her life. And she just didn't know if she'd done enough to make him proud. She had done her best. To be the heir. The first girl to inherit the responsibility of working the land, of being the one in charge. She had plans and she wanted him to approve and to be proud and…

He was in his nineties. She didn't have limitless time.

"I just love him," she said.

"Your grandfather?"

She realized that she hadn't given any context for what she had just said, but that he had picked up on it anyway.

"Yes," she said. "My grandfather. I love him more than anything. I love him… He made me who I am. He taught me to ride. He taught me everything there is to know about this place. About what we can grow here. About what we can use that grows naturally. About how free you can feel out in the middle of nowhere with no one around to talk to. How you can just be. Just you. And the ground and the trees and the sky."

"What happened with your sister that made you want to be an EMT?"

She laughed. Entirely unexpected. "Yeah. Thank God for Shelby and her broken leg."

"Why not stay an EMT?"

"I won't have time. And anyway, eventually, the ranch should be self-supporting. It's not like I'm making a ton of money with what I'm doing. It's just enough. Enough to make sure that I'm supported. Enough to make sure I have some to invest in."

"And is this where you live?"

"Yes. All the time. Rent free. Which helps. Everything of mine goes back into the ranch. I have been fixing the same pair of boots for two years so that I don't have to fork out any money that I might need."

"That's commitment."

"Yeah, well. When it's your legacy, you just do."

She hadn't meant to spill all this to him. Honestly, she never would've talked to him under normal circumstances. She never would have spent any sincerity on him whatsoever. She yawned.

And he looked at her with… Concern.

"Are you going to be all right?"

"I'm going to keep you from dying."

"Wow. Nice of you. I don't think I'm going to die, though."

"I don't think you are either. Otherwise I would've forced your ass down to the hospital. I think we've got it under control."

She hoped she did.

"I don't want to go to the hospital," he said.

And it was a strange sort of fear in his eyes that made her want to listen.

She squinted. "Do you remember something about the hospital?"

He frowned. "I don't know. It just feels like a place I don't want to be. I don't know why. But look, I don't remember anything. I don't know if I'm a good man, I don't know if I'm a bad man. I don't know if I'm on the run from the law or from the Mafia. Or from a wife."

"Maybe you aren't on the run," she pointed out.

She'd planned to mess with him tonight, but she wasn't going to hold him here. In the morning, he really did need to go somewhere. But he might just remember. He might.

His expression went opaque. "I just feel like I might be."

She sat with that. Because she knew that Chance wasn't on the run. Not strictly. But it made her wonder. Because he seemed confident in a few things, not many, and she wondered if there was a grain of truth to them or if he was just drinking his bathwater. If amnesiacs didn't actually have any kind of sense of their former life.

"Well," she said. "I can only respect that."

"Thanks. Makes me feel like I might know something."

"Well, good. Unexpected silver linings." She had another piece of bread.

"What if we take turns sleeping?" he asked.

"That seems like a potentially dangerous idea."

"Or we set an alarm. You can check on me and make sure I'm not dead."

"Great."

She was tired, though. She had been exhausted when she pulled in at the end of the shift, and it was gone nearly one in the morning now.

At least her radio hadn't gone off. She didn't think he was severe. And as long as they kept on checking in…

"All right," she said. "Let me get some sleeping bags."

She went down the hall and retrieved two sleeping bags from her closet. She laid them out on the floor. He seemed more mobile now, but she was unbearably conscious of how cold he must be.

"I swear I'm not trying to get you naked," she said, wincing slightly. "But before we settle in, we need to get you out of these clothes."

It was the look on his face that got her. Charming and a little bit wicked all at once. As if he didn't mind one bit if what she was trying to do was get him naked, after all.

"You got a blanket for me?"

"Yes," she said. "Go to the back. To my room. Strip off, and I can get your clothes washed and dried."

"That's awfully nice of you."

"What's the point of saving you from a head injury if you die of hypothermia?"

"Well, that is a good point."

She went to the hall closet and grabbed a Pendleton blanket, big and woolly with bright geometric patterns on it, and flung it in his direction. "You can hunker down in this."

"Sure thing."

He went into her bedroom, and she paced for a moment.

And when he came back out, he was holding the clothes and wrapped in the blanket, a disconcerting measure of masculine shoulder and chest revealed.

"Sorry I don't have any extra men's clothes." She migrated to the washer and dryer that were in the hallway. She chucked his clothes into the washer without examining them too closely. She didn't want to think about handling Chance Carson's underwear. Lord have mercy.

"I'm shocked you don't have an extra pair of men's jeans laying around somewhere."

"I'm not that kind of girl."

"Too proper to take a man home?"

"Too commitment phobic to let him keep a pair of jeans here. Or let him leave them behind. Once his ass is out of my bed, every trace of him better be gone, and if it's not, I'll just throw it in my burn pile."

It was true enough. The thing about taking on the mantle of being the heir to the ranch was that she had decided to go ahead and adopt all the perks that came along with it. She wasn't going to get married or have a family. She didn't care what anybody thought of her. She was going to behave the way the cowboys did. So when she wanted sex, she got it. She didn't do boyfriends. She didn't do relationships. She was a law unto herself, and that was how she liked it. Well, it could be argued that she was also a law unto her grandfather and her obligations to the ranch. And if they chafed a little more now than they had at one time…

The equine facility was the answer. It would give her a chance to show her grandfather that her own unique spin on things was right. It would give her a chance to keep her promise and then some. And it would fulfill her. The thing was, her grandfather had always been supportive of her. He was judgmental about a whole host of other people, so she knew what was involved in disappointing him. And she never wanted to do it. But she had promised him that she could do this. That she could be the thing that his own son hadn't been able to be, and she had liked that. That she had basically moved into being his favorite because she had made this vow.

And then she had discovered how difficult it was going to be to keep. The older she got, the more she questioned whether or not this was all there was to her life on the ranch. So change was the answer. Putting a stamp on it that was uniquely hers was the answer.

But then she got distracted by his shoulders and she forgot why she was thinking about her grandfather at all.

"I respect that," he said.

"You don't remember anything. How would you know not to respect it?"

He laughed. "I guess that's a good point. But I have the feeling that I'm a man who scratches an itch when the need takes him."

They looked at each other, and their eyes caught and held. And it was just a little bit too hot. She looked away, her heart pounding fast.

"Well."

"You got a deck of playing cards?"

"Are you kidding me? I have a tablet and a streaming service, we can just watch a movie."

"No way. You've already gotten the pants off me, we might as well play a rousing round of Go Fish."

"Wow."

She went back to her closet and rummaged until she came up with an unopened pack of playing cards. She tossed them to him, and he undid the cellophane on the outside, then pulled the cards out, shuffling them with ease and skill.

"You know how to shuffle cards," she said.

"Apparently. And I know how to play Go Fish."

"That's weird," she said.

"You're telling me."

He dealt the cards, and she sat across from him. And of course when he held his own cards up the blanket fell, down to his waist, revealing his whole chest.

Good grief.

If she had been told that she would be sitting with a bare-ass-naked Chance Carson in her house someday, she would have told whoever said that that they were crazy, and then gone to her room and cried because it would've made her hotter than she would have ever liked to admit.

That was the problem. Chance had always made her hotter than she wanted to admit.

He soundly destroyed her at the game, which piqued her temper, and she realized she had to keep it in check because he didn't know that they were rivals, not when it came to anything, so being generally persnickety regarding her loss had to have limits on it.

But by the time he beat her in round three, she chucked her cards at him. "I think you're cheating."

"Why would you think that?"

And he looked wicked, his blue eyes twinkling, his smile suggesting that he had never cheated at anything in his life. And he was a man who had the ability to tell himself that, because he had no memories.

No baggage. What a gift that was for a man like him, she bet.

"You're feral," he said.

"I am not."

"A little bit."

"Not."

"Come get your cards now, you gone and thrown a fit."

The cards were sitting in his lap. And he didn't think that she'd get them. Which meant that she absolutely had to.

She licked her lips, then she reached across the space, and somewhere along the way, she forgot exactly what her motivation was. If it was to prove her mettle, or if it was to be seductive.

She wouldn't say that seductive was normally in her wheelhouse. She was a woman who took a straightforward approach to sex. Because it just made sense.

It was easy enough. There was no fuss or muss required. She never felt the need to dress up or try to be anything she wasn't. But she bit her lip, looking up at him. And then slowly swiped a card from his lap. And the fire in his eyes leaped.

And she scrambled. She grabbed the remaining cards and fell back, realizing that she was overplaying her hand, no pun intended.

"Maybe Go Fish should be done now."

"I'm pretty tuckered out," he said.

"Well, let me put your clothes in the dryer."

"I don't mind sleeping nude," he said, shrugging.

Her face went hot—like she was some inexperienced virgin, and she went to transfer his clothes to the dryer, and by the time she got back, he was in the sleeping bag. In her sleeping bag, bare-ass naked. And she thought, just for a moment, about what it would be like to join him.

"We better hit the hay," she said. And she got down into her own sleeping bag. "You sleep first. I'll watch something with headphones. I'll set a timer and wake you up and make sure that you're all right."

"I feel well taken care of," he said, grinning at her.

He was so unbothered by all of it. And it turned out that, with or without memories, that was the thing that bothered her about Chance Carson the most.

He made her extremely bothered. And she wasn't sure that she could ever do the same to him in equal measure. Then she reached out and touched his forehead. "Just checking," she whispered. His jaw went hard, his blue eyes hot. And she could well imagine what was going on down in that sleeping bag. And just like that, she felt much better. Because maybe, just maybe, he was a lot more bothered by her than she thought.

And why exactly did you feel the need to prove that?

Why exactly anything. It didn't matter, though, because in the morning, all would be well. She could send him packing on back to his ranch, and forget that this ever happened. Forget that they had ever sat across from each other playing cards while he was naked. Forget that she had ever given in to the impulse to flirt.

Forget that she had ever let herself fully acknowledge the attraction that she felt to Chance Carson.

Yeah. In the morning, everything would be fine.

Chapter 4

When he woke up the next morning, he opened his eyes and felt a sense of urgency. And it took a full thirty seconds for him to realize he had no idea what the urgency was directed at. Because he didn't know who he was.

Chance.

The name echoed in his mind as he went and got yesterday's clothes out of the dryer and pulled them on.

His name was Chance, but it didn't really tell him anything that that was his name. Except that his parents had some weird tastes in names. He closed his eyes again and tried to picture... Anything. But all he could see was the liquid dark eyes of the woman who had taken care of him last night. The woman who had fed him.

Watched over him.

And when he opened his eyes and looked to his right, there she was. Her dark hair had fallen into her face, and her beautiful features were obscured. But that didn't mean there wasn't plenty to look at. He stood, and he felt dizzy, and his head hurt like a son of a bitch. But he supposed amnesia was never going to be painless.

Not that he ever had occasion to think about it before. He didn't think. He couldn't actually be sure. Since he couldn't be sure about any damn thing.

But he knew this place. He knew this woman. And he held on to that as tightly as possible.

He was a ranch hand. He walked toward the door and opened it, looked out the cabin, stunned by the view directly in front of him. The little cabin seemed to be built into the side of a mountain. Overlooking a vast and beautiful view below. The pine trees grew up tall and proud, and the patchwork of bright and dark green mountains seemed to stretch on endlessly. He could see notes of desert out before them too, flat, rocky outcroppings and deposits of porous-looking lava rock.

And it felt… It felt curiously like home. He had to wonder if he was from here originally, or if it was just that he had gotten accustomed to this place. If this was just the place he had decided to settle. But it felt too deeply ingrained to be anything quite so transient as a recent move.

It felt like something else. Something more. He took a step down the porch, and closer to the edge of the mountain, taking in a deep breath.

There was something about the air in his lungs that felt right. It felt right. In ways that he could never fathom. In ways that he could never explain.

Then he started to look around. For something to do. For anything to do. Maybe if he got back to the task at hand, any task, he would feel more like himself. He didn't know why but he had the sense that he wasn't idle. That he wasn't the kind of man to sit around and let grass grow beneath his feet.

He had a feeling that he had chosen a life of manual labor. That it was something that appealed to him. That it was something that made him feel centered. And since he couldn't really be one with himself at the moment, he would take being one with his surroundings. He would take anything, really.

He saw a stack of wood, all logs, big old rounds, and there was an ax out there.

He could chop wood. For some reason, he had no concerns about whether or not he could chop wood. And before he could put any thought to it, his body went into action. He set one log up longways on top of a larger one, then picked up the ax.

He split it with one fluid motion.

It was easy. The motion fluid, and he was right. There was something about it that made him feel accomplished. That made him feel like he was himself. Even if he couldn't remember anything, even if he didn't know who that was, or practically what it meant, he was himself. He was himself and that mattered.

So he started burning through those logs, as quickly as he could, till his shoulders and chest, the back of his arms, burned like hell.

Until he could hardly breathe, but he was getting a big old pile built up the side of him. And he didn't know why, but he had a feeling that if… If someone could see him, they would be making fun of him. For being extreme. For… For whatever thing it was that was in him that made him like this. Because this was him. He knew that. It was the weirdest thing. Like a word being on the tip of his tongue and him not quite being able to figure out what it was.

"Hey."

He looked up and saw Juniper standing there. She was wearing the same clothes from the night before, her dark hair a wild tangle. She made him ache. Not to know more about his life beyond this place. She made him ache to stay here. "What are you doing?"

"Cutting wood," he said.

"Do you think it's a good idea to be up cutting wood?"

"You're the EMT. I'm sure you can tell me whether or not it's a good idea."

"I don't think so," she said. "Hey…"

"It made me feel better," he said, cutting her off.

"It did?"

"Yes. It made me feel a little bit more like myself, whatever that is. In fact, whatever chores you have."

"Look," she said. "I need to take you somewhere. Your memory still hasn't come back and it made sense for you to be here last night, but going forward…"

"No," he said. "Do you know what anybody does about amnesia?"

She looked down. "As far as I know, they wait for it to resolve."

"Then let's wait for it to resolve. Here. I want to wait for it to resolve here." She looked hesitant. "Look," he said. "I don't know any details about myself. But I just know that I don't want to leave here. I don't know why. But it might be important."

"Chance," she said, her tone firm. "I'm not a doctor. I'm an EMT and you…"

"I don't want to," he said, his tone hard.

He didn't know why he was so certain he needed to be

here. That he needed to be with her. The world was one entire lesson he had to learn, but for some reason, this place—she—felt like the one he had to learn first.

And he might have no real basis for that conviction, but it was strong and clear and real.

"Do you have jobs for me to do? Can I be useful here?"

She hesitated. "Oh. Oh. Well. Yes," she said. "The wood. Thank you. And… Well, I've been working on restoring one of the barns."

"You have been?"

"Yeah," she said.

"Well, let me come help with that."

"Chance…"

"I am a man who knows what he wants," he said. "Even if I'm not a man who knows who he is. And I don't think I take kindly to being told what to do."

She sighed. "No. But right now what you are is a very confident man with no memory."

"I have the feeling that I'm very confident," he said.

And she bit her lip as if she wanted to say something. Yet again, he wondered at the actual details of her relationship to him. He had a response to her that seemed to be bigger than just boss-employee. But then, it could be that he had been attracted to her already, and it was just that it was exacerbated by the fact that now he couldn't remember their roles.

"I have to get ready," she said. "You will probably also need a change of clothes."

"Yeah," he said. "That is true."

He didn't want to leave here, though. Didn't want to go to his home, or lean-to, or whatever it might be. She seemed to realize that.

"Why don't you go in and have a shower?"

"Sure."

"I'll… I'll be back with whatever you need."

Juniper was cursing herself all the way down to Shelby's place. And she knew that she would be cursing herself even more once Shelby heard what she wanted, because she was going to be pissed off at her.

Chance wanted to stay. And it was one thing to haul his dead weight, but quite another to think about forcing his big, muscular frame—*oh dammit, Juniper, can you not objectify the man even in this?*—out her front door if he didn't want to go.

But what if his family worried? Granted, there were lots of Carsons and they seemed to come and go as they pleased, and she had no idea how often they all communicated.

But Chance didn't have a phone or wallet or anything on him.

You could just tell him the truth…

No, she couldn't. It could harm him. Like waking a sleepwalker.

Also, he'd know you were a liar and all the nice things that happened last night would disappear.

That wasn't the problem.

It was the cognitive issues. That was it.

"Hey," she said when she rolled up to the door.

Shelby had chin-length hair, and rounder eyes than Juniper. She also had grooves by her mouth from frowning. She was younger, but life had really worn itself into her face. Juniper doubted it had been avoidable. Shelby had had a rough couple of years. And a better moisturizer would hardly have kept the evidence of her pain away.

"Can I come in?"

"Why?"

Juniper smiled brightly. "Can't I just come visit my sister in the morning?"

"You can," Shelby said, narrowing her eyes. "You *don't*."

"I need to borrow some clothes."

"I am four inches shorter than you, Juniper."

She felt bad now, her heart squeezing. "No. I need to borrow some of Chuck's clothes." She softened her voice when she spoke of her former brother-in-law.

"Oh," Shelby said, her expression going blank for just a moment before she suddenly brightened. "Why? You got some dude naked up at your place?"

Juniper rolled her eyes. "Well. Yes."

"And he needs clothes?" Shelby smirked. "Are you a *quitter*?"

She couldn't help but laugh. Because of course her sister would take it there. "I have stuff to do. I can't lounge around naked all day."

"I wasn't suggesting lounging, J."

"I'm *aware*," Juniper said.

"Why doesn't he have a change of clothes?"

Juniper let out an exasperated sigh. "Look. It's complicated. Just indulge me. Just give me something for a man to wear."

"All right." Shelby stepped away from the door and let Juniper into the small, cozy house. It wasn't as old as her cabin, which had been built in the 1920s. This was straight out of the '70s with wood paneling and shag carpeting. It was the house they'd spent part of their childhood in, until their dad had built the sprawling, modern home their parents lived in now.

Even if it was a little dated, Juniper would always find

it warm and lovely. Homey. She wondered how Shelby felt now, though. It was supposed to be her home. Her family home, and now…

Well, *now.*

Shelby led them back to her room, and suddenly, Juniper felt strangely uncomfortable.

Everything in there was untouched. Just as it had been. And Chuck's clothes were still in the closet.

"You know, you don't have to loan me anything if…"

"I need to get rid of it," she said. "It doesn't matter whether they're hanging here or not. He's gone. He's not going to come back. I'm not going to have a séance with his favorite flannel and get him to come say *hey* from the beyond."

"I know. But if you want to keep his clothes and not have another man in them…"

"It's you. It's not me. If it were me having a sexual partner who needed some clothes, that would be weird. And I would not do that." The very fact that her room was exactly as it had been, with her wedding picture on the nightstand and a closet full of his clothes, told her that there wasn't any chance of that, since there were no men coming over anyway.

"I just… I don't know when I'd be able to get these back and…"

"I'll just give you a pair of black jeans and a black shirt. I couldn't tell you the difference between those anyway. They're all the damn same. The man had no fashion sense."

He had also been quite a bit shorter than Chance, but Juniper wasn't going to say anything. Beggars couldn't be choosers, and anyway, she wasn't bringing up the fact that it was Chance Carson who needed the clothes. All the better to let her sister think that she had picked up a guy for an uncharacteristic one-nighter.

"You're not fucking around with Jamie, are you?" she asked.

"What?" The lovely blond man that she often worked shifts with had a boyfriend. But clearly her sister didn't know that.

"You were on shift last night," Shelby pointed out.

"Right," she said. "No, look, it's not like that. It's not… No. Not Jamie. Whatever. Don't worry about it."

"I can't help it. I do worry about you. You're my only sister. And you've been… Very moody lately."

"I am not moody," she said.

"Yeah, you are," Shelby said. "You're a moody beast."

"Hey, you're the baby. I'm the one that's supposed to worry about you. Anyway, you're the prime example of stability?"

"No." Shelby shrugged. "But I have an excuse."

"Sure. Play the grief card." Gallows humor was really the only way to cope. At least, the only way Juniper and Shelby had found.

"Glaaaaadly," Shelby said, drawing the word out and finishing it with a smile. "I have to get some benefit out of this."

She didn't think the clothes would be a great fit for Chance.

Not that she was an expert on his body. Not that she had been looking. A lot. Since she was thirteen years old.

No.

Well. She *wished* that were true. She wished that she were wholly and totally immune to Chance and his looks.

And really, she wished that she were immune to the

god-awful pettiness that had made her decide she was
going to play this game with him.

But there's a point to it.

Maybe there was. Maybe there really was. Maybe it
was possible for him to begin to understand just why all
of this was so important to her.

Maybe he could understand why the land was so important to them. Maybe without all the baggage from his
own family, all of the ridiculousness, and the ridiculous
male ego nonsense that had been entrenched in him over
the course of their feud… That was it. It was that there
was so much nonsense between them.

So much.

And maybe with all of this there would be less.

He'd seemed…human last night. And that made her
feel something shift in her chest. She didn't like it.

Except, of course, when he remembered and… No. She
wasn't going to think about that. He would've gotten to
know her maybe a little bit and by then she would be…
Humanized or something.

"What is that look on your face?" Shelby asked.

"What look?"

Her lips curved upward. "Your visitor must've been
something else in the sack."

She shifted uncomfortably. "Why do you say that?"

"Because you are *spacey*."

Juniper snorted. "I don't get spacey over men."

That was true. She'd had a few boyfriends, but they
hadn't been serious. And she hadn't been heartbroken
when the relationship had ended. Hadn't missed them in
her life or her bed.

Sex… It didn't matter that much to her. She had other
things to worry about. Other things to focus on.

Her sister had been *so* in love with Chuck. He had been her one and only.

And she had acted sort of interested in the idea that Juniper had been able to have more than one partner.

But Juniper didn't see sex as anything more than a basic itch that occasionally needed scratching. And she had found often that it wasn't really all that scratched when all was said and done.

All to build up a little fanfare.

Minimal fireworks.

She didn't really know how to pretend that there had been epic fireworks.

Though, apparently, the distraction level caused by Chance was something that her sister imagined might be fireworks. Well, in fairness, it wasn't Chance himself that she found so distracting. It was the fact that she was lying to him. And that he had amnesia.

Yeah. That.

"Thanks."

"Want to have a coffee?" Shelby asked.

"I should… Get back. With clothes."

Shelby looked a little disappointed and Juniper went ahead and threw that disappointment right onto her guilt pile.

But Chance was *without spare clothing in her house* and that had to be solved.

"Right. Okay."

She scurried back out, got into her truck and began to drive back to the cabin.

And when she scampered into the house, she did so just as the bathroom door was opening, and Chance came out in nothing but a towel.

Juniper's jaw practically hit the floor. Maybe if any of the men that she'd been with had looked like this...

His body was unreal. She'd noticed that last night. Well. She'd noticed it a long time ago. But it still took her breath away. Broad shoulders, well-defined muscular chest, narrow waist with abs her grandmother could have grated cheese on for enchiladas.

All covered in dark hair that made her fingers itch with the desire to test the texture. The desire to touch them.

"Sorry," he said. "I didn't mean to ambush you."

He was *glistening*.

It was, like, not even fair.

"It's fine," she said. She took a step toward him and handed him the clothes, feeling like she could straight up sense the heat coming off of his body.

He disappeared into the bathroom, and she sat there, unbearably aware of her heart pounding in her ears.

When he reappeared, it was in black jeans that were two inches too short.

"Thank God for boots," he said.

"Sorry," she said. "They were my... They were my brother-in-law's. He wasn't as tall as you."

"Wasn't?"

Dammit. She hadn't meant to bring all this up.

"My brother-in-law, Chuck, died in a car accident a couple of years ago. My poor sister... She was devastated. She loved him. I mean." She rolled her eyes at herself. This was never easy to talk about, and it wasn't getting easier. "Obviously she loved her husband. It's just they were childhood sweethearts. It was deeper than it is for a lot of people. He was the only one for her."

"That's sad," he said. He didn't say anything for a long

time. "Kind of amazing, to have the one for you. Even if just for a little bit."

She stared at him, and she didn't know if he was like this all the time, or if this was something to do with having all the... The *Chance* wiped away.

But maybe the Chance was there. Maybe she just didn't know him.

This is supposed to be making him like you, not the other way around.

She cleared her throat. "Yeah. I mean... I don't think she would've traded it for anything. It's just really sad."

"Of course it is."

She shook her head. "I mean, I know it sounds really dumb. But it is."

"You're an EMT," he said.

She nodded.

"Were you called to the scene of the accident?"

That he'd connected those two things, and then gone ahead and asked the hard question... It made her chest hurt. Made it hard to breathe.

She took a breath. "I... Yes. Jamie, my partner. He... He recognized Chuck. He knew. He told me not to come any closer. I was desperate to, but he said... Chuck was already gone. He spared me from the worst of it. I'm thankful." She tried to swallow, her whole body seizing up. Sometimes she was angry that she'd had to do it. Sometimes she was grateful. She could never decide which. "But I will never be over having to tell Shelby."

"Has that impacted your relationship?"

"If anything, it brought us closer. I was there for her during the hardest night of her life. I had to give her the worst news. Nobody should have to tell their sister that.

And yet… Who else but your sister should tell you? Who else but your sister should be there to hold you?"

"That's an amazing perspective," he said.

"Maybe. We didn't have a choice. So we just make the best out of it. You ready?"

"Yep."

Without speaking, they walked out of the house and to her truck.

When they were closed inside the vehicle, she realized she had made another error. She hadn't fully considered what it would be like to be closed in the space with him. Hadn't fully considered the way he might smell. Or what it would feel like to be in such close proximity to him.

Her breathing became more rapid. And she felt like an idiot. Like a straight-up idiot.

And now she was basically hyperventilating. Her heart was going a thousand miles a minute, her senses were… Swamped with him.

He had used her soap. He had no other options. And it was just a generic bar brand, and it smelled so good coming off of his skin.

Like there was some magical Chance additive that had gone into it. It was him. His skin. The pheromones.

She wouldn't say she had wondered. What it would be like. If when they were done fighting they just… Fell into each other. If they tore each other's clothes off, and finished it that way. On the ground. On the floor of her cabin. Nowhere in her fantasies had they ever managed to make it to a bed. No, she and Chance Carson would never make it to a bed. They were destined to be against the wall, on the floor…

Nowhere, idiot.

Nowhere. They would never have sex anywhere.

He had never shown any indication that he might want to. Ever. And that was good. It was good.

"The barn is up here," she said, because she had to distract herself.

Good God, she had to distract herself.

"What kind of work are you doing?"

"Well, I've been reroofing."

"Reroofing?"

"Yeah," she said.

"By yourself?"

"Partly. I mean, mostly."

"Was I helping you with this?"

"No. We've mostly been… We have some cows. Not that many. And some horses, which is what I'm building up. And you mostly help with that kind of thing. Cows are mostly your thing."

The thing was, she didn't have any idea what Chance knew how to fix or anything. So she had to make sure that her lie was something he already knew how to do. Which was cattle ranching. She had a feeling he'd have the muscle memory for that. Not that she would actually let him get down to get anywhere near the cows. No. That was not going to be a thing.

"Well, I'm pretty confident I can swing a hammer as well as I can swing an ax."

"I appreciate it."

They pulled up to the old barn, and she suddenly felt self-conscious. It was nothing like the kind of barn that would be on the Carson spread. Where everything was new and perfectly kept. But then, he didn't remember that. So maybe he wouldn't judge hers quite so harshly.

He surveyed the place, and she watched his expression closely. "There's a lot of work to be done," he said.

"I know," she said.

"Don't take it personal," he said.

"About taking it personal. It's just that I have done a lot of work."

"I'm sure you have."

They got out of the truck, and she felt irrationally annoyed, and that made it feel a lot more like the Chance that she knew. It helped temper the attraction. That was the problem. He hadn't been annoying. So the way that she felt when he was around hadn't defused the fact that she wanted to punch him in his ridiculously handsome face. And now all was well. All was right with the world.

She understood herself when she wanted to punch Chance Carson in the face.

Maybe that was sad. But she didn't much care.

It was fair. It was more than fair.

She went over to the base of the ladder and picked up some tools. "Let's go," she said.

"All right," he replied.

He began to climb up the ladder ahead of her, hammer gripped in his hand. She suddenly worried about having him up there. And she wondered if she was being a little bit cavalier about his safety.

But physically, he seemed just fine. Everything seemed to be in fair working order, and it seemed as if he was capable of ladder climbing.

She came up behind him and found herself staring directly at his ass. It wasn't the first time she had looked at Chance's ass. But it was the first time she'd had such a prime view.

"You checking me out back there?"

Her head snapped up. "What?"

That had sounded more like Chance. Cocky. Exceptionally male.

"Are you checking me out?"

"I'm thinking about roof tile," she said.

"Sure," he said.

He looked back behind him, and he winked. The bastard winked.

She felt tetchy. But at least she wasn't mired in the sadness of a few moments earlier.

But then he got up onto the roof and was towering above her, and she scrambled up behind him, standing up as quickly as she could so she wasn't kneeling at his feet.

That was a bit on the nose.

"We got the nail guns all ready to go," she said. "So…"

"Let's get to it, I guess."

And he did. Making her own time on the roofing look sad.

"So you know how to do this," she said.

"I guess so. It's like the wood," he said. "I didn't know for sure if I'd ever done it before, but my body knew how to do it. So, I guess there are just some things that are like that." He looked up, and his eyes caught hers and held.

And she couldn't help but think of all the other things a person's body might actually remember how to do.

Oh. She didn't need to be thinking about that right now.

Remember how he's your sworn enemy, and you're just looking at his ass?

Yeah. She was sort of a disgrace, all things considered.

"Sorry about your brother-in-law," he said, between nails.

"Me too."

"You married?" he asked.

She huffed. "Have you seen a husband around?"

"No."

She really didn't need to be playing this brand of getting-to-know-you with Chance. And yet… She couldn't resist him.

"Ever been married?" he asked.

"Nope. Not even close."

"Why not?"

She shrugged. "Don't see the point of it. I think it's kind of bullshit, actually. I mean for me. Not for everybody else. My parents are in love. My grandparents are in love. My sister was really in love."

"So why is it bullshit?"

"It's just not for me. I don't think that I have the capacity for it. I don't know. I've never been all that worked up about any of the men I've hooked up with. Anyway, it doesn't work. Not doing what I want to do. A man can get a wife, I guess, to run his house while he works the land. I have to figure out how to do it all, and I've never met a person I wanted to try to fit into all that. On top of that, I just don't see how it would work practically." She swallowed hard. "I wouldn't respect a man who didn't have the drive I did. I couldn't be with a man who didn't have land. If he has his own land, he won't be coming to live on mine. And I certainly won't leave."

"A man ain't no kind of man unless he has land? I feel like I've heard that somewhere."

Of course, Chance didn't think he had land. But he did. A lot of it.

And that's your fault that he doesn't know, because you're a lying liar.

Yes, she was a lying liar. She felt kinda bad.

But not enough to *quit* lying.

Not enough to…

Not have him. Not have this anymore.

"Something like that."

"But?"

"If I was with a man who had the kind of ambition I did, if I was with a man who had land, then what would we do with mine? I just don't think things can work that way. Shelby and Chuck built their lives around each other. It wasn't about a ranch, or a career, for either of them. It was just about this life that they wanted to share. Everything was about each other. For my parents, it was about my dad. His business. My mom wanted to be a homemaker, and that was what she loved. She took care of us, she does beadwork, and just kind of works around all of her household duties. It's not anything she was ever ambitious with. My grandmother is kind of an extreme homemaker. She did everything joyfully, but busily. Always working. My grandfather was that way with the ranch. They share the homestead. And they were contributing toward it. If she had been doing that in one place, while he had been doing it with another, it would not work."

"And you wouldn't be happy with your horses on a different plot of land."

"No. I couldn't be. That's the thing. This is Sohappy land. And that means something to me. The heritage of it means something to me. I decided to pour myself into this at the expense of everything. I could never... I could never walk away from it."

"So, because of all that, you can't find a man who brings out strong feelings in you."

"Basically. I think that's the problem. I just... I'm not built for it."

"I wish I could tell you my story," he said. "The reasons that I think love and marriage are bullshit. But I don't even know if I think that."

"You probably do," she said. "Men who look like you…"

"Look like me?"

"Did you get a chance to look in the mirror?" she asked.

"Yeah," he said, lifting a shoulder.

"So you must know you're good-looking," she said. "I mean…" She waved her arm up and down.

"Thanks," he said. "I guess I didn't really think about it."

"Well, there's no point beating around the bush."

He laughed. "I guess not. You think I'm trouble?"

"I *know* you're trouble," she said.

And his eyes met hers again, and it felt hot and weighty, and she didn't like it.

"Just better keep moving before it gets warm," he said.

"It's funny," she said, letting herself become distracted. "It's funny the things you know."

"Yeah. I guess it is. Still don't know anything about myself." And she could feel him staring at her, long and hard, and she didn't look back. "I feel like there's something there," he said. "Between us."

Oh, that was so dangerous. And it made breathing nearly impossible, and she hated him for it as much as she wanted to launch herself into his arms.

That, at least, was normal.

But she wondered…treacherously, she wondered…if that meant that without all the anger, without all the memories, without everything…

If he felt this.

If he had.

"You work for me," she said.

"Right."

And then they let that subject drop.

They worked until the heat of the day was too much, then they climbed down. Juniper went to the bed of the truck and took out a cooler, where she had packed a couple of boiled eggs and ham sandwiches.

"I don't know if you like ham," she said, handing him a sandwich.

"Neither do I," he responded. He took a bite of the sandwich. "I do," he said. "I'm hungry as hell."

She realized that one sandwich probably wasn't going to be enough for him.

"You can have my boiled egg," she said.

A paltry offer, really. One egg. But all things considered, she owed it to him.

The lying being considered?

"Awfully nice of you."

"Well," she said dryly. "You don't know anything about me, but I am *very nice*. That's what people say about me."

"Why do I get the feeling that's not strictly true?"

She shrugged. "I don't know. Not my fault if people are sometimes incorrect."

"I don't know much, really. Literally. But I sense that a lot of people are not as observational as they should be."

"I would agree. People get entrenched in their own ways. Their own beliefs, and they never really look at anyone else. They never look around. And never challenge themselves."

She was speaking of him, of course. Him and his outrageous prejudice against her. Him and his certainty that his ancestors were being truthful about who owned that section of land.

But she felt it. She felt it resonated in her own heart. In her own chest.

And she hated that.

This was all supposed to be about him. About getting him to see things in a new way, about getting him to respect her and her family.

It wasn't supposed to change her.

"Now we get to go inside and replace the floorboards."

"Sounds like a party."

Inside, there were planks that she had precut the other day with her skill saw. They were measured out ready to go, they just needed to be nailed in.

"Fun with power tools," he commented.

She huffed a laugh.

And what was really strange was that she was having fun with him. That spending the afternoon with him was better than spending it alone.

It's not him, though.

And she would do well to remember that.

"Have I met your grandfather?" he asked, out of the blue.

"Yes," she answered truthfully.

"Does he like me?"

Well. She wasn't sure if she should answer that truthfully.

"You're taking an awfully long time. I'm wondering if I'm not going to like the answer."

"He doesn't like very many people. Or rather, I should say he's not impressed with very many people."

That was true. Her grandfather was as crotchety as they came, and he had opinions. Big opinions about who was good, who was worthy of respect and whether or not he had to pay it to them.

She liked that about him.

He was a curmudgeon. He didn't let anyone know he

had a soft spot, right at the center of his soul, that he reserved for the sky, the river and the land itself. That he was a man who loved the earth he'd walked on all his life more than most people loved anything.

He might not show his feelings, but he had them.

And it was so important to her—so very important—that she honored the trust that hard, stubborn old man had put in her.

He'd bypassed his son as the heir to the ranch.

He'd bypassed his son-in-law.

His belief was in her and it had been clear and bright from the beginning. And she'd taken the reins and promised to ride hard and true.

It was only now that sometimes…

Sometimes she wondered if she could love this ranch and this ranch alone.

Too late now.

"He doesn't have much use for you," she said. "But… That is actually true of most people. And my grandfather… He loves his family. He loves his dogs. He loves his land. Otherwise… Well, his feelings aren't all that strong."

He laughed. "I can respect that. As long as he's good to you. And recognizes how wonderful it is to have earned your admiration. I have a feeling a man could spend his whole life trying to get that, Juniper."

"Really," she said, her throat suddenly feeling dry. "What makes you think that?"

"You just seem like the kind of woman that doesn't impress easily. I like that about you. You seem like you're a whole thing."

"I am."

It was sweaty work, but they finished the flooring,

and her stomach was growling ridiculously by the time they finished.

"I'm starving," he said.

"Luckily," she said, "I have some meals my grandmother made me in the freezer. I'll just heat up a double portion."

"I will never say no to a grandmother's cooking. Another thing I know deep in my soul."

"Great."

"And what are we getting tonight?"

"Stew. And bread. It's wonderful. She makes her own sourdough."

"And you don't cook?"

"No." And then she felt a kick of sadness inside of her heart, because she didn't cook because her grandmother did. Shelby did, thankfully, but she did sometimes wonder where the recipes would go when Grandma was gone.

"It's amazing that she still bakes," she said softly. "She's ninety, and she hasn't slowed down. But I worry. I worry it won't be long before she does. That's just life, isn't it?"

Maybe that was the problem lately. Time was marching on relentlessly. Chuck was gone and it marched on. Her grandparents were getting older and older and it marched on.

She was…just her. Just here.

And it marched on.

"I don't have a lot of specific memories about how life is," he said slowly. "But it seems to me that life really is like that."

Her chest got tight. "I guess I should ask for her recipes. But part of me doesn't want to. Because sometimes

I think maybe when she's gone we don't deserve to have her food anymore. We should feel the absence there too."

"But it's heritage, right? Like the land."

"Like the land," she agreed.

They got in the truck and drove back to her cabin. And she was thankful that she hadn't run into anyone from her family. They didn't often come out this far, but it wasn't unreasonable to think that they might come to bring her some food at midday. It happened occasionally.

Her mom might not bake quite like her grandmother, but she would often bring bologna and mustard, or some chocolate chip cookies.

She didn't want to explain why she had Chance Carson working with her. And why Chance Carson didn't know who he was. And why Chance Carson thought they were maybe friends, and that he was an employee of the ranch.

No. She really didn't want to get into all that.

"It's a nice evening," he said.

"Yeah," she agreed.

"I notice you have a firepit out there. You want to eat dinner outside?"

And… She found that she did. She wanted to sit with him by the fire, and she wasn't even certain why.

"Yeah. In fact, maybe I'll get out the Dutch oven and heat the stew over the fire."

"Sounds great."

He'd said that to her more than once today.

Sounds great.

And it did funny things to her chest. Because Chance had never said that anything sounded great to her before. She might have said it to him, but that could've been when he asked if she would see something over his dead body.

Sounds great.

Except, when she had found what she thought might be his dead body, she hadn't done a dance or anything like that. In fact, she had helped him.

That made her feel a little better about her eternal soul. Sometimes she had wondered.

He got the fire going. Another one of those things he remembered, apparently. And she got the big Dutch oven, and the frozen block of stew, and got it set on a grate over the firepit.

There were little camp chairs that she set by the fire ring, and she brought out a couple of beers and handed one to him.

It didn't take long for the stew to start bubbling, and then she ladled it into tin camping bowls, and they sat and ate.

"Is this elk?" he asked.

She frowned. "Yes. How did you know that?"

"I've had it before. I mean, I just know. I don't know. I guess it's something I've had before."

"Obviously," she said. "Common out this way."

"Right."

"My dad is a big bow hunter. So we always have meat. I imagine that…" She almost said she imagined his dad was too. In fact, she was sure of it. But she shouldn't go saying things like that. Not when she was doing her best not to give him details about anything. Because it was the right thing to do, really. For the handling of the amnesia. But also she didn't need to go implicating herself in anything.

"I imagine you would've had it before." That finish was lame. And she knew it. But if he was suspicious, he didn't say anything. She stared into the fire, and then over the flames at him.

Dusk had begun to fall, and stars were punching their

way through the curtain of blue velvet above, and as it darkened, they grew stronger. The light shining all the clearer for the darkness around it.

"It's a beautiful night," she said.

"Yeah. Such a strange time of year," he said. "Beautiful. But there's something sad. In these hours just before darkness. When it's warm still but the sun has gone away. I don't know why."

She stared at him, like she'd never seen him before, and she knew that he wouldn't even find it all that weird. He didn't know that she had seen him most days for a good portion of her life. Whether it was catching a glimpse of him across the Thirsty Mule on a crowded Saturday night, or in the grocery store, or when she saw him, silhouetted by the sun, riding across Carson land.

Those moments when she wanted to hate him but felt something else instead.

"But you just know that?"

He seemed to be wrestling with it. Or concentrating hard, like it was a feat to hang on to it.

"It's a feeling. It's a feeling that I have as strong as anything."

"I see. Well... I guess maybe it's long nights?"

He shook his head and stared past her for a while. And she had the feeling when he spoke again, he wasn't speaking to her, but using words as a way to write this truth on his heart. So he wouldn't lose it. "It's something more than that. I can see a little girl. A little girl and... She's not mine. Because I'm a little boy. She's very sick."

"Oh."

"That's why I don't want to go to the doctor." He sounded far away then. "She went to the doctor all the time. Hospitals. So many hospitals. All the time. A never-ending rotation of them. When she died, it was late spring like this. One of these long nights."

The sounds around them were amplified. The flames licking over the wood, cracking. The crickets, insistent, rhythmic, somewhere in the darkness.

"Who was it?"

She didn't know. This was a story about the Carson family she didn't know.

"I don't know. I just know that I see her. And that when you asked me if I wanted to go to the hospital, I thought no. That's where people go to die. And she's why I think that. Because she was a little girl, and one day she went into the hospital and she never came out."

An overwhelming, heavy sadness pervaded Juniper's chest.

"You know, I take people to the hospital every day," she said. "They don't just go there to die. They go there to be healed. I understand that there can be bad traumatic memories connected to that. But… But the hospital can be a good thing."

"Logically I know that. But…"

"I'm sorry," she said. "I'm sorry that the first memory you're having is so sad."

"I think it's probably the strongest one I have. Because I think I felt that sadness inside of me before I ever saw her face. What a hell of a thing. That I almost died. Out there in the field. When…"

"When what?" she whispered.

"My parents have been through enough," he said. "She must've been my sister."

"Oh." The word left her body in a gust.

He knew what it was like to lose someone. He was… human.

Just the same as she was.

Just the same as they all were.

The Carsons and Sohappys weren't so different.

She was hoping he might see that during this time, but she hadn't expected it would be her own lesson.

She…she had never heard anything about that and she didn't know why he thought it. Or if it was true. And it still settled hard in her chest.

He was getting way too close to remembering things, and it was getting… Dicey. It was one thing to think that she wanted to endear herself to him this way, but him sharing something personal like this, something he never would've shared otherwise, it felt like a violation. And she had never thought that she would feel like she violated Chance Carson. But this was different. The situation with his sister.

No. He had a sister. And she was alive and well.

Callie Carson was much younger than him, and she had gone off and married a rodeo cowboy who lived in Gold Valley.

But the way he was talking about it, it sounded like he was younger.

She felt hungry for more, but at the same time she didn't want to press him. For so many reasons, but maybe the biggest one was her heart felt so tender right now. For him.

That wasn't supposed to happen.

"All right," he said.

He stood up, and she stood at the same time, ready to take his bowl from him.

"I can take the dishes."

"Oh no, that's okay," he said, and she put her hand on

the bowl, and her fingertips brushed his, and their eyes locked.

And she felt a frisson of something magical go through her. Something hot and delicious and sticky like cayenne honey, flowing all the way through her veins.

And she could hardly breathe around it. She could hardly think. All she could do was stare. And feel the thundering rhythm of her heart, like a herd of wild mustangs, the kind that you could find out here in Eastern Oregon, and she was sure that he could hear it too.

And then, gradually, that didn't worry her. Because she could see in the look on his face that he was... Hungry.

Hungry for her.

And she had to wonder if this was new, or if it had been there before.

Just like it was for her.

Maybe they felt the same.

She'd always thought she and Chance Carson felt absolutely different. About everything. But maybe not.

Maybe they felt the same.

Maybe they always had.

She opened her mouth to say something, but then he lowered his head and kissed her.

It was like an electric shock. His mouth was hot and firm, his lips certain and miraculous as they moved against hers.

She clung to him, instinctively, and it wasn't until she heard the bowl clatter to the ground that she realized she had let go of the metal vessel. And she was glad it wasn't glass.

But it was a metaphor. A metaphor for how precarious this was. Because she was forgetting. And she was letting herself get caught up in all the wrong things.

But she couldn't help but be caught up now. In his hold, in the searing kiss, the magical pressure of his mouth on hers. She'd had any number of kisses. But they had just been something to do.

Because when you thought a man was attractive, you might as well kiss him. Because even though it wasn't like she had gone to bed with that many men, she had never found it to be that big of a deal, and if she was in a relationship, she was all right taking it to its natural conclusion.

A kiss had never scalded her like fire, searing her and leaving her feeling empty, a hollowed-out vessel forged by flame.

But his did.

She was so hot. Everywhere. And she ached. Not just between her legs, but in her chest. It hurt how badly she wanted to be close to him.

How much she wanted to tear away their clothing that stood between them, how much she wanted to press herself flush against him with nothing between them.

She had never wanted like this. This quickly. This violently.

It was a sickness.

But it was a beautiful one.

She clung to his shirt, then pushed her fingers through his hair, arching against him, rubbing her breasts against his solid chest like a cat.

He growled, and then rolled his hips forward, and she could feel the insistence of that hard length between them.

On the floor. Against the wall.

She had thought about this.

And she wanted him. But… He didn't know who she was. He didn't know who he was.

She jerked away. Horrified. And she realized that she was snared in a net entirely of her own making.

"I'm sorry," she said. "I'm sorry. You work for me and…"

"But that's not all there is between us, is there?" he asked, his voice going husky.

No. Of course it wasn't all there was between them.

Of course it wasn't.

But she couldn't say that. She couldn't explain. Anyway, the explanation didn't make things any clearer. The explanation was even more confusing. He wasn't her employee. And they weren't having a secret assignation.

They were enemies. Caught between a family feud, and nothing more. Two people who had driven each other nuts for an age. Not anything deeper than that. How could they be?

"It's just… I'm sorry. It's not right. It's not right."

"I'm a man," he said. "And I know that. For certain. Whether or not I have all my memories. I know how to cut wood. I know how to fix a roof. I know how to put in a floor. I think I can figure out how to…"

"That's not what I'm worried about. I am worried about taking advantage of you."

As she stood there with her head coming up to the middle of his chest, she realized that what she was saying sounded ridiculous. But she understood.

Way to go, Juniper. Caught in the net of your own idiocy.

"I'm sorry I…"

"It's all right," he said. "Look, I can leave if you want. I don't need to stay here. I can go back to my own cabin if it…"

"No. I'm fine. I don't… It's not you. I promise."

"I'm not going to hurt you," he said.

"I know that," she said. "I trust that. You have never…"

You've never given me any indication that you would. No matter… No matter what. Even if we were fighting."

"All right." He nodded slowly. "As long as you trust that."

"I do."

Chapter 5

Sleeping on the living room floor in Juniper's place was more uncomfortable tonight than it had been the other night. Because he was hard as a rock and unlikely to find sleep. But he had meant what he'd said to her. He wouldn't make any advances on her. No matter what. Not if she wasn't interested.

It was hilarious, her being worried about his consent. He had made his pretty clear. But then, she had concerns about his memory. Or whatever.

Even if we were fighting.

That word came flooding back to him.

Fighting? Had they fought? The way she said that made it sound like they had. Sometime.

And he couldn't help but wonder why. What about. She had acted like she only vaguely knew him, but he was starting to get the impression that wasn't true.

He was up before the sunrise and set about fixing coffee and eggs.

Juniper woke up not long after, dressed in utilitarian gear, clearly ready for her shift as an EMT.

He found her fascinating. And beautiful.

"I'll see you later," she said. "I have to work. I... I'll bring you back some more clothes."

"Sure," he said.

"Sorry you just had the one spare outfit. Sorry about... Everything."

"None of it's your fault."

"How are you feeling about staying here?" she asked.

"It's still what I want," he said. "If you don't mind."

"No," she said. "Not at all. If this is where you want to be, then... Great. I... I'm happy to have you."

"Hey, can I head over to the barn and do some finish work for you today?"

"Sure," she said.

"I'd like to keep helping out. I'd like to make myself useful in my invalid state."

"I appreciate it. You don't need to do that."

"But I enjoy it," he said.

And that was that.

He left the cabin and went out walking. There wasn't a vehicle left up at her cabin, so it was up to him to make it there on foot, but he didn't mind. He remembered the route to get down there, and it was a pleasant walk.

The stormy weather of a few days ago had vanished now. Spring flowers making themselves known, dots of yellow and orange in a brilliant field of green.

His mind was pleasantly empty. And right now, it felt pleasant. It was strange, how he knew that this was different, even though he couldn't quite remember what it was like to have his mind be full. Last night had maybe been a preview of that. He had been so preoccupied thinking about the things that had happened with Juniper, that thing that was niggling at him that she'd said, that he hadn't fully marinated on that memory from his childhood. The little girl. His sister. He was sure. Even though he didn't know her name. Even though he didn't really know his own name—not beyond what Juniper had told him—he felt a sense of certainty over the images there. In the feelings they created. He had been a child. There was something different about his eyes and those memories. And there was something about the pain in his chest. The way that it bruised. As if it was a fresh betrayal brought on by life. Not just another of life's bullshit moves.

No, this had been something unique. Something special. The pain that was the first of its kind. Back when the world seemed bright and full of possibility, this had been his first indicator that things could go terribly, horribly wrong.

It had shaped him, this pain. It had changed him. There was a before, and there was an after.

Even without his memories, he was still living in the after.

But he chose to focus on the day around him, and not on those memories, and he wondered if that was what he did. If he was the kind of man who didn't dwell on hurt, if he was the kind of man who simply walked forward.

He walked across the field and made his way over to the barn. He climbed the ladder, ready to do the work now. He began to nail more tiles into the roof surface, and right as he was finishing one section, he stood, and his boot heel wrapped around the edge of the cord. He pitched forward, and he saw the ground far below rising up to meet him. But he didn't fall. He caught himself. But still, it took him back to a moment, and suddenly, he could see another fall in his head.

He had fallen off the horse. His horse. He had fallen off of his horse and hit his head on the ground. While he had been riding the line between Carson land and Sohappy land.

Carson land.

He had been on Carson land, because he was a Carson.

And Juniper Sohappy was his rival.

By the time Juniper pulled into her sister's property, she was exhausted. She had stopped at the Thirsty Mule and had picked up burgers to go, and had had a difficult time making eye contact with Cara Thompson, who was Jace Carson's best friend, so even though she would never be outright rude to Juniper while she was in the woman's place of business, she didn't like Juniper, and she didn't do a very good job of hiding that fact.

If only she knew. If only she knew that Juniper had Chance squirreled away up at her cabin, and Chance didn't know who he was.

She had worried about his family and their concern for him before, but now that she knew about their loss, it…

It ate at her.

As soon as Juniper closed the door to her truck, her sister's front door flung open, and her sister came bounding outside. "What the hell?"

"What?"

"I saw Chance Carson up on the roof of your barn today, wearing Chuck's clothing. And so you have to answer my question."

"I do not guarantee that I will answer your question," Juniper said, her mouth going dry.

"Are you going to pound town with Chance Carson?"

"Don't say *pound town*," Juniper said, practically covering her ears.

"Doing the horizontal Macarena?"

"Stop it."

"*Screwing.* Are you *screwing* him?"

"I am… I am not *screwing* Chance Carson."

Of course, the truth was so ridiculous she should probably stick with the story that she was…banging the man, because her sister was never going to believe that Chance Carson had amnesia, and that she had lied to him, and they were currently doing a modern-day dramatic reenactment of *Overboard* with him as Goldie Hawn to her Kurt Russell.

No. That wouldn't go over very well at all.

But she had to try and explain. Somehow.

"He…" She scrunched her face. "He got hurt."

"He got hurt?"

"Yes."

"Why was he naked at your house?" she pressed.

"He wasn't naked at my house specifically. I mean, he has been. You know, when he was showering or changing his clothes. Not *with me.* But he fell. Off of his horse or something, the details are fuzzy. And I found him in the field unconscious. I took him back to the cabin because it was the middle of the night and we're so far away from the hospital, and I am a professional, so I looked at his head, and he had a concussion…"

"None of this explains what he is doing there, and why he is wearing my husband's clothes."

She hedged. "He can't remember anything."

"He can't *remember anything*?"

"No," she said. "Least of all that he hates me. I mean, that he hates all of us."

"Oh, Juniper."

"I might have… I might have a little bit told him that he's working for me."

"Do you have a death wish?" Shelby practically shrieked that question.

"No. I don't have a death wish. I don't wish to be dead at all."

Shelby's dark eyes were wide. "He's going to kill you."

"No, he isn't."

"When he finds out that you were lying to him, that you made him do menial tasks for you while he didn't remember who he was, he is going to *kill you*. Strangle you with his big, capable, roof-repairing hands."

"You are being a drama queen." But there was a thread of truth to her words that disquieted Juniper.

"I'm not being a drama queen, you're being a sociopath. And, I grant you, Juniper, I really admire the brand of crazy that you're being. Because this is petty on a level that I could never even aspire to. And I value pettiness. I value it with all of my being. I am so deeply impressed by this, but I worry for your safety. Because if you are by yourself when he finds out…" She suddenly stopped talking, and her eyes went wide. "But are you *sleeping with him, though*?"

"I'm *not* sleeping with him," she said.

"Not even a little?"

"How do you *a little* sleep with someone?"

Shelby huffed a laugh. "Oh please. You're the one who has had multiple sex partners."

"Don't say it like that!"

"More than me anyway, and I think you know exactly how you can a little bit sleep with someone. Are you sucking his…"

"No." She needed Shelby to not finish that sentence. Badly. "I kissed him. Once. I told him that it couldn't happen again. Because I'm not actually a sociopath, Shelby, and I cannot sleep with a man who thinks that he works for me, when he is in fact my mortal enemy. I will screw with my mortal enemy all the livelong day, but I will not take advantage of him physically in that way."

"Well, thank God you have some scruples remaining in you. But this is deeply disconcerting."

"I don't know what to tell you. I just… It just happened, it tumbled out of my mouth. I was very tired, and then there was no going back."

"I don't even know what to say."

"Get me some clothes for him, or…"

"He's going to have to walk around the cabin naked."

Her face went flushed. She could feel it. "No," she said. "He will not be walking around naked."

But what a visual that was.

"I have deep concerns for your safety. You need to have your walkie-talkie on you at all times. When he finds out, and he literally tries to kill you."

"He isn't. He isn't going to try to kill me. He's… Look, the worst part is I kind of like Chance. I mean, Chance without his memories."

"It's *not* Chance," Shelby said insistently. "We're not who we are without our memories. If I didn't remember all the horrible shit that happened in my life over the last couple of years that…"

"It might be nicer?"

She sighed wearily. "It might be nicer. But I probably wouldn't be me. And the minute that he remembers, he will be him, and he's going to go back to being the person that he always was. This isn't really him. You have to remember that."

"I know. I promise you I'm not going to get hurt."

Shelby sighed. "Right." She said nothing for a moment. "But how good of a kisser is he?"

There was a keen sort of interest shining in Shelby's eyes and Juniper knew why. But they never talked about it. Ever. It was an unspoken law.

Never mention Kit Carson, or the way Shelby looked at him.

So she didn't. Even though she wanted to.

Juniper growled. "Just get me some clothes, please."

Shelby returned with a stack of clothes and handed it to her with a skeptical expression. Juniper snatched them close to her chest and looked at her sister's hopeful expression.

"He kisses like a dream," she relented.

"Oh, that is really good to know. The Carson men are… Well, they are problematic."

"Agreed."

"So are you," she said.

"Noted," Juniper shouted as she ran out of the house, ignoring her sister's further calls to not get murdered by Chance.

She got into her truck and drove back up to the cabin. And when she got there, Chance was standing in the doorway.

But it wasn't Chance, the man that she had spent the past several days with.

It was Chance Carson.

The *real* Chance Carson.

And he did in fact look like he might have murder on his mind.

Chapter 6

He could see the moment she registered what was going on. He could see the second she realized that she was looking at him. Really him, not the man that she had been playing around with for the past few days.

No.

She was well aware of who she was looking at in that moment, and he was fascinated. What would she do? How would she try to talk herself out of this? Would she? In his experience, Juniper was confrontational. A hellcat if ever there was one, and the little creature was more likely to bite than anything else.

He looked at her face, and he waited. Then she held up a bag that was in her hand and smiled. "I brought hamburgers."

Interesting. That's how she was going to play it.

She was going to make him say it.

"I'm not in the mood for hamburgers," he said, crossing his arms and leaning against the post on the porch.

"That's too bad," she said, her grin somehow brightening. "I would've gotten you a salad if I would've known."

"I don't want a salad."

"Well. I guess there is some middle ground between a hamburger and a salad. But I didn't realize. I'm sorry."

"You know what I would like?" he said.

"What exactly?"

"I'd like an explanation."

Her eyes darted left, then right, and she put him in the mind of seeing her as a scared bull, trying to figure out which way to scurry.

There was no way to scurry. Not from him.

"Well, I finished my shift, I am quite tired, but I stopped at the Thirsty Mule anyway to grab some hamburgers from Cara. You don't know who Cara is, though." That smile became all the more determined.

"I don't?"

"Not as far as I know," she said, smiling sweetly back.

And that was the thing, the weirdest thing. What hit him then was that while he hadn't known who she was, she had known who he was the entire time. She had been well aware that he was Chance Carson, that they theoretically hated each other, and she had kissed him.

Enthusiastically.

Had pressed that tight little body up against him and practically begged for his touch. In fact… He had a feeling that if it hadn't been for his memory loss, she would've taken it all the way.

She had weird lines, did Juniper. Apparently, there was no issue lying to him and using him for manual labor, but she wasn't going to take advantage of him sexually.

He supposed he should be grateful for that. Not that he would've felt overly taken advantage of.

"Not as far as you know," he repeated. "You know, I've been thinking," he said.

"Have you?"

"Yes. I've been thinking about the kiss the other night."

"Oh."

"It was good."

"I… Yes." Her face was scarlet red, and he could see her doing the dance. He could see her uncertainty. Maybe she wasn't entirely sure if he remembered or not, and it was making her nervous. Making her uncomfortable. Good.

He took a step toward her. "I'm not in the mood for hamburgers. I'm in the mood for another kiss."

He knew that his voice had a dangerous edge, and he could see her respond to it. Could see her pupils widen, could see her breath get shallow. She was afraid of him, but she was also intrigued. She was aroused. Turned on, and more than a little bit interested by what was happening between them.

He felt a smile curve his lips, and he knew it wasn't a kind one.

"I told you it wasn't a good idea," she said.

"Right," he said. "You're so worried about taking advantage of me."

Rage thrummed through his veins as he advanced on her, as he moved to cup the back of her head with his hand.

Her hair was so soft. She was soft.

And he never would've thought that Juniper Sohappy was soft.

He'd've thought she would be like embracing a cactus. All prickles and spikes, and maybe hard steel underneath.

But no. She was a woman.

She smelled like honeysuckle and the warmth of the sun. She was impossibly beautiful. And he wanted her.

And dammit, he felt owed.

She had been screwing with him. Laughing her ass off having him do her chores while he couldn't remember anything.

All over a piece of land?

And he had told her things that… Things he didn't talk about. Because he didn't remember that he didn't talk about them.

It was a damn shame.

But nothing he couldn't correct by getting some of his own back.

He watched as her pulse fluttered wildly at the base of her throat.

She was a beautiful creature. He wanted to lick her there. Run his tongue along the smooth column of her neck.

And he realized right then that what he wanted more than anything, more than punishing her, more than making her pay, was to make her scream.

Beneath him. Above him. However she wanted it.

He had buried that. All these years he had buried that. He had acknowledged that she was beautiful, but he had never allowed himself to fully give in to the desire that arced between them every time they fought. But her kissing him back had proved that she felt the same, and it had opened the floodgates of his own need.

And honestly, the worse she was, the more of a little weasel she was, the more he wanted her. Angry and hard and complicated.

Chance didn't do angry, he didn't do hard, he didn't do complicated.

Chance liked a bar hookup with a pretty, easy girl who didn't have any connections to his actual life. Chance liked a woman who was there for a good time, not a long time. He liked to keep it easy. Because he didn't like complications. Because complications meant entanglements, and entanglements meant attachments, and attachments were just something he wasn't willing to do.

For all the reasons he remembered now. Deeply. Keenly.

"Don't you want to kiss me again just a little bit?"

"No. I was being stupid. I was being crazy. And I…"

He closed the distance between them, kissing her hard.

And there was no way that she wouldn't be able to read the difference between this and the previous kiss. Because they were nothing alike. In this kiss, he poured all of his frustration. All of his rage that she had tapped into something emotional inside of him that he preferred to never acknowledge. Into this kiss, he put every ounce of withheld desire. All of the need that he had chosen to shove down deep for all of these years. Because he couldn't sleep with Juniper. She was the bane of his existence. She was…

She was the damned sexiest woman he had ever held in his arms, and his body felt like it was on fire.

He had never been so angry at a woman in his entire life, and at the same time he was utterly and completely helpless to battle the desire that he felt for her.

So he kissed her. Kissed her hard, held her face and angled her head just so he could take it deep. His tongue sliding against hers, stoking the fire in his midsection that left him shaken to his core.

And he didn't do shaken. He didn't do anything like this. "Kiss me back," he demanded.

And she whimpered, wrapping her arms around his neck. He felt the bag of burgers hit him square between the shoulder blades, but he didn't really care.

He arched his pelvis against hers, let her feel the intensity of his arousal.

"Chance…"

"Tell me," he said.

"Chance…"

"Tell me what you did," he said, reaching down and cupping her breasts, squeezing one, rubbing his thumb over her nipple until she gasped with desire.

"Tell me what you did, Juniper."

"I didn't… I didn't do anything."

He arched his hips forward, grinding the evidence of his arousal against the cleft between her thighs, and she shook, shuddered.

"You're a little liar," he said.

"And you," she said against his mouth, "are a fucking asshole."

"Am I? Am I the one who lied to a man that couldn't remember who he was?"

"Am I the person that is trying to steal somebody's land out from underneath them?"

"I told you to get a fucking surveyor, Juniper," he said, curling his fist into her hair and pulling, angling her head back as he kissed her deeper. "Did you think about doing that?"

"You pay for it," she spit, then launched herself up on her toes and kissed him again.

He picked her up, just a couple of inches off the ground, and walked them both backward into the house. He slammed the door behind them, grabbed the bag of hamburgers from her hands and flung them down onto the couch.

Then he set her back down, staring down into her eyes. "Too far," he said. "You went too far."

"I saved your ass, Chance."

"Well, thank you for not leaving me out there to get eaten by coyotes, what a fantastic example of your humanitarianism. You truly are the best of us, Juniper."

"Screw you," she said.

"I'd rather screw *you*," he said.

And he grabbed the top button on that EMT uniform and flipped it open.

Then he did the next button, and the next, revealing golden-brown curves that made his mouth water.

"You always knew it would end here, didn't you?" he asked.

"You're such a bastard," she said, reaching out, her hands working the buckle on his belt. She undid the snap on his jeans, then reached inside, and the breath hissed through his teeth that she curled her fingers around his cock, squeezing him tight.

"Such a bastard," she said, but this time the words had no heat.

And her mouth dropped open, a small whimper escaping. She licked her lips, then looked up at him. "You're so big," she said.

And that did it. That absolutely undid him. Juniper looking at him and talking about his size, the venom gone from her voice... There were spare few novelties left in the world for him.

He had experienced loss, grief, he'd had well more than his share of sex, but this... This was a truly new experience.

And he hated that he was betraying to her that he was

so damned basic. That all it took to get his engine revved was for a woman to say something like that.

Not a *woman. Her.*

It's the fact that it's her.

"And you are the sexiest little demon I've ever seen," he said. "Shame about your personality."

"Shame about yours," she said, still gripping him tight and running her hand up and down his aching shaft.

"Let's get you out of this," he said, undoing the rest of the buttons on her top and flinging it down to the ground.

Her bra was simple, black, but displayed her glorious cleavage to perfection.

He lowered his head, licking the plump skin there, tugging down one side of her bra and revealing her nipple, sucking it deep into his mouth until her head fell back and she gasped.

She held on to his head as he sucked, teased her. With his other hand, he smoothed down her back, moving to grab her ass, squeezing her as he continued to tease her.

He could feel her begin to tremble. Her whole body on a razor's edge.

"You're gonna call my name so many times that neither of us will ever forget it," he said against her mouth.

"I'll make sure to spell mine," she said. "That way it gets in there good."

He did away with the matching navy pants she was wearing, and with the bulky uniform dispensed with, he could see that she was all woman, all curves.

Her underwear did not match her bra, and there was something about that that got him hot.

This wasn't a woman who had been expecting to have sex.

Black bra, white panties with little red roses.

"Cute," he said. "I didn't take you for a delicate little flowers kind of girl."

"It's not that deep. I bought a package, white, beige and floral."

"You are something else," he said.

"Don't fall in love with me."

He laughed. And kissed her again. "No worries," he said. "I'm not in any danger. We're going to have a lot of fun, though."

And he hauled her up off the ground again, this time lifting her completely so that she could wrap her legs around his waist.

While he walked her back to her bedroom, she grabbed the back of his shirt and tugged it up over his head. He let go of her with one arm, then the other, so that she could free the entire garment. Then she cast it onto the ground. She put her hands on the center of his chest, running her fingers down his body.

"It is such a nice chest," she said.

"I like yours too." He reached around and unhooked her bra, freeing her breasts and revealing them to his gaze. "Fuck," he said. "You're so damn sexy."

"Good," she said, and she had that same wicked smile on her face that he felt on his own when she'd said he was so big.

There was just something about it. Knowing that the person who hated you more than anything was completely spellbound by your body. Couldn't do anything to fight this. Because, dammit, if they could, they would. She had done something that was unforgivable. But he didn't like her anyway.

Sure, for a minute, he thought he did. But then he remembered himself. And it had been different. It was all different.

And he wasn't worried about it.

He was going to have her.

He was going to have his way with her until neither of them could walk.

He flung her down onto the bed, then kicked off his boots and took the rest of his clothes off along with it.

Her eyes went round. She gripped the edges of her underwear, and she made them down her legs, leaving her spread out and naked for him on the bed.

He growled and came down over her. "Little witch."

"Asshole," she said, putting her hand on his face.

And then he kissed her. With all the pent-up hunger inside of him. And this wasn't as angry as the rest. Because he was past anger now. All the fire in his blood was desire. And he was desperate for wanting her. She sighed and arched against him, her legs falling open, and he put his hands between her thighs, stroking the wet seam of her body, moving his thumb in a circle over that sensitized bud there.

And then he pushed a finger into her, then another, working her as he kissed her. Until he couldn't take it anymore.

He didn't take a slow, leisurely trip down her body. He just moved quickly, dragging her hips up to his face and licking her deep, making her body arch up off the bed. "Yes," he said, lapping at her with all the need inside of him.

He tasted her, licked her, sucked her until she was sobbing, until she was begging. He pushed two fingers inside of her and stroked her until she whimpered. He added a third slowly and she started to shake, her thigh muscles trembling as he sucked her deep into his mouth while pushing deep.

And she broke. She grabbed hold of his hair, pulling hard as her internal muscles pulsed around his fingers. As her release ripped through her, seemingly going on and on.

He was so hard he could scarcely stand it.

He had never believed in blue balls before, but he did now.

If he didn't have her, he was going to combust. Or something was going to fall off. And he didn't want that.

"Please tell me you have some condoms," he said. "I don't have any of my shit."

"I do," she said.

She hurried off the bed and into the bathroom, and he heard her rummaging around. It took her a minute, but she finally returned with a strip of protection.

"It's been a while," she said. "I don't really need to just keep them by the bed."

"I'm not judging either way. I'm just glad that you have them."

It hadn't been a while for him. Or maybe it had. Maybe it had been forever. Maybe this was the first time. Maybe this was the only thing that mattered.

He wasn't sure anymore. Everything was mixed up and jumbled up inside of his head, and the only thing that really made sense was her.

She went back down onto the bed, and he took one of her arms and pinned it up over her head. Then he did the same with the second, the pose trapping her beneath him and raising her breasts up like an offering. He lowered his head to them again, sucked one briefly into his mouth, then another.

He positioned himself at the entrance of her body, and she was so tight and wet he groaned.

"Please," she begged. "Chance."

"Say it again."

"Please, Chance," she said.

And he thrust home. She arched up off the bed, a rough cry rising in her throat. And she met his every stroke, thrust for thrust.

Her nails digging into his skin as he drove them both to the edge of sanity.

And then when he couldn't hold on anymore, he pressed his face into her neck and bit her.

And that was when he felt her lose her grip.

Her climax took him off guard, the force of it tearing through him like a wildfire. Her internal muscles clenched tight around his cock, and he lost it completely.

He moved his hand down to her hips, gripped her tightly as he thrust into her three more times, hard and fast, before spilling himself.

"Juniper," he said, unable to hold back the exultation of her name. Unable to do anything but simply… Praise her.

He lay down beside her, his chest pitching with the effort of breathing.

"Hell," he said.

"I can't move," she said. "You killed me."

And then she laughed.

"What?"

"My sister said you would kill me."

"Your fucking sister knows?"

"My fucking sister *saw you*," she said. "I ended up having to tell her."

"You owe me," he said.

"I'm… I what?"

"I'm not kidding. You crossed the line."

"We have to talk about this right now. Have you ever heard of an afterglow?"

"I don't think you get an afterglow with hate sex," he said.

"Was it hate sex? Or was it just undeniable sex?"

"A good question," he said. Because he had to wonder if maybe it was more undeniable than he would like. He had to wonder if maybe they'd been headed this direction the whole time. So maybe not as directly, all things considered.

"In what way do I owe you?"

"You're going to have to come work for me."

"I am not working for Carsons," she said.

"You have no choice. You slept with me. You lied to me. And there are quite a few things I could do with that."

"Are you… Blackmailing me?"

He hadn't really intended to. And he didn't quite know what all was going on inside of him just at the moment.

But it seemed reasonable. It seemed reasonable, the idea that he would bring her to Carson land and force her to do the same amount of labor that he'd done for her.

Or maybe it's not that at all. Maybe you're just trying to get your own back because you spilled your guts about Sophie and now she knows.

"I'm not working for you."

"I could probably call the police, Juniper."

"And tell them what? You had amnesia and I made you work for me? Yeah. I'm sure that Deputy Morton would be very interested in that. She is my friend, by the way."

"Then maybe your grandfather would be interested to know that you have a hard time keeping your hands off me."

"You… You're horrible," she said. "I cannot believe that I just did that with you."

"You can't?"

Their eyes met, and she looked away.

"Maybe you should just do it because you feel bad."

"I will never feel bad for you. I will never feel bad for any Carson."

"Let me know when you have a day off coming up," he said.

She rolled out of bed and stepped away from him, and he watched the gentle jiggle and that rounded curve of her ass as she stalked into the bathroom.

She was soft. Curvy. He liked it.

And he hadn't had sex with her to enact any kind of revenge. It was just that it was… Convenient.

She came back in a moment later, fully dressed. "How about this?" she said. "I'll come work for you. I will debase myself as your farm girl. But in the end, you agree to look into what happened between our great-great-grandfathers. And into the way the card game happened. If your family has a record…"

"I'm sorry, I don't think you're in a position to negotiate," he said.

"Maybe not," she said.

And he realized that they were at the end of everything. Of common sense, of dignity. He had been filled with an insane amount of rage, and rightly so. But it had led here. And now he was trying to use it against her. And maybe they did need to settle it, once and for all. But his pride wouldn't allow him to do it for nothing.

"All right, Juniper Sohappy, you have yourself a deal."

"You know I don't have time to come work for you."

"I know. Maybe use some vacation time."

"You…"

"You'll get your evidence, if it exists."

"Good," she said.

"Get time off."

"Get out of my house," she said.

"Now… I'm going to need a ride," he said.

She reached over to the nightstand, grabbed her keys and threw them at him. "I'll have my sister drive me, and I'll pick up the truck tomorrow when I report for work."

"Well, then. See you bright and early."

And he began to collect his clothes, and he had a feeling it was going to take a hell of a long time to sort through everything that had happened over the last few days.

Chapter 7

She had to submit for time off and she was furious about it. But that was a good thing, because when she wasn't furious she felt overcome by the memories of what it had been like to be in bed with Chance.

The way that he had touched her, the way that he had... The way that he had filled her.

And that bastard had gone ahead and proved her own fantasies were wrong. Oh, it had been intense. It had been angry. But he carried her right to bed, and there was something in that, when her previous, shame-filled fantasies had always been centered around them not making it to a bed.

No, it infuriated her.

And also left her hot and bothered in a way that...

Sex had never been like that for her.

Forget multiorgasmic, she had never even been consistently orgasmic. And even then, often it had felt muted.

She had always been more concerned about how she looked, the way that she was reacting. All these little things that really shouldn't matter, but did.

And she found herself stalking over to Shelby's house, because she was going to have to explain her absence. And she... Well, she would rather have Shelby be the keeper of the information, and not her parents. And definitely not her grandparents.

"Still alive, I see," Shelby said.

She laughed bitterly. "Oh yes. But he knows."

"Oh no," Shelby said. "What happened?"

And she felt... She didn't want to talk about sleeping with him.

Because what did it say about her? She had been... She had been angry and so turned on when they had been fighting. She should've resisted him, but it had never even entered her mind to do that. She had just... She had just wanted him. And what kind of insanity was that? Just wanting a man who so clearly hated her. The malice in his eyes as he had advanced on her...

But then he'd kissed her. And gradually the quality of the heat between them had changed.

Gradually it had become about something else.

And by the time he had buried his head between her legs and...

Well, she could honestly say no man had ever done that quite like that before.

He was a beast.

And she had... She had loved it. She had always sort of considered herself practical about sex. Not that she would say she wasn't sexual. She got the urge like anyone else. Just that it wasn't a driving factor in her life, or anything she needed all that frequently.

But after all that with him, she was ruminating on it quite a bit more than she would like to admit.

"Well, I am being blackmailed," she said.

Shelby sputtered over her coffee. "You're being blackmailed."

"I guess that's a little bit dramatic. But he is making me work for him. Tit for tat."

"Well," Shelby said. "All things considered... It could be worse."

"Don't tell me you're taking his side."

"There's not really a side here. You play games with dangerous predators and you win... Well, you win whatever the predator is going to do."

"You don't know anything about this. You don't know anything about predators."

She laughed. "Maybe not. But I'm smart enough to know I wouldn't screw around with one of the Carsons."

"Right. Well. So I'm just imagining the fact that your cheeks get pink when Kit Carson goes by?"

She felt guilty. She really did. Because Kit Carson was a closed subject, and Juniper knew it, and yet here she was, talking about him.

"There's nothing between me and Kit Carson," Shelby said.

"Doesn't mean you don't look at him."

"I'm not dead," Shelby said. "That's the thing."

And she knew that she was dancing dangerously close to things that she ought not to touch.

"Fine. I just wanted to let you know, in case anyone asked. I am doing some work on a friend's ranch."

"A friend."

"Well." She sighed. "And I'll get Chuck's clothes back for you."

"Thanks," Shelby said. "I probably shouldn't hold on to them."

"You love him," Juniper said.

"I do," Shelby agreed. "I do love him, but I think that that isn't… Isn't helping. It doesn't do anything. It doesn't bring him back." She shook her head. "Any more than hanging on to his clothes or his pocket knives or… Or anything."

"It doesn't make it go away," Juniper said.

"No," Shelby said. "It doesn't. It would give me more space, though."

"Well, I guess at a certain point you'll decide what you need more. His things or space."

"True," Shelby said. "Right now… I don't really need the space. You be careful."

"What do you mean? You keep acting like Chance is dangerous. We may not like each other, we may be involved in a feud, but…"

"No, the problem is I think you do like him. I think you always have. You have a conflict with him. But if you didn't…"

"It doesn't matter. I do. Grandpa hated Chance's grandfather. Until Chance makes it right, what Grandpa feels like…"

"Why is it up to Chance to make it right? And why is it up to you to fix it? Your great-great-grandfather caused all this bullshit."

"It was Chance Carson's great-great-grandfather and…"

"Hey, maybe he cheated him. Maybe he took advantage. What happened happened."

"That's easy for you to say, Shelby. This isn't up to you."

"Why is it up to you?"

She nearly exploded. "Because I promised. I promised

him. And I said it would be easy and I could do it. I have to be the one because there isn't another one."

Shelby looked like she pitied her then, and Juniper could hardly stand it. "If our great-great-grandfather couldn't fix it. Or our great-grandfather. Or our grandfather. Or our father… Why do you think you can?"

Because then she'd know. She was right.

She'd done right.

"Because," she said, knowing she sounded frustrated and childish. "Because somewhere, deep down, I kind of assume he *does* care about what's right."

"I see. And it's not just about the Carsons, it's about him. That's what it always comes back to. The way the two of you fight about this."

"It does not always come back to the two of us."

"It does, Juniper. It always has. Like I said, what if there was no feud? How would you feel then?"

"It doesn't matter."

"You kissed him."

"Well, yes," she said, her cheeks going hot.

"And?"

"It doesn't matter. Because he is who he is, and I'm who I am. And all that matters is that this might finally settle things between us. He agreed to get the property assessed. Based on old records…"

"You don't have the money for that."

"He does. He agreed to pay."

Shelby arched a brow and crossed her arms. "I'm worried what that's gonna cost you."

"Again, you're acting like…"

"It's your emotions, Juniper. I am worried about your emotions. I am worried that you have feelings for this man. And if you spend more time with him, something is going to happen and..."

Juniper's face went hot.

Shelby's eyes narrowed. "Something already did. You're not telling me something."

"It doesn't matter."

And then her sister's eyes widened. Comically. "You *slept with him*."

"Maybe. Well, there was no sleep. He stormed out after."

"Oh."

And suddenly, Shelby took on the manner of an indecisive squirrel. Her body jerked one way, then another, and Juniper wondered what the hell was happening with her sister.

"What?"

"I'm trying to decide something."

"What are you trying to decide?"

"I'm trying to decide if I want to know the details."

"Why?"

"Because I would be lying if I said that I wasn't curious about...well. There are a lot of Carson men."

Juniper narrowed her eyes. "Kit. You are curious about Kit. And you think hearing about his brother will give you insight."

"Why are you fixated on Kit?"

"Because you're fixated on Kit. I'm not an idiot. He has made you into a little bit of a stuttering mess since you were sixteen."

Her sister's face flushed, but this time it was with anger. "I was with Chuck when I was sixteen. The fact that I got embarrassed around an inarguably cute boy is not an indicator of anything."

Except she thought it probably was. She thought it always had been.

But there was no having the discussion. And maybe there was really no point. Juniper had never been very good at letting things go. The entire incident with Chance being a prime example of that.

"Tell me you've never had a sex dream about him."

"Get out of my house," Shelby said, only a little bit kidding.

"It's really big," Juniper said.

Shelby bit her lip. "Thank God."

"Right?"

There would've been nothing sadder. Nothing sadder at all than evidence that all those tall, handsome men were over there and they were... Lacking.

But she could say with certainty, Chance was not lacking at all.

"It's just good to know," Shelby said pragmatically. "That there are some things in the universe that make sense."

"I guess. Though, if I hadn't made a very bad choice and slept with a Carson, I might've found it amusing if they had all been cursed with teeny-weenies."

"Yeah. But a handsome man is a handsome man. And a waste of all that...would be a waste of all that. Feud or not."

"Yeah. Fair," she said.

"I'll cover for you."

"Thank you."

"Don't have sex with him again."

"I won't. It was a onetime thing. The truth is, it had been... Brewing. And the whole explosion when he got his memory back was the tipping point. And I don't think it's going to combust like that again."

"It better not. Protect yourself."

"Aye, aye, captain."

And as she left her sister's house, she purposed in her mind to let go of fantasies of Chance. She purposed in her mind to rid herself of impure thoughts entirely.

She was going to work. She was going to keep the goal in mind.

With any luck, this feud would finally be over. Or maybe it would still simmer beneath the surface, but she would be proved right.

And as far as she was concerned, Chance Carson could die mad.

Chapter 8

"I don't see any cattle."

That was Chance's greeting when he got back to Evergreen Ranch.

"Well, that's because I didn't go get them," Chance said. "Where the hell is my horse, by the way?"

"Hell if I know," Kit said. "Keep track of your shit."

"Yeah, I don't know," Jace said.

"Is she here?"

"Why don't you know?" Boone asked.

Well, he was going to enjoy *this*.

"I don't know," he said, "because I have had amnesia."

His brothers exchanged a glance. Seated around the table outside one of the barns, where they all took their lunch, they had been eating sandwiches and planning the day when Chance showed up.

He had stopped off at his cabin and taken a very long shower.

Put on some of his own clothes that actually fit, and tried to make absolutely certain that he had his thoughts together.

"You do not have amnesia," Boone said. "That is idiotic. That's like the time we told Kit that Dad was going to sell him to a traveling band to play the washboard and set him out at the edge of the property at ten p.m. He believed it because he was eight. We're not eight."

"I did," he said. "I spent days not knowing who I was, and I don't know what happened to my horse."

His brothers looked at each other. "Seriously," Boone said.

"Seriously. I don't know what happened to my horse, who I can only assume ran back here. But I'm a little concerned about her."

"Well. I don't know. It's entirely possible one of the hands did something with her."

"Great," he said. "Not only did you assholes never try to contact me, and get concerned about me, you don't know where my horse is."

Flint frowned. "Where *have* you been?"

"It's a long story," he said. "However, it ends with the fact that Juniper Sohappy is going to be working here. She owes me."

"Well, I need to hear the long story," Kit said, kicking back in his chair. "Because you're claiming to have been struck down with amnesia and now I hear Juniper Sohappy is involved. So it is story fuckin' time."

This was the part he was looking forward to less.

"Fine. She found me, she rescued me. But I didn't remember who I was. And she told me that I was her ranch hand."

Boone just about fell out of his chair. Kit was laughing so hard that Chance thought he might choke, while Jace was shaking his head, his eyes wide. "Well, damn," Jace said.

"Yeah. So."

He noticed they were happy to believe the amnesia thing now.

"I knew she hated you," Boone said, wiping tears off his face, "but that is really something. So she held you hostage all this time?"

"Yeah. Torture every hour."

"Really." Boone and Flint looked at each other.

"Shut the fuck up," Chance said. But he couldn't even really be mad, because they were right.

He had in fact slept with her. That was in fact a thing that had happened.

"We'll behave ourselves," Flint said. "When she gets here. Unless you don't want us to. Which would be fair."

"She and I have an agreement."

He wasn't going to get into the whole thing with the card game and looking for evidence that may not exist.

Because then they really would ask what the hell he was doing.

Because why he had agreed to meet any of her demands, he really couldn't explain. She didn't deserve it. That was the thing. That was the bottom line. She didn't have any kind of high ground. She didn't have any kind of upper hand. It made no earthly sense that he was giving it to her.

"I'll see you guys around. I'll be devising torture for Juniper."

"Return torture," Boone said. "My favorite."

"You're a dick," Chance said as he walked away.

And right when he got to the main through road for the barn, Juniper pulled in.

"Howdy," he said when she rolled her window down. "Welcome to Evergreen Ranch."

"Thanks," she responded.

"You can park over this way."

Thankfully his brothers had cleared out by the time he got to the barn. He didn't want to deal with them on top of having to deal with her.

"All the trainees start here," he said.

She rolled her eyes, then rolled the window of the truck up. She killed the engine and got out, and his gut went tight at the sight of her.

She was wearing a tight black tank top and a pair of formfitting jeans.

Much more flattering than the EMT uniform.

And he knew what her body looked like underneath all that now.

Knew that the promise of the spark that had burned between them all this time was barely even a preview of what it could be like between them.

He was a lot taller than her, nearly a whole foot, he reckoned. And yet they had fit together perfectly.

And he was trying to keep his mind on the task at hand, and not on her, but it was difficult. Because last night was still fresh in his mind.

"I'm investigating to see if my horse actually made it back," he said.

"Oh," she said. "I didn't know you fell off your horse."

"I did. I can't remember quite what happened. Something. Something must've spooked her. She's a good mount, and normally steady, but..."

They went into the barn and went down the stalls. Most

of them were empty, because his brothers had taken their horses out for the day, but there she was.

"Geneva, you turncoat," he said. "You left me to die."

"Now, you leave her alone," Juniper said. "I think she's a discerning woman."

"She's not discerning of shit," Chance said, shaking his head. "She's a termite is what she is."

"I won't hear a word said against her."

"You can choose any of the horses that are left," he said. "Lefty is pretty good. Cheech has a bad temper."

"Well, so do I. I guess I'll settle for Cheech."

She did so, and while they were getting ready, she ran her hands over the horse lovingly. "Ex-rodeo horses?"

"For the most part. Not all."

"I never did know how I felt about the rodeo."

"Believe me when I tell you, nobody cares more about their animals than the people who breed them for those events. They're worth more than the cowboys. Trust me."

"I guess I can understand that. In the sense that I know a lot of people don't get that cattle ranchers care about cows more than just about anybody."

"Damn straight," he said. "We're connected to the way everything in the world works. To the way it's fueled. Life, death and the cost of all of it."

"I never would've thought we have something in common."

"Well, there you go, we have a couple things in common. Caring about our animals, and a mutual enjoyment of having sex with each other."

She frowned deeply. "How do you know I enjoyed it?"

"Please. You were basically putty."

"Maybe I'm easy," she said.

"Somehow, I don't think so. Somehow, I think you're

a little bit of a tough nut, Juniper Sohappy. And I think I cracked you."

"Please. Men really do think highly of themselves."

"I think pretty highly of you too."

"So highly that you're forcing me to do manual labor for you?"

"Payback for the work I did for you."

"Fine," she said. "That's fair enough."

"Yeah. Sometimes I am. And if you would stop being mad at me for the sake of it, you might see that."

He got on his horse, and she mounted behind him, and the two of them took off, with him leading the way.

They walked the horses down over a bare rocky ridge that ran along the river.

This was high desert.

The rocks ran the gamut from pale tan to adobe red.

The sagebrush that was scattered throughout the landscape was scrubby and vile. The deer liked to eat it, but it gave them a particular flavor that Chance had never been fond of.

Because of course he actually did know the taste of venison, the taste of elk and the different regions where they tasted different, because of what they ate.

Because now he understood himself, and his memories, and it was no longer a mystery.

He felt a strange… A strange stab of envy for the man he had been just two days ago who hadn't known a damn thing. Who had been strangely excited by the things that he knew, and unencumbered by… Everything. The only thing he had known for sure was Juniper.

And that had been interesting.

To say the least.

Great. He missed being a simpleton. That was really something.

He shook his head.

"There's a whole bunch of lava rock down in here, and you can find agates," he said. "Me and my brothers used to spend hours down here hunting rocks. It was our favorite spot to go."

"I can imagine you running wild around here. And getting into all kinds of scrapes," she said.

"Oh hell, yeah. One time Boone got bitten by a rattlesnake."

"Really?"

"Yeah. Oh man, he held off on telling Mom and Dad as long as possible, because he was sure that he was going to get his hide tanned. And he was right. Dad was so pissed off."

"He was mad that Boone got bitten by a rattlesnake. At *Boone*."

"Yeah. We weren't watching. We weren't being responsible. We knew better."

"Still, that seems a little odd."

"It's just that they had so much to worry about, what with…"

He cut himself off. Because he didn't really intend to talk about Sophie.

He never did. It was just that he had already told her, in a roundabout way. And that was the problem.

He had already explained certain aspects of that part of his past, even without the details.

And it had made him feel freer now.

"Well, at the time my parents had a lot on their plate."

"Right. Well, I never got bitten by a snake. But Shelby

and I used to run all over the ranch too. It's funny, how we didn't really run into each other."

"You stay to your side, we stay to ours. It stands to reason."

"Yeah." She chewed her bottom lip. "My grandfather really hated yours."

"A lot of people did," Chance said. "He was a difficult bastard. It doesn't surprise me that your grandfather hated him. I'm not sure that any of us were ever especially fond."

"Really?"

He shook his head. "Yeah. I don't know. To hear my dad tell it, he was mean. Mean as a snake."

"That isn't how I imagined you would feel. And if that's true…why do you care so much about the land? I know why I do. I love my grandfather, what matters to him matters to me."

"Because we're not carrying this on for him," Chance said. "We're carrying it on for us. To be more, bigger, better than the name he established for us. To be stewards of the land and everything that inhabits it." He grinned. "To get rich."

"Ha!" She belted that laugh and it echoed around them.

"Hey, in my estimation, my grandfather did one valuable thing. He had my father. And whatever his father was like, I don't know, but it's because of them that we are here. My mom and dad… They're good parents. Getting mad about rattlesnakes notwithstanding. They love us."

"Yeah. So do mine. We just want different things. We care about different things."

"You care about the ranch," he said.

"Yes," she said. "Just about to the exclusion of everything else, if I'm honest."

"Why do you care about it so much?"

"I remember once in school I was doing a group project, and this kid got mad at me for having an opinion. And he told me to go back to where I belong. You know, my country." She held her arm out in front of her, showing her brown skin. "And I didn't know what to say at the time. All these things stuck in my throat, chief of which were how stupid he was. But… I realize that the ranch was where I was from. It rooted me. Grounded me. And even when people were ignorant or assholes or whatever… They can't take that from me. I belong here. I love it here."

Chance's stomach turned. "You might've told him to go back to where he came from."

She laughed. "Yeah. I thought about it later. Unfortunately, at the time I was just… Shocked. And sad. But the truth is, even though I didn't give him the thousand comebacks that I have inside of me now, I found my sense of resolve that day."

"I'm sorry that happened to you."

"Don't you think there's a little bit of that in this whole dispute?"

He stopped his horse and turned to face her. "Not for me."

"With our grandparents."

He looked surprised. "I don't… Probably. Probably. I can't say no."

"I think your grandfather, your great-grandfather, thought they deserved it more. Because they think they're more important."

"I'm sorry," he said. "It never occurred to me."

"Why would it?"

The simple question was a stinging indictment.

"Look, this is dumb. Why don't we figure out how to share?"

"No," she said. "I want to know. I really want to know. If you have paperwork that says anything about the ownership transfer, I want to see it. If you have family history. I don't want you to give me something because you feel guilty. And if…if he lost it fairly, if there's a way to know that…" She sucked in a breath. "I'll buy it back."

"You don't have the money," he said pointedly, and he saw her flinch as he did.

"I know. But I'll figure it out."

"What if there are no answers, anywhere?"

"There have to be some," she said. "Talking helps."

"Usually we just end up yelling."

"Yeah, I guess this is a step toward being functional adults. What a novel concept."

"We behaved like adults the other night," he pointed out.

And he regretted that, because he didn't need to bring it up. It just made it far too easy to imagine everything that had passed between them. And how damned good it was.

"Right," she said. "Except the aftermath."

"You have to admit," he said, because the reminder of her behavior brought him right back to reality, if nothing else would, "that what you did was…"

"All right. Lying to you wasn't my best move. But honestly, I couldn't tell you everything. You're not supposed to do that, because of shock. I needed you to have realizations on your own. Also, I sat up with you all night, I made sure that you were okay. I didn't leave you out in the middle of that field."

"I know," he said.

"What bothers you the most? That you did some labor for free? Or that I had to take care of you? Because I think maybe that's part of the problem. That and the fact that maybe you don't hate me."

"If I don't hate you, then you really don't hate me," he said.

"Well, I had to see you as a human being for a few days."

"Must've been a trial," he said.

"No. It wasn't. That's the problem."

"Well, I didn't know who you were."

"I wanted you to understand," she said. "I wanted you to understand why it was important. Not with all of what you think you know sitting there in your head. So I'm sorry if I made a weird choice. I'm sorry if I made a bad choice. But the land means the world to me. My grandfather means the world to me."

"And what would your grandfather say if he knew about us?"

"There's not an us," she said.

"I meant the fucking, Juniper, but I was trying to be a gentleman."

"He'd die," Juniper said, looking at him straight on. "Then and there. My grandfather will not be knowing about us. Not ever. He can't. I've given up too much to have a romp in the sack ruin my relationship with him."

"A romp in the sack? Wow."

"Oh, don't give me that, it's not like sex is sacred to you."

He looked at her long and hard, and what he hated most was that the word she'd used just now felt more right for this thing between them than any other he could think of.

He said nothing. He just snorted. "Well, I'm not in any hurry to spread it around."

"My sister knows," Juniper said. "But I can't keep anything from her. It doesn't work."

"My brothers know too, but it's not because they're insightful, it's just because they're assholes, and I didn't tell them anything. But they're going to think what they think no matter what. And they've always thought that…"

"They've always thought what?"

Sacred.

No, just sex. And sex he'd wanted for a long time, in fact. Maybe that was why it was notable. Maybe that was the only real reason why.

"They've always thought that I wanted you."

"I see," she said. "And are they right?"

"What do you think?"

"What's your favorite spot on the whole ranch?" she asked.

He looked around and pointed down at the watering hole below. "That spot. All the good agates are there. And you can jump right in from those rocks. And the water goes way over your head. You feel like you're never going to touch the bottom. We used to play here all the time."

"It's nice," she said.

"Yeah. That's one of the last memories I have of all of us together. Before Buck…"

"What happened to Buck? I barely remember him, because he's older."

"He had that accident. He… He didn't want to stay after that."

He could never understand his brother's decision to leave.

Buck hadn't been the one drinking. He'd been badly injured all the same.

But it had something to do with his friend's death, he knew that.

But he had never understood what required Buck

to leave home, to leave his entire family when they all would've supported him. But it was like he just didn't want to be here anymore.

And his absence had created some strange, hard feelings around town.

Especially with the family of his friend.

"Yeah. It's been rough without him. But I have a surplus of brothers."

"Well, you were all close."

And he thought about Sophie again, in spite of his best efforts.

"Yeah," he said. "We are close. We don't take family for granted. You can't take family for granted when…"

He stopped talking. And she didn't push him.

"How close are we to the border of your land?"

He knew she would know.

"Not far. Maybe two hundred yards."

"I want you to show me your favorite spot."

"I haven't done any work so far," she pointed out.

And he realized that he'd lost the thread of what today was supposed to be. He was supposed to be punishing her or something. He was supposed to be making her work. And they should've gone the rest of the way along this trail to get to the fence that needed fixing. But they could also do it later. They could do it later and it would be just fine.

But suddenly none of it seemed as important as this.

And it wasn't just because he was attracted to her, though he was. There was something else.

Something about the way the sun glinted off of her hair, and the way she smiled. Or the way she frowned.

There was just something about her.

"Show me," he said.

"Okay," she responded. "If you really want me to."

"I do."

She moved her horse forward, leading the way, jogging the animal down the side of the trail.

He laughed and took off after her. It was an easy ride. Not for beginners. It was for people like them, who knew what they were doing, knew the land and knew how to push the limits.

"You actually ride in the rodeo?" she asked when they were on a flatter part of the trail, moving into the more lush part of the land, pine trees suddenly becoming thicker and more prevalent.

"Yep," he said. "I can't say that I was the best. But I had a good time. Saddle bronc, mostly. That is generally my family's game."

"Oh. Not bulls."

"Boone rode bulls."

"Maybe I should've slept with Boone."

He shot her a look, and she grinned.

"Oh, so it's like that," he said.

"I'm a woman of discerning tastes," she said.

And he didn't think they had ever gone this long without acting like they were going to kill each other. So that was something.

They pushed their way through the trees, and the trail narrowed. "This is out way far away from anywhere my parents ever go to. And my grandpa quit moving through the whole property a long time ago. His mobility just isn't what it used to be. But this was my and Shelby's secret spot. The trees seem to grow over the trail, like a rounded entrance into some kind of enchanted world, and we imagined that if you were a child, that was exactly what you would see."

Especially what two girls would see.

"We always said there were fairies," she said. "There was a movie about that. Fairies in an English garden? And we were obsessed with it. And we used to imagine that they were here. I love this place."

There were purple flowers and ferns growing beneath the trees, and it was just entirely different to the landscape they had just come from.

There was running water nearby, and it took him a while to realize that it was a stream. It probably fed into the larger river that they had just come from.

And at the end of the stream was a little pool. "Not deep enough to jump in," she said. "But perfect for floating. Which is what we used to do."

"It's beautiful," he said.

"This place means so much to me," she said.

Then she got a mischievous glint in her eye, turned around and pulled her shirt up over her head.

She didn't know what she was thinking. Stripping while still on the back of a horse. It was crazy. And she had decided that she wasn't going to touch him again. Because it was foolishness. Absolute lunacy.

Because it wasn't anything that she needed to do, and it was in fact something she absolutely shouldn't do.

But then, she didn't know why they were out spending time together. Riding around their favorite childhood spots rather than working or sniping.

And then she'd done that.

Oh well. She was committed now. She dismounted, unhooked her bra and threw it down where the shirt was. Then she stripped off the rest of the way and slipped into the translucent green water. It was like an emerald here under the trees, and the still pool with its large rounded stones at the bottom had always ignited her imagination. Had always made her feel like she was part of something wonderful. Part of something bigger than herself.

Part of something magic.

Her grandmother believed so strongly that there were things in the world that no one could understand. That nature itself had breath, and it was constantly speaking to them, flowing through them.

And it was here that Juniper could feel that for herself. Here that she felt touched in a spiritual way. And she had brought Chance to this spot. She really didn't know what she'd been thinking.

She felt vulnerable, exposed, and it wasn't just because she was naked.

"Join me?" she asked.

He got off his horse and pulled his shirt up over his head, revealing that delicious body to her gaze.

How could she ever go back? To hating him. She wanted to. It was simple.

Even just admiring his body, she had hated him.

But now he had touched her. And he was a generous lover, she couldn't overlook that. And what it said about him.

He wasn't a man who just took. He was a man who gave with talented fingers and a wicked tongue. He was a man who seemed to derive as much pleasure from hers as he did from his own.

That's just sex. It has nothing to do with the content of his character.

Well, that was a good reminder. But it wasn't doing much to penetrate her thinking right now.

He was completely naked in a moment, and then he joined her in the pool, his eyes intent on hers.

"Normally, I wouldn't be too thrilled about being in a pool of cold water in front of a beautiful woman. But thankfully, your beauty far outweighs the cold."

"Well. That is… Bizarrely flattering," she said.

"In the absence of anything else, always take bizarrely flattering."

"I'm not sure what to make of this," she said. "Given that you're my mortal enemy and all."

"Yeah, why me specifically?"

She knew the answer to that question. Because she was supposed to hate the Carsons, and from the first moment she had ever seen Chance Carson, hate was not the dominant emotion. She had been fascinated by him. She had been completely and utterly transfixed from day one, and there was something about the directive given to her by her grandfather, and that feeling that had made her feel violently angry with him in that first moment. When she had been eight and he was ten.

She remembered it so clearly. It may not make sense. And it may not be fair, but it was the truth.

She had liked him, and she wasn't allowed to. And she loved her grandfather more than she loved any other person on earth, and wanting a Carson was a violation of their family. Of their name.

Of all the promises she'd made to be worthy of being the one who took over the family legacy.

So she had done her best to turn that all into anger. She had done her best to turn it all into outrage.

But it hadn't worked. At least, not consistently.

And here she was. Naked in the water with him again.

"Chance…"

"You're beautiful," he said, closing the distance between them. And he kissed her lips, the heat of his body cutting through the icy water and making her tremble.

He wrapped his strong arms around her, crushing her breasts to his chest. "Dangerous," he gritted against her mouth.

"Why?"

"I don't have a condom."

"I'm on the pill," she said. "As long as you're... As long as you're good."

He nodded. "Yeah."

"Me too."

The fact of the matter was, she always doubled up on her protection. This felt alarming and like a step into something new. But she wanted him. And she didn't want to wait for him. Because if they waited, they might come to their senses. If they waited, then they might realize that they shouldn't do this.

But she didn't want that realization. She wanted to feel him against her. Inside of her. She wanted to kiss him until neither of them could breathe. She wanted to chase down her pleasure with him.

Only him.

"I always use..."

"Me too," she said.

He understood. He didn't say anything, but he understood. That she'd never let a man do this before. And she felt breathless with the anticipation of it.

She waited for him to shift their positions and surge inside of her, but he didn't. Instead, he angled his head and kissed her. It was maddeningly, achingly slow, something completely different to the way they had come together in anger only recently. It was painful, almost. The care that he took with each corner of her lips. To make sure he kissed every inch. And then he began to look into her. Slowly. She moaned as he took the kiss deeper and deeper. As the desire between them became a burgeoning flame, and he kept it banked. It was the control. The absolute, maddening control that got her.

Because she felt like she was going to vibrate out of her skin, and he seemed to enjoy it. Didn't seem bothered. Not in the least.

His big hands roamed over her body, all of her curves, and he made them feel beautiful. Made them feel precious. She wasn't toned. Wasn't insanely physically fit, but she liked the way that it felt when he squeezed her tight; he made her softness feel sexy, and it was a novelty.

It was more than a novelty. She couldn't pretend that's all it was. Some simple fascination and nothing more. No. It was everything.

This moment was everything.

She moved her hands down his chest, his damp chest hair. He was just really beautiful.

And she was going to take this moment and drink it all in. Drink him in, because she didn't know if it would ever happen again. She didn't know if she would come to her senses. She should… Go now. She should come to her senses and put a stop to all of this. But she really didn't want to.

No. She wanted to savor it. To live in it.

And so she would. Now. Because now they were past the point of no return. Now there was no going back.

It didn't matter what anyone would think. Because it was only the two of them, here in the fairy grove, here in this place that was the closest she had ever gotten to showing any other person the deepest part of her heart.

She wondered if he realized. She wondered if he knew.

She watched as her fingertips skimmed over his ab muscles, over the ridges and dips and hollows in those beautiful, corded muscles.

He was hard. Solid from all the work that he did. And she loved the contrast between their bodies.

Loved that he was masculine to her feminine. And she couldn't recall ever having luxuriated in that before.

She didn't think about her femininity much. It didn't matter to her.

He deepened the kiss, pulling her up against him, and she parted her thighs, wrapping them around his waist and moving her hips restlessly against him, trying to do something to soothe the ache there.

"Be patient," he said, nipping her lip.

"No," she said. "I'm not patient. I want you."

"Say my name."

And she realized that if there was ever a taboo fantasy, for her, this was it. It had been.

"I want you, Chance Carson."

It couldn't be any more blatant if she had asked him to take her on their disputed property.

He shifted their positions, and she felt the blunt head of his arousal pressing up against the entrance to her body. Then he surged inside of her, bare and hot, and she could tell even there in the water like this. She gasped. And his eyes met hers, intense and beautiful. And it terrified her then, how well she knew that face. How close it was to hers, and how much she wanted it to stay that way.

She wasn't really in conflict with herself, not anymore. And she had spent a whole lot of time wanting to see him only so they could fight, while the underlying issue was that she wanted to see him.

But she wasn't lying to herself. Not now. She just wanted to be close to him.

He began to move, his movements hard and intense, his mouth set into a firm line as he began to push them both closer and closer to paradise.

She gripped his shoulders, digging her fingernails into his skin, digging her heels into his thighs as she was pressed firmly against the rock wall of the pool while he took her.

She put her hands on his face and his jaw went slack, his thrusts getting harder, more intense. And all she could do was cling to him. This man. Her storm, her porch, and how could one person be both? It didn't make any sense. And she wished for a moment that she could be the one with amnesia. That she could just forget absolutely everything and have this moment. But he was Chance, and it was complicated. And there was never a scenario where it wouldn't be.

And it was just… It was too much. It was all too much.

And still, her climax rose inside of her. Threatening like an impending storm.

And she knew that if it broke open, it would drown her completely. But she didn't have the strength to deny him. Didn't have the strength to turn back now.

Then he kissed her and began to whisper against her mouth. Dirty promises that shocked her, that amped up her arousal. That made her slicker still and created a delicious friction between their bodies.

She met his every thrust, and when they went over the edge, it was together. And he spilled inside of her on a growl, the unbearable intimacy of the moment creating aftershocks within her.

And he didn't draw away from her when he was finished. Rather, he stayed like that, looking at her, stroking her hair back away from her face.

"I promise I really did mean to give you work to do today."

"Well, now I can't work," she mumbled, resting her forehead on his shoulder. "I don't think I can walk."

He chuckled. "It's touch and go for me too."

Then they both turned their heads at the same moment, looking at the horses, who were standing there placidly. "I can honestly say I haven't performed a live sex show for a pair of horses before," he said.

She laughed. "That kind of surprises me, given that you are a rodeo cowboy. I would've thought there was ample opportunity for you to be playing around with women in various paddocks."

"Hell, no," he said. "I'm a grown-ass adult past the age of having to have sex in strange places. I have a house, I have a bed, I have money for hotel rooms."

"That's awfully mature of you."

"Apparently, I'm not all that mature with you."

"Well, we've known that."

"I guess so." He sighed heavily. "What are we going to do about this?"

She lifted a shoulder. "Burn it out."

"Makes as much sense as anything."

And maybe on the other side of that, none of this would be there. Not the simmering anger or the burning desire. She could handle that. Lord knew she would actually be much happier.

She moved away from him, swimming to the shore and going to gather her clothes.

It was harder this time. Without the cloak of anger to

do away with the tender feelings left behind by the connection created during sex.

Not that she'd ever been superaware of it before. It was worse, she decided—or better, she supposed, depending on how you wanted to look at it, but worse was the best descriptor for when it was with Chance—when it felt amazing. When you had an orgasm together. Because she felt somehow united with him in his pleasure, rather than an observer of his superior, easy-seeming male pleasure, which was how it had always been in the past. She was a participant. And he didn't go to where he couldn't bring her along.

A strange thing that it was with Chance she had found that.

"We ought to maybe go repair a fence or something," he said.

She laughed hollowly, tugging her shirt back over her head and then deciding to go hunt around for her shoes.

He was halfway dressed, and by the time she found her shoes, he had completed the job.

"Yeah. I guess that would be the responsible thing to do. If your version of revenge is just give me multiple orgasms, I have to say, it's not very good revenge."

"My bad," he said.

"Did you just say *my bad*? What year is it, and how old are you?"

He grinned. "Sorry."

She didn't know what to do with him when he was like this either. Good-humored and light and in general enjoyable rather than a big pain in her ass.

It was making compartmentalization nearly impossible. Because he wasn't just a little bit different when they were in the throes of passion.

He was a little bit different all around. Like they were finally able to drop some kind of guard they normally had up when they were with each other. And it made her wonder if he saw her as different too.

"I suppose we should go back and work on the fence now," he said.

"That would have been easier before you killed me," she said.

"Sorry," he responded, grinning. He did not look sorry.

She narrowed her eyes, but she couldn't really be mad. Mostly because the sex had been so good.

"I don't know very much about you," he said.

"You've known me forever."

"Yeah, I guess. But I don't really know much about you."

She realized the same was true of him.

"I don't know. I had a pretty normal childhood."

"Except people were gross to you at school sometimes."

"Yeah. But I don't really know any different than that. I'm tough, I was raised to be tough. We both were. I have both my parents, and I have my grandparents. We have it pretty good."

"But that's not the extent of it, is it? That's just surface stuff."

"It's all I really know about you."

"I want to know about the men in your life," he said.

She frowned. "There aren't any notable men in my life."

"Good," he said, his gaze assessing.

"What do you care?"

"I don't know. But I do."

"What about you? What about the women in your life?"

"I've never been serious about anyone. On purpose. I'm a ho."

"Well, points for honesty," she said, laughing.

"I never wanted anything permanent." He shook his head. "My parents do all right, especially with their life-style. Living out of an RV for part of the year while my dad travels around for the rodeo. But we've made it into our thing. Something we can rally around. I'm like you. I have both my parents… I guess in the end that makes me pretty lucky."

"Who was the little girl?" She shouldn't be asking this, because he had told her when he didn't remember any-thing, and it didn't really feel fair to fling this at him now.

"Yeah. So we came to that part. I'd rather we talk about how I'm probably the best sex you've ever had?"

She rolled her eyes. "Settle down, boy, you're all right."

"Why haven't you found anyone?"

"I told you already."

"That feels like an excuse."

"It's not an excuse. It's my life. What I want and what I dream of doing isn't an incidental. It's everything."

He nodded slowly. "My sister Sophie," he said. "We were close to the same age. She was always very sick. We loved her. I mean, we just doted on her. It was really some-thing. The only girl among all those boys. We couldn't play with her, not the way that we could play with each other, because we had to be really careful with her. But it was all right. Nobody minded. Boone used to carry her around on his shoulders. Buck and Kit made a little cart just for her. With a princess canopy on it. She was in and out of the hospital all the time. And one time… She went and she never came back. And I remember… I remember standing in front of the hospital, in front of the doors, and my dad was grabbing my jacket sleeve and telling me to go inside, telling me to go visit. I couldn't. I couldn't go in.

I just was frozen. Was some kind of terror that I couldn't quite sort out. But it was real, and it had me completely shaken. So I waited in the car, and then my sister died. She never came out of that hospital, and I wasn't brave enough to go in."

She hadn't expected that. She would've thought that anything that serious she would know about. She would've thought that it would've been something that people spoke of.

"Callie came along sometime after. And at first I was afraid. Afraid of what might happen to her. But she was this rowdy, rambunctious delight."

"But you can't replace somebody that you've lost. Not like a straight-out trade."

He shook his head. "No. It couldn't be clearer that they weren't the same person. It's funny, it's been so long. But I remember her on her birthday, and I remember how old she would've been. And you know Callie… She's great. My mother wanted that little girlie girl, though. And Callie isn't that. She ran roughshod with us over everything."

"I'm so sorry," Juniper said, feeling everything inside of her twist and turn onto its head.

She really didn't know him. She had never allowed him to be a full person. Not ever. She had always just seen him as her sworn enemy.

"It's all right. It's been a long time, like I said."

She thought of Shelby, and Chuck. "All time does is change wounds," she said. "Makes them into something different. It doesn't take them away, or turn you back into the person you were before. I know it isn't the same, but my brother-in-law was a lot like a brother to me. He and Shelby were together from the time I was fifteen. And he was always around. I can't remember my life without him. And then he was gone. She's devastated by it. She'll never be the person she was before. He was her other half. And then... I don't know. There's my grief. Which is real, but it isn't hers."

He hung his head. "Sharing grief can be a good thing," he said. "But there is something about it. When someone else feels it also much more than you. When someone else has a claim to the greater grief in the moment. But it doesn't make yours any smaller. It just means you're afraid of hurting them with yours."

"It must've been hard to watch your parents go through that."

"Yeah," he said. "It was. And my brothers. And it's been hard to watch Callie too in some ways. I envy her. Because she was never touched by the grief of it, not personally. But some of it... Did a decent enough job of messing her up. Because you know... You can't replace what you've lost."

She felt bruised for him. Cracked open inside.

"I'm sorry, I really didn't know."

He looked into the distance. Like he might find answers there, or at least find some break in the intensity between them. "It happened before we came here."

"Well, how inconvenient that you're a human being." She tried to say it with a laugh but she couldn't.

He aimed a lopsided grin at her. "I hate to be an inconvenience."

They got back on their horses and began to go back to the ranch. They found that fence line and set about to repairing it. "You're the best I've ever had," she said, because it felt a fair trade after he'd shared this.

"Tell me more," he said.

"I dunno. I thought sex was all right, but not worth jumping up and down over. I haven't always been able to…"

"You mean to tell me you were sleeping with guys who couldn't make you come?"

"Yeah, but I figured women don't really expect to come every time."

"Honey, I expect a woman with me to come every time. More than once."

"Well, so far, promise fulfilled. So, thank you for that."

"You're welcome."

She looked up and smiled at him, and her stomach went a little bit tight. And she didn't even feel like fighting it, or telling herself it shouldn't be like this. That it shouldn't be so easy to like him, or work his dadblasted Carson land.

She liked being beside him.

And she let it be.

When they finished the fence, it was dinnertime, and her hopes of sneaking away were dashed.

Because all of his brothers were sitting outside at a table in front of the barn, with a big dinner spread in front of them.

"What's this?"

"We had dinner sent up from the fancy hotel."

She blinked. She forgot sometimes that the Carsons were rich. Rich enough to cater a random dinner.

"Hey," one of them said. "Come join us."

She looked at Chance. He shrugged. "You're hungry?"

"Obviously."

And her stomach fluttered, because of course she was obviously hungry because they had burned so many calories not just fixing the fence, but with the activities from the swimming hole.

"Well, sit down and eat."

"Did you really order food from a fancy hotel just for a random dinner?"

"Yeah," Boone said. "I'm starving. And pot roast, mashed potatoes and dinner rolls sounded like the ticket to me."

"I guess with this many of you to feed…"

"Oh, my mom gave up being the person that tried that a long time ago. When we were high schoolers she resorted to basically throwing bologna our direction and running the other way."

"That's a lie," Kit said. "She threw bologna packages our direction and said make it your damn self."

Her stomach growled, and she took her seat at the table, Chance seated alongside her, his thigh touching hers.

The brothers were loud and boisterous, and she hadn't actually spent time with them in a group since school. Even then, it had been more being adjacent to them than actually being in the middle of them.

They were a lot. A lot of personality, a lot of tall, handsome cowboy.

And she couldn't pretend anymore that she was immune.

She looked over at Kit. Kit, who she knew Shelby was attracted to. And she couldn't blame her. He was a handsome man, though he didn't do for her what Chance did. That was the thing. Objectively, every single one of the Carson men was stunningly attractive, with mixed and matched features from each other, hair ranging from dark brown to near blond. Brown eyes, hazel eyes, charming smiles, large hands.

But it was more than just finding him handsome. It was… Some kind of chemistry that seemed to defy everything else.

"I don't think I have ever seen you when you weren't scowling," Flint said.

"Well, normally I have something to scowl about if I'm around this many Carsons. But you're feeding me. So I'm not going to be a bitch."

Flint laughed and tossed another dinner roll her way. She caught it and started to slather it with butter.

And when she was done, she realized that she was smiling, and laughing, and eating seconds of berry pie while Jace encouraged her to put all the whipped cream that was left in the can over the top of it.

It was weird to recognize that they were a family. Like hers. That she had more in common with them than not. It had been so easy to make them enemies. To paint them something other, something less, than her own family. But here they were, sitting together, eating together, being immature at each other. It was just so shockingly normal. When they got up from the table, Chance put his hand on her lower back, and she stiffened. He dropped his hand, as if he had sensed the reaction.

They got closer to her truck, and he looked at her. "You want to spend the night?"

She laughed. She couldn't help it.

"What?"

"I haven't been asked for a sleepover in quite some time."

"Do you need to get your mom's permission?"

"They wouldn't give it."

"Then it's best if we don't ask."

"You are going to get me in a lot of trouble," she said.

"You started the trouble."

"Maybe we need to make sure your head injury didn't dramatically change your personality."

"No. Sleeping with you might have done that."

She flushed. "I have to go home and grab some things. I won't be a minute."

"I know. We're neighbors, after all."

Yes. They were neighbors. Feuding ones at that. And she would do well to remember that. Because at the end of the day, no matter how much the Carsons were like the Sohappys, no matter how much she liked him, no matter how much fun it was to kiss him, no matter how exhilarating it was to have him inside of her, her grandfather would never get over the betrayal. And that was something that could simply never happen.

Chapter 9

It had been two weeks of sneaking around with Juniper while she worked his land. And he really enjoyed it. He did.

But he'd been thinking. A lot. About the proposed endgame of all of this. He wasn't angry at her, not anymore. It was impossible to be. But what he wanted was to speak to her grandfather. He had decided that that was what he had to do.

What had become clear to him was that the biggest issue between him and Juniper was they could only see things one way. They saw the way their great-grandfathers had seen things, and had passed down that perception. And he was completely mired in that. He had to hear their side of the story. He needed to speak to her grandfather.

He could tell her, but…

He didn't want her to worry or have unnecessary anxiety about it, because he knew she was so protective of that relationship.

He'd be careful.

Because he was being careful with her.

He pulled up to the old farmhouse that was situated nearest the road on the ranch. There were two old cars in the driveway, and everything around the property was immaculate. No leaves, no debris. No nothing. The porch was spotless, with hanging plants all around.

Everything showed its age, but it also showed the incredible care that the owners put into it.

He parked, then walked up the steps, pausing for a moment before knocking firmly on the door.

He heard dogs barking, and then the shuffling of feet. The door opened to reveal a tiny gray-haired woman who was wearing a denim housedress and had her hair back in a low ponytail. "Yes?"

"Mrs. Sohappy," he said. "I was hoping I might be able to speak to Mr. Sohappy."

"Ron is sitting in his chair," she said. "What's your name?"

"I'm Chance Carson. I wanted to ask him a few questions."

The woman's eyes narrowed. "A Carson." Then the door slammed in his face, and he heard those same footsteps moving away from the door.

Well. Shit. Juniper hadn't been kidding. Her grandparents really did hate the Carsons, and he couldn't just show up and start talking to them, apparently.

He turned and started to walk down the steps, but then he heard the door open again. "Where you going?"

"I thought I wasn't welcome."

"I had to see if you were welcome," she said. "I wouldn't say *welcome*. But he will speak to you."

He nodded. "Thank you."

He walked back up the steps and followed the woman into the house. "I'm Anita," she said.

"It's nice to meet you, Anita," he said.

"We'll see if it's nice to meet you, Chance Carson."

He walked through a narrow hall and into a sitting room, where an old, gray-haired man was sitting in a mustard-yellow recliner. "What is it you want, Chance?" The man's voice was rough.

"I wanted to ask you some questions. About what you know about what happened between my great-great-grandfather and your grandfather."

The man looked at him then, his dark eyes serious. "You want to know what I think happened?"

"Yes."

"He wasn't of our blood. Our family. He married my grandmother. He was too fond of alcohol and card games. He lost a portion of the ranch playing cards with your great-great-grandfather. He was drunk and I think your great-great-grandfather was a cheat. There were witnesses that said he had an ace up his sleeve."

Chance nodded slowly. "And how is it... How is it you have the Sohappy name? If your grandfather wasn't part of the family."

The old man smiled. "I changed it back."

There was something in that simple statement that challenged a deeply held wall inside of Chance. Left it cracked.

That simple.

If something wasn't right, you changed it.

"Why are you asking now?" the old man asked, his eyes piercing. "Why now?"

"Because I realized just how wrong it is to hold on to your assumptions. When you could just ask. That's what we do, isn't it? We stay steeped in our own perspectives, and we never challenge them. We never looked to see what anyone went through. Juniper told me… She told me about something that happened at school. Someone who treated her badly because of her skin. I never saw anything like that. Not because it didn't happen, but because I wouldn't. Because people wouldn't do it in front of me, and they wouldn't do it to me. And you think then that that means things don't exist. Things you don't see. You think that your slice of the world is the whole thing, rather than just being a piece. I don't want to be like that anymore." He took a breath. "She has made me question a lot of things."

The old man's stare was sharp. "And now what will you do?"

"We need to redraw the boundary. We need to move the fence."

"Just like that?" he asked.

"Yes. Just like that."

"We should see if we can find proof."

He looked at the old man and saw pride radiating from him. And he knew he was never going to talk him out of that.

"All right. If that's what you want, then that's what we'll do."

He nodded.

"I had already agreed to see if my family had any records of what happened. I talked to Juniper about it."

"She's a good girl," her grandfather said. "She's going to make this place great."

"It looks to me like it's already pretty great. Because there's been a lot of great people here for a long time."

"It's family that helps make you who you are. But it seems to me that your great-grandfather, your grandfather... They didn't have an influence with you."

"Family does make you who you are," Chance said. "And sometimes, when what it would make is a bad thing, you have to make a decision to change it. My dad did that. I'm grateful to him. You have to break cycles or they just carry on. We need to break this cycle. We are neighbors. We don't need to hate each other."

Then the old man stuck his hand out, and Chance took it. And they shook.

Chapter 10

"I heard that Chance had a conversation with Grandpa," Shelby said.

"What?" Juniper popped around the rack in the clothing store she and her sister were in.

"Yeah. Apparently, he came to get his side of the story. He told Dad about it, and Dad was floored. He couldn't believe it. He said he didn't think one of those, and I quote, *arrogant sons of bitches* would ever do something quite that reasonable."

"I... I don't even know what to say."

"You must be good in bed," Shelby said. Then she grinned.

"Don't say that out loud, and don't ever say it so Mom and Dad can hear you. Or Grandpa."

"Well, Grandpa has new respect for at least him. So... Maybe things wouldn't be so bad if he found out."

"I have no desire for that to happen."

"Yeah. Fair. I mean, it would be somewhat horrifying."

"More than somewhat."

"So what exactly is going on with him? He must really like you to do that."

"I don't think so," Juniper said, suddenly feeling uncomfortable. "I think he's just… A lot nicer than I give him credit for. Or maybe *nice* is the wrong word. He's more reasonable. But there are things about him that I didn't know and…"

"Such as?"

"He… He had a sister that died. When she was really little. And he was just a kid and… I don't know. There's just more to him. There's sadness in him. And hearing him talk about his family, about the way that he loved her, it just made me feel…" She felt almost guilty telling Shelby about his pain, but…

If anyone understood loss, it was Shelby.

"Are you falling in love with him?"

She jerked up. "No. That would be impossible. Completely and utterly impossible. How would that even work?"

"I don't know. You seem to like him, plus you enjoy sleeping with him…"

"And that is not love," Juniper said.

"It's pretty close," Shelby responded. "Trust me."

"Surely there's more to it than that."

"Marriage is long. You have to find the person that you like to be around most in the world. Who you most like to see naked."

Her sister smiled for a second, and then her smile dimmed. "Of course, marriage is long unless it isn't. I so forget sometimes."

"I'm sorry," Juniper said.

"Hey," Shelby said. "It's not your fault. And you don't need to keep yourself from being happy because of me."

Juniper laughed. "I'm not that benevolent."

"You actually are much more benevolent than you need to be. I mean, why are you in a feud with him to begin with? Why are you doing any of this?"

"What do you mean?"

"I'm just curious. What would you be doing if you didn't feel obligated to Grandpa?"

"I don't feel obligated," she said. "I agree with him about what's important. I care about it. I want to do the same things, because it matters to me."

"All right, I believe you. But I do wonder…"

"What do you wonder?"

"Are you keeping yourself from being really happy?"

Juniper frowned. "I don't understand."

"It's something I've been thinking a lot about," Shelby said. She got a faraway look in her eye.

"What?"

"How many things I do just because I'm already here. Just because I started doing something, and I don't know what else to do."

"I want to establish an equestrian program here at the ranch. It's what I want to do, it's what I care about."

"But do you really care about border disputes and all of that, or is that just something that you're holding to because Grandpa was mad about it?"

"Those things matter. I'm not letting it go."

"At this point, what I wonder is if you're not letting it go because you feel more comfortable having that line drawn between yourself and Chance."

"I don't have any issues with Chance. Obviously."

"You lied to the man and kept him stowed away in

your cabin when he got a head injury. And I feel like you do have some issues. With him, and maybe with relationships in general."

"I don't have issues with relationships."

"You're so dedicated to the land, Juniper. But why? At the exclusion of everything else? You wanted to do other things at one time…"

"But I realized I couldn't and still stay here and give it my all, and I needed to."

"Why is that? Is it because of Grandpa? Is it because you don't think Mom and Dad take his concern seriously enough? I know you love him, I know you have a really particular relationship with him. But it's not up to you to dedicate your whole life to this place. You can have the equestrian stuff without sacrificing everything else."

"I don't know how to do it. Anyway, I'm not in love with him, so it isn't an issue."

"Okay."

"Are you thinking about leaving?"

Shelby shook her head. "No. I'm not going to leave. But I'm thinking of going back to school. My life just isn't any of the things that I thought it would be. We were supposed to have kids, you know? And then that never happened, and I wish I would've done something, but we were just in a hurry to get married, and all I wanted was for us to have a family. Now he's gone too. That's the thing. He's gone too. And whatever I thought… It's not what I'm getting. It's not what I had. So, I need to figure out how to make something new. And thinking about that got me thinking about you. I don't know how you imagined your life at this point…"

"I didn't, really," she said. "I have the ranch. And that's what I care about."

"But you also have Chance."

"Stop saying that. I don't really have Chance. He's not… He's not a factor. He's just a dude. And he's not worth upending my life over. Good sex is hardly something to go crazy over."

"It's not nothing. Take it from someone who's been without for a good long while."

"Well. I appreciate the fact that you dreamed of that. Of the family and all of that. I just… I never did."

"Why not, Juniper?" she asked.

"Because you can't have everything, can you? You have to choose. You have to decide what manner of life you're going to make. And for me, the ranch is my primary baby."

"And who will you pass it on to?"

She looked at her sister, and she realized that right now… They were the last of the generation. The last of all the generations.

"I don't know. It doesn't matter. We'll be dead. So I won't care."

"It doesn't work like that. You don't care about generational legacy and then magically not care when you're old."

"Future Juniper's problem. I'll fuss about it when I'm a hundred."

"Well, I think you should worry about yourself a little bit now."

"Thank you for your feedback. I'll be sure to take that on board."

Shelby rolled her eyes and made a scoffing noise.

"What?"

"What is the point of even being your sister? You don't listen."

"You're the baby. It won't work. At least you tried."

"I did," Shelby said. She shook her head. "It wouldn't hurt you to try, you know?"

"I guess not."

Juniper grinned and went back to browsing.

The thing was, she heard what Shelby was saying. That Shelby didn't understand. She didn't want to do all this with the property. She didn't want to make the ranch her life. So, they were just different. They wanted different things.

And that was okay.

Juniper couldn't imagine a scenario wherein she could make room in her life for a relationship that superseded the ranch. Shelby couldn't imagine a life where enjoying some hot sex with a good-looking man wouldn't end in love and marriage. That was fine. It was just the differences between the two of them. That was all.

There was nothing wrong with Juniper.

Nothing at all.

Chapter 11

He hadn't had dinner with his whole family for quite some time. But Callie was visiting from Gold Valley, and they had determined to have a dinner with all the siblings—except Buck—and their parents.

Dinner was loud and boisterous, as it always was when their family got together; it was just how they were.

"We need to talk for a second," he said, once everybody had dessert in front of them.

"What about?"

"I had a talk with Ron Sohappy," Chance said.

His dad scowled. "You mean he yelled at you and threatened to unleash his dogs on you?"

"No. I had a talk with him. About what happened initially with the ranch."

"And you think that he's going to tell you the truth?"

"I think he did, and I told him we'd try to find some sort of proof."

"How are we going to do that? Look for the smoking ace?"

Chance shook his head. "I've decided I don't want that. Why can't we share water rights? Why can't we work together? This feud has gone on long enough, and it's pointless. I want to be in a situation where I'm not fighting with my neighbor."

"That's noble of you, son," his dad said, "but I wonder what brought about the change of heart."

"It just seems like the right thing, Dad," Chance said. "And I care about it. I want us to do better than the generations that came before us, and I think we have. You know Grandpa was an asshole. Why are we on his side? Why do we listen to that story of how this ranch came to be, and how everything just is? I don't really understand. We have a chance to be better than those that came before us, and I believe that we need to do it. Because it's just right. Because it's fair."

"Hey, whatever you say, Chance, but I doubt you're ever going to join the two families together or anything like that," his dad said. "Some things are just too ingrained."

He nodded slowly. "I get that you feel that way. Because that's just how it's been. But I don't see why we gotta keep doing things one way just because it's how they've been."

"Well. If you say so."

"I do. Actually, I want to have them over for a barbecue."

"Damn," his dad said. "You really are trying to break ground."

His sister, Callie, smiled. "I like it, Chance," she said. "As you know, I'm all for shaking things up."

Being that she was responsible for the movement of

women breaking into new events in the rodeo right now, he absolutely knew she'd understand.

"You're a good one, Callie," he said.

"I agree," said her husband, Jake.

"Well, I'll get planning," he said.

Of course, he was going to have to get Juniper to agree.

He wanted to make it right. He needed to. The journey they'd been on...

He felt suddenly like he was standing in front of old, familiar doors that were too forbidding to ever walk through.

They couldn't go on like this.

But he'd made his mind up.

And he could give her this.

"How good of a mood are you in?" he asked when she came through the door of his cabin that night.

She was no longer working at Evergreen Ranch; there was no need to keep up the pretense anymore. The fact of the matter was, he just wanted to spend time with her, and anyway, they just did when they wanted that.

"I don't understand how to answer that question," she said.

"Should I get you naked before I start asking you for things or..."

"Well, I'm always for being naked with you." She smiled.

It was the easy camaraderie between them that never failed to surprise him.

Because it was just there, and they didn't have to try, after all that time of sniping at each other for so long... This was just there.

They had way more in common than they had different. They both loved this place equally, and they were both willing to work to make it better.

They were both absolutely and completely stubborn, hardheaded pains in the ass. But they appreciated it about each other. So there was that.

"You better go ahead and pitch it now," she said, sighing heavily.

"I want to have a barbecue," he said. "With both of our families."

"What the hell?"

"I want to make some things clear. I don't want to fight with your family anymore. I want to fix it."

"Why?"

"Because it makes no earthly sense. All this bullshit. All this hanging on to things in the past. It doesn't make any sense."

"That's..." She sighed. "I mean, I guess you're right. Honestly, I can't pretend that you're wrong. It's been a long time with all this stuff, and... I don't know that it benefits anyone."

"It doesn't. Your closest neighbors, and we should be allies, not enemies. We need to share the water rights."

"That's... I mean, it would definitely help."

"It would help us both. And I get that...that might seem like a bullshit thing to offer if your family was cheated." And he realized then, no matter what, there was only one real way this could go. "I want to sign the land back over to the Sohappy family. If you'll allow us water access, great. But it needs to go back to you. It's your land. Your blood."

Her eyes went glossy and he felt something terrible and fierce tighten his chest.

"I trust you," she said. "You don't need to sign the land over to us."

He felt like those words had cost her.

"You really are something," he said.

"Well, so are you. Something kind of undeniable, whether I want that to be true or not."

"It should be yours," he said, speaking of the land again.

She nodded. "Okay."

"So let's have a family barbecue. And let's put the bullshit feud to rest."

"I'd like that."

"I would like to get you naked also," he said, lowering his voice and moving toward her. And he kissed her, and it was like taking a full breath for the first time all day.

Because she was wonderful, brilliant. Amazing. Because she was everything that he had ever wanted.

Those words came out of nowhere and struck him like a thunderclap, and he chose not to pay them much mind. He chose not to think about them at all.

Instead, he just focused on her. On the way she looked, the way she tasted. He let the desire between them carry him somewhere else.

And it was like having amnesia again. Like being free of all the shit that weighed him down day in and day out. When they were together, it was like they both forgot.

And it was a gift. A blessing.

And he didn't normally use words like that or even think he needed them. But right now he would take them. Right now he would feel them.

But when she ran her hands over his skin, he tried to keep himself from feeling it too deeply.

When it was done, she curled up against him. "So when is this barbecue going to be?"

"I'd like to have it before my sister and her husband go back to Gold Valley. So as soon as possible."

"Well, my dad is retired, as he likes to remind me, so that means he's probably available whenever. Though, it'll be interesting to see if he will willingly sit in the same room as your dad. He doesn't feel the same way about the ranch that my grandpa does, but he's not neutral on the subject of the Carsons."

"We're going to do our best to change that. I don't want them to be neutral. I want him to actually have some nice feelings for us. Let's be neighborly."

"You and I might be someplace past neighborly," she said.

"Yeah, maybe." He moved over top of her and kissed her. "Spend the night with me."

She nodded. "Okay."

But for the rest of the night there was no need for talking.

It hadn't been easy to convince her family to come to a barbecue hosted by the Carsons. And, of course, her grandmother had refused to go empty-handed, so that meant a rally to make mass amounts of fry bread.

And keeping it hot on the drive over was everyone's burden.

Juniper, Shelby, their mother and father and their grandparents all drove separate trucks over to the ranch. And when they pulled up to the grand main house at Evergreen Ranch, Juniper knew a moment of disquiet.

The Carsons were something else. They were wealthy,

they were extravagant with it even, and her family had a much more modest existence.

But when Chance broke away from his brothers and his parents to come and greet them, she felt some of her disquiet dissipate. She just hoped that her family didn't see the connection between the two of them. Because that was something she didn't want to have to explain on top of everything else.

But he was so... Oh, he was wonderful and she couldn't keep the smile off her face. The way he spoke to her parents, her grandfather and grandmother. The respect and manners, and she really didn't know that would make her swoon, but it did.

Her family mattered.

And he was treating them exactly as she wanted them to be treated.

"Thank you for coming," he said. "We really appreciate it." He shook her grandfather's hand first. Then went to her grandmother.

After that, he greeted her parents.

Then he moved to Shelby, who treated him to a sly look. "You must be Shelby," he said. "Haven't seen you in a while."

"No. Neither. Except I did see you from a distance a few weeks ago."

"I see."

"Yeah," she said.

Juniper elbowed her.

"What?" she asked.

The brothers all took their turns making introductions, and then they all got to setting out food.

Her grandfather, who wasn't shy at all, immediately engaged the senior Carson.

"Your son is a good man," he said.

Abe Carson nodded. "He is."

They talked about cows, they talked about water, they talked about the rodeo.

Once the rodeo stories started, they didn't stop.

At the big table, which was laden down with meat, and her grandmother's fry bread, she was seated next to Callie, Chance's sister.

"Hi," she said. "I know who you are, but I don't think we've ever really met."

Callie was bright and chipper, and she made Juniper feel old. But then, she had to be somewhere around five years older than her.

"Yeah. It's good to see you."

"I think it's great what Chance is doing. That he cares about getting everybody together, and making sure they're getting along."

"Yeah. I never would've thought it about him, but he seems invested in it."

"He seems to like you," she said.

And Juniper stiffened. She wasn't sure how anyone could get that from their interactions.

"Does he?"

She shrugged. "Just a feeling I get. When he looks at you."

"Oh. Well. He's a good guy. He really is."

"I think so."

At some point, half the people bundled up and went to target practice, and everybody ended up out by the gravel pit on the property, sitting in lawn chairs and drinking beers and shooting rifles.

And there was a time when she would've worried about her grandfather having a rifle around the Carsons, but things seemed to be just… Different now. Was it all because of the way that Chance had gone to talk to Grandpa?

Had it really been enough to change the tone of the relationship between their families?

Maybe respect was the first, most important step. And then listening.

It forced her to see him differently, watching this interaction with his family.

Yet again.

And what she couldn't quite believe was the way that things had changed between them in these past weeks. The way that her ideas had been challenged.

When she went back home, her dad commented how they were actually such a nice family.

And she didn't… She didn't know what to do about that.

All of a sudden this barrier had been lifted, one that had once existed between herself and Chance. And yes, it could be argued that that had been dispensed with the minute they started sleeping together, but that had been something else. And this was… This was something emotional, and she didn't quite know what to do with it.

"Thank you," her grandfather said. "Your commitment to the ranch is truly commendable. I feel like you must've done something to make him change the way that he saw things."

Oh, that made her feel terrible.

Because it had been so momentous for her to be given the chance to run the ranch, and it meant the world to her to do right by her opportunity.

But what would they think if they found out that a huge reason Chance had changed his mind about everything was because she'd slept with him? Even if that was a simplified version of events, it was how it would look. Like she'd bought the land back with her body. By sleeping with the enemy.

"I just care about the ranch," she said. "It's my life, Grandpa, you know that."

He nodded his head. "I know."

"I'll honor it."

"I know," he said again. He patted her hand. "You're a good girl."

There. She was a good girl.

That was everything she had ever wanted to be. And now that she had it, she didn't know quite what to make of it.

Except… She really had no reason to continue on being with Chance.

And it wasn't sad or anything like that. There was no reason for it to be. They were at a conclusion. She was actually really happy. It might've all happened in a strange roundabout way, but she had accomplished something. She had changed some things. For the better. And she was just so grateful for that. Because they didn't need each other anymore.

And they didn't hate each other. And surely that was progress. Surely.

"Good night," she said, giving her grandpa a half wave.

"Good night."

And then she went back to her cabin and went to bed alone, and tried to tell herself that it was just fine.

Chapter 12

Juniper went down to the First Bank of Lone Rock the very next day. She was ready to try to get her loan to get the barn built.

A newer barn. A bigger one.

Yes, she would continue to work on restoring the one that she and Chance had worked on together, but she wanted something state-of-the-art, cutting-edge. She had her money saved up for the first of her horses, and this, she would be getting some help on.

Her plan was also to rent out space for people to board their horses, helping turn more of a profit at the ranch.

So a state-of-the-art facility was important.

And she finally had all of the years at her job required to go for a loan this size.

It was a big deal. Because this was debt. Real debt. Attached to her name. This was all the real stuff, as real as it got, in fact. This was her marriage. Her dream.

She laughed hollowly.

Then she walked into the banker's office, and two hours later, she was fully approved for the loan.

Now she would just need to line up construction workers and all of that. She had her plans, which she had needed before she could present them to the bank.

It felt big. And the first thing she wanted to do was… Call Chance.

She didn't need to. He wasn't a key part of this enterprise or anything like that. He wasn't even a factor.

She could call Shelby, and she did want to talk to Shelby about it. But she found she wanted to share the triumph with him, and she didn't quite know what to do with that.

They didn't talk on the phone, not very often. Mostly it was just texts back and forth. And then they were together. To hook up, not anything else. They'd never been on a date. Of course, when you had held a man captive while he had amnesia, she supposed you didn't really need to go on a date.

That was just kind of silly.

"Stupid," she muttered, and took her phone out, and found Chance's name in her messages.

"Hey," he said. "Everything okay?"

"Everything is wonderful," she said. "I got a loan. I'm building a new equestrian facility."

"That's… That's good. You want to do that, right?"

"Yes," she said. "I do. I really do. Chance, this is the biggest… It's the biggest thing. Nothing else has ever been this big."

"We should go out and celebrate," he said.

And her heart swooped inside of her chest. "Really?"

"Yes. We should. We should go out and celebrate that you're amazing."

"I… Okay."

And that was how she found herself at Shelby's. "He wants to go out," she said.

"You've been sleeping with the guy for like a month."

She nodded. And she didn't tell Shelby that she had just been thinking about how she needed to end things with him. About how she needed the two of them to get back to some semblance of sanity.

Because all that they were was a little bit intense.

Because there was no point. Because they had that whole reconciliation with the family, and her whole goal of having him see her and her family as people had been realized.

"And you need a dress," Shelby said.

"It's dumb, right? That I would want to wear a dress for a man?"

"It's not dumb," Shelby said. "It's normal. I know you don't have a lot of experience with this…"

"Well. It's because I… I've been trying so hard to live up to the fact that I'm the first girl to get this opportunity."

"Juniper," Shelby said. "That's ridiculous. Grandpa doesn't care that you're not a boy."

"No. And he totally thinks I can do anything that a boy could do. That isn't what I mean, it's just… I'm the first. And our great-great-grandpa who lost the ranch was the first to not be part of the family by blood and make a mistake and…and then it was why Grandpa didn't want Chuck to have the ranch. Why he wanted it in the family. So I can assume if I screw up…"

"First of all," Shelby said, "you'll be in charge. So you'll get to decide who carries it all on. Second, he wouldn't have given it to Chuck. Not ever. He'd have always trusted you with it, no matter the family history."

"But…"

"And if you have to love this land more than everything else, who will you pass it to?"

"I was counting on you reproducing."

Shelby laughed. "Well, that's blown to hell, isn't it? You might have to make your own life." Her tone softened. "You have to do what you want, you can't just be the fulfillment of Grandpa's dreams. He isn't going to live that much longer, Juniper. He's ninety-four."

"He could live another ten years," Juniper said. And it made her feel panicky, because she really did love him more than just about anyone or anything else.

"I know that you love him," Shelby said. "And I know that all of this comes from how much you love him. But he wants you to be happy. You didn't ever have to be a boy. You didn't ever have to love nothing more than this ranch."

She did her best not to let her sister's words sink too deep. "I still don't own a dress. And I would like to wear one to go out with Chance."

"Well, I can accommodate you. Especially because my dresses don't get any use these days."

Her sister tried to smile, but it came out a little bit thin.

She grabbed a stack of dresses, and after she had tried on two, Juniper suddenly understood why women were often upset about the shapes of their bodies.

Some of them showed off too much of her hips, some of them were too low-cut. And some of them emphasized that she had a little bit of roundness to her stomach.

"These are instruments of torture. Mental torture," she said.

"It's fine," Shelby said. "Wear the red one. You look amazing in it."

"What if I'm wrong?" she said, staring at her reflection. "What if he just wants to go to a bar and have a beer? Like friends?"

"Well, you'll be the best-looking bitch in the bar."

"Oh no, I'll feel really stupid. What if I have all of this wrong?"

"I thought you didn't want it to turn into anything."

"I don't," she said, her heart pounding heavily. "I don't want it to be anything else. I want it to be… What it is. I actually wanted it to be over." She was always meaning to not tell her sister things, and then accidentally blurting them out.

"You wanted it to be over?" Shelby asked, her eyes wide.

"Yes. I just wanted things to get back to normal. Or, not normal, better. Because I did it, right? I mean, I showed Grandpa that the Carsons could be good people, and I showed Chance that we weren't wrong about the situation with the land and how it wasn't fair. I did that. So, the two of us don't need to be together anymore."

"Did you stop being attracted to him?"

"No. Not at all. He's gorgeous…"

"I know," she said. "I've seen him."

"He's gorgeous, and I like being around him… And don't say anything. It's not that, it's just that today when I got the loan I just wanted to talk to him."

"You care about him," Shelby said.

"I like him. And I don't know what to do with that. I've never split my focus from the ranch. I do the EMT thing because it's necessary, and it was… Look, it wasn't really being a doctor, but it helped with the ranch instead of taking from it. I needed it for the money. But I need to love the ranch more than I love anything else. It needs to be the thing that I focus on, it needs to be…"

"You're a human being," Shelby said. "And it doesn't matter whether you were born you or born a man. You're just you. And you get to be a human being."

"I don't know how. I don't know how to have balance. I don't know how to have… Any of this. All I know is the ranch, all I know is obsession."

"Maybe this is a great opportunity to try and not just be obsessed. With him or the ranch."

"I guess. Do you have lipstick? Who am I?"

"You're my sister," Shelby said. "And will figure this out."

Chapter 13

He pulled into Juniper's driveway at five, because while she had asked if they could meet in town, he had decided that was bullshit, and he needed to take her, since they were celebrating something, and… Hell. He just wanted to. He couldn't recall the last time he had felt compelled to take a woman out, and in fact, he wasn't sure he ever had.

Maybe this was the chance to…finish it.

Not that he was going to end things tonight, but it might be a good chance to draw a line under things.

The issues with the family were resolved.

Maybe this would tie up the unfinished business with them.

Maybe you just want to be with her...

He shrugged that off.

And then when she came out of the house, his stomach went tight. She was beautiful in a red dress that hugged her figure and stopped just above her knee. She had on red lipstick, her black hair loose and hanging around her shoulders.

He had never seen her look quite so... She was always beautiful. He didn't care what she wore. She was the damn sexiest woman he had ever seen. That was just a fact. But right now she was testing him. Testing the limits of his restraint.

He got out of the truck and rounded to her side, opening the door for her. She looked up at him, her dark eyes wide. "What..."

And then he leaned in and kissed her. Hard.

"You look beautiful."

Her face went scarlet. "Thank you."

"No problem."

It was a bit of a drive down into Lone Rock, and he had been thinking of taking her to the Thirsty Mule, but he was going to have to take her to the Horseshoe. The old saloon building was restored to its original glory, with luxurious private dining rooms, and all kinds of things that hearkened back to the Gold Rush era of Lone Rock.

It was a favorite of his family, and they ate there every Christmas Eve.

"You like the food here?"

"There aren't many options in town," she said.

It was true. Lone Rock was tiny, a little gold speck out in Eastern Oregon, with very little surrounding it. The main street of the town was all original buildings, restored over the years to keep the look of the late 1800s alive.

It was certainly never going to modernize.

"Well, it is the best food in town," he said. "But don't tell Cara I said that, or she'll start a riot."

"The food at the Mule's great," she said. "It's just that, you know, it's..."

"Bar food?"

"Yes."

"You've never really lived anywhere else, have you?" he asked.

"No," she said.

"I have," he said.

"Where all have you lived?"

"Well, if I'm honest, mostly in an RV in different locations." They got out of the truck and walked toward the restaurant. "You know, until we had to slow down for Sophie. The nearest hospital. We lived on the outskirts of Portland for quite a while. Sophie needed to be near Doernbecher so she could receive specialized care. The Children's Hospital there is one of the best in the country."

"Oh wow. That must've been very different."

"It was. But… We were willing to do anything for her health. And then after that… Well, my grandpa died, and Lone Rock seemed like the place to go. With Evergreen Ranch available, that was just where we went. It was the best thing. For all of us."

They walked inside the restaurant, and Janine, the hostess, who he'd known since he was a kid, greeted them.

"Your usual table?"

His family often rented private dining.

"It's just the two of us tonight," he said. "We can sit out in the main dining area."

The carpets were a rich cranberry color, with the original lights, covered in carnival glass, turned low to give the place a romantic ambience. The tables were covered in white tablecloths, the walls red brick.

"I've actually never eaten here," Juniper said when they took a seat.

"Never?"

"It's not really our…"

"Hey. I get it. We're from different experiences."

"Well, I appreciate that you understand that."

"I do. I more than understand it."

He decided to go for an expensive bottle of champagne, in spite of her protests, and encouraged her to order exactly what she wanted, no matter what the cost was. She gave him a slightly wicked look. "I have always wanted to pretend like ordering something expensive meant I was afraid I'd have to pay for it with my body."

"I am happy to accommodate that fantasy," he said, his voice getting gravelly.

She ordered the fillet.

He gave thanks.

He loved watching her eat. Loved watching her smile and sigh over every bite. And he encouraged her to order a couple of different desserts after they brought out the tray with all the examples of the evening's selections.

"You can take the extras home," he said. "But it really is the best."

After much pushing, she agreed.

When they were finally finished, he had several boxes for her to take back home with her.

And he liked that. He liked giving her things. He liked seeing her happy. And he couldn't remember the last time he'd ever felt like that. Like sharing in somebody else's enjoyment was as good as having his own.

"Why don't you come back to my place?" she asked.

And he wasn't going to argue.

Something felt different between them tonight, and she didn't know if it was the dress or the dinner. She just didn't know. She felt different.

And she was… Electrified with it.

All the way back to the tiny cabin, she let herself get more and more wound up. She wanted him so badly she could hardly stand it. Maybe it was the adrenaline rush of having him again when she had been determined to break it off and never experience the pleasure of his hands on her skin. Maybe it was that she wanted him in a way that made her entire body ache. In a way that made her feel like he had been worth the wait, even though she would've said that she wasn't waiting for him. And tonight she felt completely and utterly one with her womanhood, and that was another thing she had struggled with. Even with him. Even as he had made her feel like her curves were a good thing. Like her body was special. Wonderful. Valuable. She couldn't say that she had felt purely feminine, or purely comfortable with it. But something about the dress, that lipstick, the whole night, made her feel a connection with herself that she hadn't before.

They got out of the truck, and her hands were shaking as they went up the front steps into the house. Then she turned and launched herself into his arms. She kissed him like she was dying, parted her lips and let him consume her.

And he did.

"I hope you know you don't actually have to pay for the steak," he said.

She laughed. "Maybe I just like the fantasy?"

"Do you?"

"Because I never felt like I was one of the pretty girls. Because I never felt like I was allowed to be. Because I never… Because always for me it's been about being convenient, not caught up in passion."

"I want you," he said. "You. This has nothing to do with feuds or anything else. I just want you."

"Thank you," she breathed, and she kissed him again, pouring all of her desire, all of her passion, into it.

He moved his hand around her back and unzipped her dress, leaving her in the borrowed high heels she was wearing and her underwear, leaving her feeling more feminine than she ever had in her life.

She stood back, leaning against the wall and arching her hips forward. He growled, pressing his hand to the front of his jeans, to where he was already hard and in desperate need of her.

"You want this?"

She nodded.

Then she went over to him and put her hands on his chest, slid them down his body as she dropped to her knees.

She had never done this before. Because she had never been in a relationship long enough to think that the man merited this kind of special treatment, and she knew that some women treated it like a free and easy thing. A little bit of action without the commitment of full-on sex, but she had always felt like there was something a bit more intimate about it, and she had always hesitated to try it.

But not with him. Not with him at all.

She undid his belt buckle, undid the zipper on his jeans and freed him, wrapping her hand around his heavy arousal, looking up at him as she leaned in and stroked him from base to head with the tip of her tongue.

His breath hissed through his teeth, the glint of desire in his eyes nearly undoing her completely. She felt powerful. Female. Incredible.

She took him into her mouth, as deep as she could,

and began to suck him like he was her favorite flavor of Popsicle. The taste of him was… Amazing. And she would never have thought that. But then, she thought he was singularly beautiful. She could write poetry about his anatomy, without ever having been all that impressed with the look of a naked man before this.

But she loved the look of him.

He was glorious. The most incredible man she had ever seen in her life. And she reveled in just what she was making him feel now. What she alone seemed to be able to make him feel. If there was anyone else, she didn't want to know about the bitch. She wanted to be the only one.

It made her feel desperately sad that she wasn't… That she couldn't be… That it couldn't be forever.

Why not?

Because it couldn't be. It couldn't be so easy.

And to just decide that you wanted forever when, before, you didn't think you did. To just decide that you loved a man when, before, he was your sworn enemy. To be able to love something more than her family land when she'd committed to not allowing herself that. Not ever.

It couldn't be that easy.

She shut her brain down and continued to lick, suck and stroke his masculine body.

She brought him to the brink, until his thigh muscles were shaking, and then he grabbed hold of her hair and moved her away from him, nearly lifting her up off the ground by her hair and bringing her in to kiss him. "I have to have you," he growled.

"No complaints from me," she said breathlessly. He lifted her against him and kissed her. Wildly. Recklessly. Then he carried her back into the bedroom, and she stopped him, pulling him up against her, pulling them both against the wall.

"Is that how you want it?" he growled.

"Yes," she whispered.

He pulled her panties aside, pushing his fingers between her legs, then dropping to his knees, taking her with his mouth, putting her thighs over his shoulders and eating her diligently as he pinned her body against the wall.

She arched against it, pushing her hips more firmly against his mouth as he continued to consume her.

She dug her fingers into his shoulders, tugged at his hair.

"Please," she begged. "Please."

"Not until you come for me," he said.

His words, electric, magic, set off a spark inside of her body that started deep within, shivering outward as it bloomed into a deep, endless climax that left her gasping. Left her breathless.

Then he rose up and, keeping her pinned against the wall, thrust into her, her hands pressed back against the drywall, held firmly in place by his ironclad grip, as he thrust, hard and fast, into her body. And it was a funny thing, because this was how she had always thought it would be between them. Desperate and needy, and not with the civility of a bed.

But their first time had been in a bed, and now here they were against that wall, when there was no more hate between them. When there was no more distrust.

But they had made it here. And somehow, something in her had always known they would.

She had always known that they would. And as her eyes met his, she knew why.

Because she loved him. She felt it clear and loud inside of her. She loved him.

She loved Chance Carson, and it didn't matter if it felt impossible. Because she would do whatever it took for the two of them to be together.

She wasn't only a rancher.

She didn't only love this ranch. She didn't only love her family name. She loved him. And it felt like a powerful realization. One that made her feel like she could scarcely breathe. Scarcely think.

He thrust into her, and her climax hit her like a wave, and then his own overtook him just a split second later, like a lightning bolt had gone through them both at once.

He held her while he shook, while he spent himself inside of her, and she clung to him. And she knew.

She knew. She had no idea what he would say. No idea what he would do. But it was the truth, and she could no more keep it in than she could ever keep in the animosity that she had once felt for him.

Because above all else, between herself and Chance Carson, there wasn't room for any more lying.

She had lied to him once already, and she would never do it again. "I'm sorry," she said, stroking his hair, and she hadn't meant to say that. Hadn't meant to say that she was sorry, but it had come out, and she realized once it did that it had been an important thing for her to say. "I should never have lied to you. When I found you. I should've taken you straight back to your family. I'm so sorry that I did that. It was selfish. I was blinded by the fact that the only thing that I thought mattered was the ranch, was getting even, was getting what I wanted. I wanted to force you to see something... And it was wrong of me. I swear I will never lie to you. Not again."

"It's okay," he said, looking slightly mystified by her intensity.

But he would understand. Eventually, he would understand.

"And the thing is," she said, touching his face, "I love you, Chance Carson. And I need you to believe me. I need you to trust me. I love you, Chance, and I would be willing to do anything, absolutely anything, to get you to love me back. Because I've never wanted anything but this ranch, and now that I've committed myself to it, now that I'm in debt for it, all of that… Now that I have that, what I want more is you. But it's a good thing. I want you. And I will split my time anywhere. And I said I'd never do that. But I would. For you. For you I would."

"Juniper," he said, his voice rough.

"You don't have to say anything," she said. "You don't have to say anything now. It's just… I'm kind of blown away by how strong I feel about this. By the fact that for the first time… For the first time I know what I want. Not what someone else wants for me. And not what I think I have to do. Just what I want. So. It's okay if you can't feel the same. It's okay if you can't answer me yet. I'm just glad that I know. I'm glad that I know." But her mouth was dry, and her whole body felt like it was poised on the edge of a knife, and it did matter. It did fucking matter what he said. What he wanted. It mattered because if he didn't want her… Well, if he didn't want her, then everything was just going to be kind of terrible.

"Juniper, I…"

"You're going to say something anyway. You hard-headed asshole."

"I'm not going to leave you thinking that I might be

able to… That I might change my mind. That I might change who I am. I won't. I can't."

"You're right about one part. You won't."

"You don't understand…"

"I understand what it's like to live your whole life so afraid that you're going to do the wrong thing, and then the person that you love most in the world will tell you that you want what they wanted. I know that fear. But you know what, if that's how my grandfather feels, then that's how he feels. And if that's how you feel… That's the thing, I can't control what anyone else feels. I can't control what you say or do or want. I can only control myself. I love you." She swallowed hard, tears springing into her eyes, and normally, she would despise that weakness. But right now she couldn't. Right now she didn't.

Right now all that mattered was she knew how she felt. And she wasn't afraid. She felt more herself than she ever had. She felt like… She didn't need to perform. She didn't need to do anything but be. And this was who she was. She loved the ranch, and she wouldn't compromise. She loved Chance, and she wouldn't compromise there either.

This was the most vulnerable she'd ever been, but also the most certain. And as difficult as she could feel the coming moment would be, she didn't resent it. Because it had brought her to this place of being one with herself. Certain of herself.

"Juniper, this isn't what I want. I watched my parents' lives be torn apart by losing a child, and I… I lost my sister. And I can't… I can't."

It broke her. But she wasn't angry.

She had been angry with this man so many times over things that weren't justified, and she had a feeling she would be a little bit justified in being angry about this. But she wasn't. She just wasn't.

Because she could see that he believed it. Deep down in his soul, and she understood that. She knew what it was to believe something so deeply about yourself.

It was all fear. That was what it was. Fear of losing the thing that you had, all that you had managed to make for yourself, in exchange for something that felt uncertain. Something you had lived without all this time, so maybe you didn't even actually want it, maybe you didn't need it.

"I want you to remember something," she said. "That I loved you. Even when you said you couldn't. That I care about you. I want you to remember that."

"Juniper…"

"No. I don't want your apologies. I don't want your speeches. You know what you can and can't do. You know who you are. And if you don't, I hope you find out. And then I hope you come find me. But if not, I want you to know… I think we really could've been something. Something I didn't even think I believed in. But now here I am, asking for it. Demanding it."

"I can't."

"Then you have to let me go," she said.

And she looked at him, and realized his face had become the dearest thing in the world to her, and it hurt to walk away. It hurt worse than anything ever had. Than she'd imagined anything ever could.

But she would let him go anyway.

Because she wouldn't compromise. And she finally realized she didn't have to.

Because she didn't need to be in service to what her grandfather wanted in order to be loved. Any more than she needed to leave the ranch to love Chance. Any more than she needed to keep her feelings to herself, or to stand there and compromise.

She had meant it when she'd said she didn't need him to say anything now. It was true.

But if he insisted on ending this, she would accept it. And she felt... Impossibly brave making that choice. To speak her heart to the person she loved most in the world and risk losing him.

And he left.

And her home felt empty, and so did she.

She sat in her pain for a long time, tried to sleep and failed. Marinated in her pain all day the next day until she finally drove from her cabin, to her grandfather's house. Her heart in pieces.

She walked up the steps and went inside, her heart thundering heavily. "Juniper," he said when he saw her. "What brings you here?"

"I have something to tell you."

"Yes?"

"I'm in love with a Carson. And I love the ranch. And I love you. I'm not a son, and I'm sorry. I'm a granddaughter. But I love this place, and I will take care of it. I'll take care of it even if I end up living at Evergreen Ranch. I'll take care of it if Chance doesn't love me back and rejects me. And I'll love you even if that makes you angry. But I need you to know. I need you to understand."

"Juniper," her grandfather said, his voice rough. "You thought that I wouldn't love you?"

"It isn't that. But I promised you I'd do this. Perfectly. And I was just so afraid... I was just so afraid. That I couldn't quite be what you wanted. That I wasn't quite what you needed. And I wanted to prove myself. I gave up on my dreams of medical school. Of being a doctor.

I threw myself into everything I could do here. All this time. And the problem is I liked Chance, from the first moment I saw him, and I wanted to hate him with the fire of a thousand suns, so I did everything I could to make that happen. But I didn't. I've always wanted him."

"I never wanted you to not be true to yourself," her grandfather said. "Not ever. I love you, and I want you to be happy. I'm sorry if an old grudge made you feel that you had to do anything differently."

Juniper laughed, but she wasn't mad. She wasn't. The risk had been hers to take all along, to be honest about herself and who she was, and she hadn't taken it.

And now she had taken the risk, she had spoken her truth. She had faced down her fears, with Chance, and now with her grandfather. And she might've lost Chance for now, but her grandfather was looking at her with love, and she knew that she'd made the right choice. She knew that things would be okay. They would be.

"Juniper," her grandmother said. "Will you stay for dinner?"

She could wait to dissolve. She would dissolve. Because she wanted Chance, and right now, he didn't want her. Or at least, he didn't think he could.

"Yes," she said. "I will."

Because there would always be time for her to dissolve. Because the grief would be waiting for her when she got up from this table.

But right now she had her grandparents. She had her family. And she had herself. And she would take a moment to celebrate that.

Chapter 14

He couldn't sleep. Or worse, he could. And when he did, he dreamed. And he was back there. Standing in front of the hospital, unable to go through the doors.

Because whatever was behind there was so terrible he couldn't face it.

He couldn't bring himself to stand. Couldn't bring himself to move over there. He was completely blocked. Bound by an invisible force that he couldn't see. That made it impossible to breathe.

Grief. His body whispered the truth of it even as his brain resisted giving it a name. Grief.

So much grief, and his feet felt like they were encased in cement. And he couldn't take a single step. His breathing was labored, and when he did finally wake up, he was in a cold sweat.

Grief. This unending grief.

But it wasn't Sophie he was thinking of. It was Juniper.

He had really told her that he couldn't do it. That he couldn't love her.

You already do.

Maybe that was true. But how? He didn't understand.

He felt like she was there, just on the other side of that door, but for some reason, for some damned reason, he couldn't get there. He didn't understand it. He didn't know how the hell to make sense of it. He wished that there was someone he could talk to, but he found he only wanted to talk to Juniper.

And he had sent her away, so, that was going to work out real well for him.

He loved her. It was the reason he had been motivated to talk to her grandfather. The reason he'd wanted to bring the families together for a barbecue. And he knew that he did. He knew that rejecting her was cowardice.

But what had he been thinking? That she wouldn't want it to be love? That it wouldn't come down to this? Of course it had. It was inevitable. It had always been fucking inevitable between the two of them. There had never been any other option. And yet he was running scared of it. Running scared of it like a child, not acting at all like a man.

Why can't you go through the damned hospital doors? And it took a while to realize he'd said it out loud. Why couldn't he go?

He had regretted it. All of this time he had regretted it, and here he was, doing it to himself again. Ruining things for himself again.

You will regret it always if you don't do it. That's all you have to do. Just have the balls to move forward.

It was the hardest thing. But this was different than

having his sister behind those doors, dying, with no chance of survival.

This was an unknown. And maybe on the other side there would be joy. Maybe there would be struggle. Maybe there would be pain. But it would be worth it. It would be worth it.

For her. And suddenly that made all the difference. Imagining her walking forward with him. Imagining her there, taking his hand and leading him through.

And yeah, all the bullshit he'd ever had to deal with was right there still. Behind those doors.

But so was the potential for everything else. For joy, for love, for happiness. The kind that he had let himself believe he didn't want, let alone need.

But he did.

And most of all, he needed her.

Walking with him.

But he had to take that first step on his own.

He got out of bed, and then Chance Carson took a step forward.

Juniper was out working when Chance showed up.

She recognized the sound of his truck now. Recognized him.

Just the feel of him.

It was because she was different now. Because they were different.

She dropped the stack of wood she was holding and stood there, watching as he crossed the space and made his way to her.

"What are you doing here?"

"I walked through the door," he said. "And I'm ready. For whatever's on the other side of it. I'm ready. I recognize that it's been what's holding me back. I punished myself for all those years, for not being able to go and see my sister one last time. And I felt like it meant I wasn't going to be able to go any kind of distance for anyone. I felt like I deserved to sit in that same loneliness she might've felt because I wasn't there. But you know what, that's self-protective bullshit. It was never about me. That's the thing. It never was. It's always just been about love. I loved her, and I was a kid, and it kept me frozen. Loving you kept me frozen too. But I remember what it was like to forget. To forget that I'd ever been hurt, to look at you without any of that weighing me down, and it made me want to change."

His breath was unsteady and it made her heart seize up, but he kept on talking. "It makes me want to reach out. Makes me want to walk through the door. Because there I was, when you walked away, standing on the outside just like I was then. I don't want that. I don't want to stand on the outside anymore. I don't just want to be looking in. I want to be with you. Even if it hurts. I want to be with you no matter what's on the road ahead of us. For a while I got to forget. And that was a powerful thing. But it's so much more powerful to stand here remembering all of it. Every fight we've had, every shitty thing I've been through, and want to be with you anyway. Because I do. Please believe that. It just took me a long while to realize.

"Juniper, I know how much it hurts to lose somebody. I've held it close for all these years. But I almost chose to lose you, and I can't accept that. I can't accept that choice I nearly made. Because it isn't living. When I have all this, when I have you, standing there wanting me, how can I choose any different? How can I choose not to love you when I already do? How can I choose to walk away like it would be the best thing? It wouldn't be. It wouldn't be living. Yes, I'm living with grief, but I'm still living. And so many people are, so many people do, every day, and they still choose to love. My parents chose to keep on loving. They had another child, even after all that. It's the lesson I missed. That love is worth it. Every time. No matter what. Love is always worth it."

"I love you," she said, flinging her arms around his neck, her heart pounding heavily.

"I love you too," he whispered, his breath hot against her ear.

And she wept. She thought maybe he did too. "We can live here," he said, his voice rough. "Whatever you want."

"Really?"

"Yes. We can live here. We can live in Evergreen Ranch. Hell, we can live at both. Or away. You could go to medical school. Be a doctor like you wanted. Stay here, make the equestrian thing happen. Do both. Do everything. Do nothing. Just be with me, and I'll be with you."

He was so earnest, so…him. The man she'd rescued, who had no memory. The man who'd had it all come blazing back. He was both.

And he was willing to give up the thing that stood between them: the land.

And she realized in that moment she was too.

"You would live here, in my tiny little house?" she asked.

"Home is wherever you are. Love is where you are. I… I only just realized… I didn't need to be in the hospital. Because my love was there already. Love goes before you. And it always goes with you. It's not a place. And for me, it's you."

"For me, it's you."

"You said you couldn't compromise."

"Well, that was back when I would've told you I couldn't have loved a Carson."

"And when was that?"

She smiled. "You know what, I can't remember. Maybe I have amnesia."

"As long as you never forget how much you love me."

"Oh, Chance, I could never forget that."

"Do you still want me to be your ranch hand?"

"I wouldn't say no."

"What if I was just your husband?"

"I can't imagine what our grandfathers would say about a Carson and a Sohappy getting married."

"It doesn't matter what they would say," Chance said, grinning.

And she smiled, because it was true. "You know, all that really matters is that we want it."

"And I do."

"I do too."

She kissed him, and she could only ever marvel about the fact that she loved him now far more than she had ever hated him. And one thing she knew for sure, it wasn't his ranch or hers that would be their greatest legacy.

It was love.

It was the only thing that had ever made their land worth anything. Love.

And it was the thing that made life worth living.

Always and forever.

* * * * *

CLAIM ME, COWBOY

November 1, 2017
LOOKING FOR A WIFE—

Wealthy bachelor, 34, looking for a wife. Never married, no children. Needs a partner who can attend business and social events around the world. Must be willing to move to Copper Ridge, Oregon. Perks include: travel, an allowance, residence in several multimillion-dollar homes.

November 5, 2017
LOOKING FOR AN UNSUITABLE WIFE—

Wealthy bachelor, 34, irritated, looking for a woman to pretend to be my fiancée in order to teach my meddling father a lesson. Need a partner who is rough around the edges. Must be willing to come to Copper Ridge, Oregon, for at least thirty days. Generous compensation provided.

Chapter 1

"No. You do not need to *send pics*."

Joshua Grayson looked out the window of his office and did not feel the kind of calm he ought to feel.

He'd moved back to Copper Ridge six months ago from Seattle, happily trading in a man-made, rectangular skyline for the natural curve of the mountains.

Not the best thing for a man who worked at an architecture company to feel, perhaps. But he spent his working hours dealing in design, in business. Numbers. Black, white and the bottom line. There was something about looking out at the mountains that restarted him.

That, and getting on the back of a horse. Riding from one end of the property to the other. The wind blocking out every other sound except hoofbeats on the earth.

Right now, he doubted anything would decrease the tension he was feeling from dealing with the fallout of his father's ridiculous ad. Another attempt by the old man to make Joshua live the life his father wanted him to.

The only kind of life his father considered successful: a wife, children.

He couldn't understand why Joshua didn't want the same.

No. That kind of life was for another man, one with another past and another future. It was not for Joshua. And that was why he was going to teach his father a lesson.

But not with Brindy, who wanted to send him selfies with "no filter."

The sound she made in response to his refusal was so petulant he almost laughed.

"But your ad said…"

"That," he said, "was not my ad. Goodbye."

He wasn't responsible for the ad in a national paper asking for a wife, till death do them part. But an unsuitable, temporary wife? Yes. That had been his ad.

He was done with his father's machinations. No matter how well-meaning they were. He was tired of tripping over daughters of "old friends" at family gatherings. Tired of dodging women who had been set on him like hounds at a fox hunt.

He was going to win the game. Once and for all. And the woman he hoped would be his trump card was on her way.

His first respondent to his counter ad—Danielle Kelly— was twenty-two, which suited his purposes nicely. His dad would think she was too young, and frankly, Joshua also thought she was too young. He didn't get off on that kind of thing.

He understood why some men did. A tight body was hot. But in his experience, the younger the woman, the less in touch with her sensuality she was and he didn't have the patience for that.

He didn't have the patience for this either, but here he was. The sooner he got this farce over with, the sooner he could go back to his real life.

The doorbell rang and he stood up behind his desk. She was here. And she was—he checked his watch—late.

A half smile curved his lips.

Perfect.

He took the stairs two at a time. He was impatient to meet his temporary bride. Impatient to get this plan started so it could end.

He strode across the entryway and jerked the door open. And froze.

The woman standing on his porch was small. And young, just as he'd expected, but… She wore no makeup, which made her look like a damned teenager. Her features were fine and pointed; her dark brown hair hung lank beneath a ragged beanie that looked like it was in the process of unraveling while it sat on her head.

He didn't bother to linger over the rest of the details— her threadbare sweater with too-long sleeves, her tragic skinny jeans—because he was stopped, immobilized really, by the tiny bundle in her arms.

A baby.

His prospective bride had come with a baby.

Well, hell.

She really hoped he wasn't a serial killer. Well, *hoped* was an anemic word for what she was feeling. Particularly considering the possibility was a valid concern.

What idiot put an ad in the paper looking for a temporary wife?

Though, she supposed the bigger question was: What idiot responded to an ad in the paper looking for a temporary wife?

This idiot, apparently.

It took Danielle a moment to realize she was staring directly at the center of a broad, muscular male chest. She had to raise her head slightly to see his face. He was just so...tall. And handsome.

And she was confused.

She hadn't imagined that a man who put an ad in the paper for a fake fiancée might be attractive. Another anemic word. *Attractive.* This man wasn't simply *attractive...*

He was... Well, he was unreal.

Broad shouldered, muscular, with stubble on his square jaw adding a roughness to features that might have otherwise been considered pretty.

"Please don't tell me you're Danielle Kelly," he said, crossing his arms over that previously noted broad chest.

"I am. Were you expecting someone else? Of course, I suppose you could be. I bet I'm not the only person who responded to your ad, strange though it was. The mention of compensation was pretty tempting. Although, I might point out that in the future maybe you should space your appointments further apart."

"You have a baby," he said, stating the obvious.

Danielle looked down at the bundle in her arms. "Yes."

"You didn't mention that in our email correspondence."

"Of course not. I thought it would make it too easy for you to turn me away."

He laughed, somewhat reluctantly, a muscle in his jaw twitching. "Well, you're right about that."

"But now I'm here. And I don't have the gas money to get back home. Also, you said you wanted unsuitable."

She spread one arm wide, keeping Riley clutched firmly in her other arm. "I would say that I'm pretty unsuitable."

She could imagine the picture she made. Her hideous, patchwork car parked in the background. Maroon with lighter patches of red and a door that was green, since it had been replaced after some accident that had happened before the car had come into her possession. Then there was her. In all her faded glory. She was hungry, and she knew she'd lost a lot of weight over the past few weeks, which had taken her frame from slim to downright pointy. The circles under her eyes were so dark she almost looked like she'd been punched.

She considered the baby a perfect accessory. She had that new baby tiredness they never told you about when they talked about the miracle of life.

She curled her toes inside her boots, one of them going through a hole at the end of her sock. She frowned. "Anyway, I figured I presented a pretty poor picture of a fiancée for a businessman such as yourself. Don't you agree?"

The corners of his lips tightened further. "The baby."

"Yes?"

"You expect it to live here?"

She made an exasperated noise. "No. I expect him to live in the car while I party it up in your fancy-pants house."

"A baby wasn't part of the deal."

"What do you care? Your email said it's only through Christmas. Can you imagine telling your father that you've elected to marry Portland hipster trash and she comes with a baby? I mean, it's going to be incredibly awkward, but ultimately kind of funny."

"Come in," he said, his expression no less taciturn as

he stood to the side and allowed her entry into his magnificent home.

She clutched Riley even more tightly to her chest as she wandered inside, looking up at the high ceiling, the incredible floor-to-ceiling windows that offered an unparalleled mountain view. As cities went, Portland was all right. The air was pretty clean, and once you got away from the high-rise buildings, you could see past the iron and steel to the nature beyond.

But this view... This was something else entirely.

She looked down at the floor, taking a surprised step to the side when she realized she was standing on glass. And that underneath the glass was a small, slow-moving stream. Startlingly clear, rocks visible beneath the surface of the water. Also, fish.

She looked up to see him staring at her. "My sister's work," he said. "She's the hottest new architect on the scene. Incredible, considering she's only in her early twenties. And a woman, breaking serious barriers in the industry."

"That sounds like an excerpt from a magazine article."

He laughed. "It might be. Since I write the press releases about Faith. That's what I do. PR for our firm, which has expanded recently. Not just design, but construction. And as you can see, Faith's work is highly specialized, and it's extremely coveted."

A small prickle of...something worked its way under her skin. She couldn't imagine being so successful at such a young age. Of course, Joshua and his sister must have come from money. You couldn't build something like this if you hadn't.

Danielle was in her early twenties and didn't even have a checking account, much less a successful business.

All of that had to change. It had to change for Riley.

He was why she was here, after all.

Truly, nothing else could have spurred her to answer the ad. She had lived in poverty all of her life. But Riley deserved better. He deserved stability. And he certainly didn't deserve to wind up in foster care just because she couldn't get herself together.

"So," she said, cautiously stepping off the glass tile. "Tell me more about this situation. And exactly what you expect."

She wanted him to lay it all out. Wanted to hear the terms and conditions he hadn't shared over email. She was prepared to walk away if it was something she couldn't handle. And if he wasn't willing to take no for an answer? Well, she had a knife in her boot.

"My father placed an ad in a national paper saying I was looking for a wife. You can imagine my surprise when I began getting responses before I had ever seen the ad. My father is well-meaning, Ms. Kelly, and he's willing to do anything to make his children's lives better. However, what he perceives as perfection can only come one way. He doesn't think all of this can possibly make me happy." Joshua looked up, seeming to indicate the beautiful house and view around them. "He's wrong. However, he won't take no for an answer, and I want to teach him a lesson."

"By making him think he won?"

"Kind of. That's where you come in. As I said, he can only see things from his perspective. From his point of view, a wife will stay at home and massage my feet while I work to bring in income. He wants someone traditional. Someone soft and biddable." He looked her over. "I imagine you are none of those things."

"Yeah. Not so much." The life she had lived didn't leave room for that kind of softness.

"And you are right. He isn't going to love that you come with a baby. In fact, he'll probably think you're a gold digger."

"I am a gold digger," she said. "If you weren't offering money, I wouldn't be here. I need money, Mr. Grayson, not a fiancé."

"Call me Joshua," he said. "Come with me."

She followed him as he walked through the entryway, through the living area—which looked like something out of a magazine that she had flipped through at the doctor's office once—and into the kitchen.

The kitchen made her jaw drop. Everything was so shiny. Stainless steel surrounded by touches of wood. A strange clash of modern and rustic that seemed to work.

Danielle had never been in a place where so much work had gone into the details. Before Riley, when she had still been living with her mother, the home decor had included plastic flowers shoved into some kind of strange green Styrofoam and a rug in the kitchen that was actually a towel laid across a spot in the linoleum that had been worn through.

"You will live here for the duration of our arrangement. You will attend family gatherings and work events with me."

"Aren't you worried about me being unsuitable for your work arrangements too?"

"Not really. People who do business with us are fascinated by the nontraditional. As I mentioned earlier, my sister, Faith, is something of a pioneer in her field."

"Great," Danielle said, giving him a thumbs-up. "I'm glad to be a nontraditional asset to you."

"Whether or not you're happy with it isn't really my concern. I mean, I'm paying you, so you don't need to be happy."

She frowned. "Well, I don't want to be unhappy. That's the other thing. We have to discuss…terms and stuff. I don't know what all you think you're going to get out of me, but I'm not here to have sex with you. I'm just here to pose as your fiancée. Like the ad said."

The expression on his face was so disdainful it was almost funny. Almost. It didn't quite ascend to funny because it punched her in the ego. "I think I can control myself, Ms. Kelly."

"If I can call you Joshua, then you can call me Danielle," she said.

"Noted."

The way he said it made her think he wasn't necessarily going to comply with her wishes just because she had made them known. He was difficult. No wonder he didn't have an actual woman hanging around willing to marry him. She should have known there was something wrong with him. Because he was rich and kind of disgustingly handsome. His father shouldn't have had to put an ad in the paper to find Joshua a woman.

He should be able to snap his fingers and have them come running.

That sent another shiver of disquiet over her. Yeah, maybe she should listen to those shivers… But the compensation. She needed the compensation.

"What am I going to do…with the rest of my time?"

"Stay here," he said, as though that were the most obvious thing in the world. As though the idea of her rotting away up here in his mansion wasn't weird at all. "And you have that baby. I assume it takes up a lot of your time?"

"He. Riley. And yes, he does take up a lot of time. He's a baby. That's kind of their thing." He didn't respond to that. "You know. Helpless, requiring every single one of their physical and emotional needs to be met by another person. Clearly you don't know."

Something in his face hardened. "No."

"Well, this place is big enough you shouldn't have to ever find out."

"I keep strange hours," he said. "I have to work with offices overseas, and I need to be available to speak to them on the phone, which means I only sleep for a couple of hours at a time. I also spend a lot of time outdoors."

Looking at him, that last statement actually made sense. Yes, he had the bearing of an uptight businessman, but he was wearing a T-shirt and jeans. He was also the kind of physically fit that didn't look like it had come from a gym, not that she was an expert on men or their physiques.

"What's the catch?" she asked.

Nothing in life came this easy—she knew that for certain. She was waiting for the other shoe to drop. Waiting for him to lead her down to the dungeon and show her where he kept his torture pit.

"There is no catch. This is what happens when a man with a perverse sense of humor and too much money decides to teach his father a lesson."

"So basically I live in this beautiful house, I wear your ring, I meet your family, I behave abominably and then I get paid?"

"That is the agreement, Ms. Kelly."

"What if I steal your silverware?"

He chuckled. "Then I still win. If you take off in the dead of night, you don't get your money, and I have the benefit of saying to my father that because of his ad I ended up with a con woman and then got my heart broken."

He really had thought of everything. She supposed there was a reason he was successful.

"So do we… Is this happening?"

"There will be papers for you to sign, but yes. It is." Any uncertainty he'd seemed to feel because of Riley was gone now.

He reached into the pocket of his jeans and pulled out a small, velvet box. He opened it, revealing a diamond ring so beautiful, so big, it bordered on obscene.

This was the moment. This was the moment when he would say he actually needed her to spend the day wandering around dressed as a teddy bear or something.

But that moment didn't come either. Instead, he took the ring out of the box and held it out to her. "Give me your hand."

She complied. She complied before she gave her body permission to. She didn't know what she expected. For him to get down on one knee? For him to slide the ring onto her fourth finger? He did neither. Instead, he dropped the gem into her palm.

She curled her fingers around it, an electric shock moving through her system as she realized she was probably holding more money in her hand right now than she could ever hope to earn over the course of her lifetime.

Well, no, that wasn't true. Because she was about to earn enough money over the next month to take care of herself and Riley forever. To make sure she got permanent custody of him.

Her life had been so hard, a constant series of moves and increasingly unsavory *uncles* her mother brought in and out of their lives. Hunger, cold, fear, uncertainty…

She wasn't going to let Riley suffer the same fate. No, she was going to make sure her half brother was protected. This agreement, even if Joshua did ultimately want her to walk around dressed like a sexy teddy bear, was a small price to pay for Riley's future.

"Yes," she said, testing the weight of the ring. "It is."

Chapter 2

As Joshua followed Danielle down the hall, he regretted not having a live-in housekeeper. An elderly British woman would come in handy at a time like this. She would probably find Danielle and her baby to be absolutely delightful. He, on the other hand, did not.

No, on the contrary, he felt invaded. Which was stupid. Because he had signed on for this. Though, he had signed on for it only after he had seen his father's ad. After he had decided the old man needed to be taught a lesson once and for all about meddling in Joshua's life.

It didn't matter that his father had a soft heart or that he was coming from a good place. No, what mattered was the fact that Joshua was tired of being hounded every holiday, every time he went to dinner with his parents, about the possibility of him starting a family.

It wasn't going to happen.

At one time, he'd thought that would be his future. Had

been looking forward to it. But the people who said it was better to have loved and lost than never to have loved at all clearly hadn't *caused* the loss.

He was happy enough now to be alone. And when he didn't want to be alone, he called a woman, had her come spend a few hours in his bed—or in the back of his truck, he wasn't particular. Love was not on his agenda.

"This is a big house," she said.

Danielle sounded vaguely judgmental, which seemed wrong, all things considered. Sure, he was the guy who had paid a woman to pose as his temporary fiancée. And sure, he was the man who lived in a house that had more square footage than he generally walked through in a day, but she was the one who had responded to an ad placed by a complete stranger looking for a temporary fiancée. So, all things considered, he didn't feel like she had a lot of room to judge.

"Yes, it is."

"Why? I mean, you live here alone, right?"

"Because size matters," he said, ignoring the shifting, whimpering sound of the baby in her arms.

"Right," she said, her tone dry. "I've lived in apartment buildings that were smaller than this."

He stopped walking, then he turned to face her. "Am I supposed to feel something about that? Feel sorry for you? Feel bad about the fact that I live in a big house? Because trust me, I started humbly enough. I choose to live differently than my parents. Because I can. Because I earned it."

"Oh, I see. In that case, I suppose I earned my dire straits."

"I don't know your life, Danielle. More important, I don't want to know it." He realized that was the first time he had used her first name. He didn't much care.

"Great. Same goes. Except I'm going to be living in your house, so I'm going to definitely…infer some things about your life. And that might give rise to conversations like this one. And if you're going to be assuming things about me, then you should be prepared for me to respond in kind."

"I don't have to do any such thing. As far as I'm concerned, I'm the employer, you're the employee. That means if I want to talk to you about the emotional scars of my childhood, you had better lie back on my couch and listen. Conversely, if I do not want to hear about any of the scars of yours, I don't have to. All I have to do is throw money at you until you stop talking."

"Wow. It's seriously the job offer I've been waiting for my entire life. Talking I'm pretty good at. And I don't do a great job of shutting up. That means I would be getting money thrown at me for a long, long time."

"Don't test me, Ms. Kelly," he said, reverting back to her last name, because he really didn't want to know about her childhood or what brought her here. Didn't want to wonder about her past. Didn't want to wonder about her adulthood either. Who the father of her baby was. What kind of situation she was in. It wasn't his business, and he didn't care.

"Don't test me, Ms. Kelly," she said, in what he assumed was supposed to be a facsimile of his voice.

"Really?" he asked.

"What? You can't honestly expect to operate at this level of extreme douchiness and not get called to the carpet on it."

"I expect that I can do whatever I want, since I'm paying you to be here."

"You don't want me to dress up as a teddy bear and vacuum, do you?"

"What?"

She shifted her weight, moving the baby over to one hip and spreading the other arm wide. "Hey, man, some people are into that. They like stuffed animals. Or rather, they like people dressed as stuffed animals."

"I don't."

"That's a relief."

"I like women," he said. "Dressed as women. Or rather, undressed, generally."

"I'm not judging. Your dad put an ad in the paper for some reason. Clearly he really wants you to be married."

"Yes. Well, he doesn't understand that not everybody needs to live the life that he does. He was happy with a family and a farmhouse. But none of the rest of us feel that way, and there's nothing wrong with that."

"So none of you are married?"

"One of us is. The only brother that actually wanted a farmhouse too." He paused in front of the door at the end of the hall. He was glad he had decided to set this room aside for the woman who answered the ad. He hadn't known she would come with a baby in tow, but the fact that she had meant he really, really wanted her out of earshot.

"Is this it?" she asked.

"Yes," he said, pushing the door open.

When she looked inside the bedroom, her jaw dropped, and Joshua couldn't deny that he took a small amount of satisfaction in her reaction. She looked… Well, she looked amazed. Like somebody standing in front of a great work of art. Except it was just a bedroom. Rather a grand one, he had to admit, down to the details.

There was a large bed fashioned out of natural, twisted pieces of wood with polished support beams that ran from floor to ceiling and retained the natural shape they'd had in the woods but glowed from the stain that had been applied to them. The bed made the whole room look like a magical forest. A little bit fanciful for him. His own bedroom had been left more Spartan. But, clearly, Danielle was enchanted.

And he shouldn't care.

"I've definitely lived in apartments that were smaller than this room," she said, wrapping both arms around the baby and turning in a circle. "This is... Is that a loft? Like a reading loft?" She was gazing up at the mezzanine designed to look as though it was nestled in the tree branches.

"I don't know." He figured it was probably more of a sex loft. But then, if he slept in a room with a loft, obviously he would have sex in it. That was what creative surfaces were for, in his opinion.

"It reminds me of something we had when I was in first grade." A crease appeared between her eyebrows. "I mean, not me as in at our house, but in my first-grade classroom at school. The teacher really loved books. And she liked for us all to read. So we were able to lie around the classroom anywhere we wanted with a book and—" She abruptly stopped talking, as though she realized exactly what she was doing. "Never mind. You think it's boring. Anyway, I'm going to use it for a reading loft."

"Dress like a teddy bear in it, for all I care," he responded.

"That's your thing, not mine."

"Do you have any bags in the car that I can get for you?"

She looked genuinely stunned. "You don't have to get anything for me."

It struck him that she thought he was being nice. He didn't consider the offer particularly nice. It was just what his father had drilled into him from the time he was a boy. If there was a woman and she had a heavy thing to transport, you were no kind of man if you didn't offer to do the transporting.

"I don't mind."

"It's just one bag," she said.

That shocked him. She was a woman. A woman with a baby. He was pretty sure most mothers traveled with enough luggage to fill a caravan. "Just one bag." He had to confirm that.

"Yes," she returned. "Baggage is another thing entirely. But in terms of bags, yeah, we travel light."

"Let me get it." He turned and walked out of the room, frustrated when he heard her footsteps behind him. "I said I would get it."

"You don't need to," she said, following him persistently down the stairs and out toward the front door.

"My car is locked," she added, and he ignored her as he continued to walk across the driveway to the maroon monstrosity parked there.

He shot her a sideways glance, then looked down at the car door. It hung a little bit crooked, and he lifted up on it hard enough to push it straight, then he jerked it open. "Not well."

"You're the worst," she said, scowling.

He reached into the back seat and saw one threadbare duffel bag, which had to be the bag she was talking about. The fabric strap was dingy, and he had a feeling it used to be powder blue. The zipper was broken and there were four safety pins holding the end of the bulging bag together. All in all, it looked completely impractical.

"Empty all the contents out of this tonight. In the morning, I'm going to use it to fuel a bonfire."

"It's the only bag I have."

"I'll buy you a new one."

"It better be in addition to the fee that I'm getting," she said, her expression stubborn. "I mean it. If I incur a loss because of you, you better cover it."

"You have my word that if anything needs to be purchased in order for you to fit in with your surroundings, or in order for me to avoid contracting scabies, it will be bankrolled by me."

"I don't have scabies," she said, looking fierce.

"I didn't say you did. I implied that your gym bag might."

"Well," she said, her cheeks turning red, "it doesn't. It's clean. I'm clean."

He heaved the bag over his shoulder and led the way back to the house, Danielle trailing behind him like an angry wood nymph. That was what she reminded him of, he decided. All pointed angles and spiky intensity. And a supernaturally wicked glare that he could feel boring into the center of his back. Right between his shoulder blades.

This was not a woman who intimidated easily, if at all.

He supposed that was signal enough that he should make an attempt to handle her with care. Not because she needed it, but because clearly nobody had ever made the attempt before. But he didn't know how. And he was paying her an awful lot to put up with him as he was.

And she had brought a baby into his house.

"You're going to need some supplies," he said, frowning. Because he abruptly realized what it meant that she had brought a baby into his house. The bedroom he had installed her in was only meant for one. And there was no way—barring the unlikely reality that she was related to Mary Poppins in some way—that her ratty old bag contained the supplies required to keep both a baby and herself in the kind of comfort that normal human beings expected.

"What kind of supplies?"

He moved quickly through the house, and she scurried behind him, attempting to match his steps. They walked back into the bedroom and he flung the bag on the ground.

"A bed for the baby. Beyond that, I don't know what they require."

She shot him a deadly glare, then bent down and unzipped the bag, pulling out a bottle and a can of formula. She tossed both onto the bed, then reached back into the bag and grabbed a blanket. She spread it out on the floor, then set the baby in the center of it.

Then she straightened, spreading her arms wide and slapping her hands back down on her thighs. "Well, this is more than we've had for a long time. And yeah, I guess it would be nice to have nursery stuff. But I've never had it. Riley and I have been doing just fine on our own." She looked down, picking at some dirt beneath her fingernail. "Or I guess we haven't been *fine*. If we had, I wouldn't have responded to your ad. But I don't need more than what I have. Not now. Once you pay me? Well, I'm going to buy a house. I'm going to change things for us. But until then, it doesn't matter."

He frowned. "What about Riley's father? Surely he should be paying you some kind of support."

"Right. Like I have any idea who he is." He must have made some kind of facial expression that seemed judg-

mental, because her face colored and her eyebrows lowered. "I mean, I don't know how to get in touch with him.
It's not like he left contact details. And I sincerely doubt
he left his real name."

"I'll call our office assistant, Poppy. She'll probably
know what you need." Technically, Poppy was his brother
Isaiah's assistant, but she often handled whatever Joshua
or Faith needed, as well. Poppy would arrange it so that
various supplies were overnighted to the house.

"Seriously. Don't do anything... You don't need to do
anything."

"I'm supposed to convince my parents that I'm marrying you," he said, his tone hard. "I don't think they're
going to believe I'm allowing my fiancée to live out of one
duffel bag. No. Everything will have to be outfitted so that
it looks legitimate. Consider it a bonus to your salary."

She tilted her chin upward, her eyes glittering. "Okay,
I will."

He had halfway expected her to argue, but he wasn't
sure why. She was here for her own material gain. Why
would she reduce it? "Good." He nodded once. "You probably won't see much of me. I'll be working a lot. We are
going to have dinner with my parents in a couple of days.
Until then, the house and the property are yours to explore. This is your house too. For the time being."

He wasn't being particularly generous. It was just that
he didn't want to answer questions, or deal with her being
tentative about where she might and might not be allowed
to go. He just wanted to install her and the baby in this
room and forget about them until he needed them as convenient props.

"Really?" Her natural suspicion was shining through
again.

"I'm a very busy man, Ms. Kelly," he said. "I'm not going to be babysitting. Either the child or you."

And with that, he turned and left her alone.

Chapter 3

Danielle had slept fitfully last night. And, of course, she hadn't actually left her room once she had been put there. But early the next morning there had been a delivery. And the signature they had asked for was hers. And then the packages had started to come in, like a Christmas parade without the wrapping.

Teams of men carried the boxes up the stairs. They had assembled a crib, a chair, and then unpacked various baby accoutrements that Danielle hadn't even known existed. How could she? She certainly hadn't expected to end up caring for a baby.

When her mother had breezed back into her life alone and pregnant—after Danielle had experienced just two carefree years where she had her own space and wasn't caring for anyone—Danielle had put all of her focus into caring for the other woman. Into arranging state health insurance so the prenatal care and hospital bill for the delivery wouldn't deter her mother from actually taking care of herself and the baby.

And then, when her mother had abandoned Danielle and Riley...that was when Danielle had realized her brother was likely going to be her responsibility. She had involved Child Services not long after that.

There had been two choices. Either Riley could go into foster care or Danielle could take some appropriate parenting classes and become a temporary guardian.

So she had.

But she had been struggling to keep their heads above water, and it was too close to the way she had grown up. She wanted more than that for Riley. Wanted more than that for both of them. Now it wasn't just her. It was him. And a part-time job as a cashier had never been all that lucrative. But with Riley to take care of, and her mother completely out of the picture, staying afloat on a cashier's pay was impossible.

She had done her best trading babysitting time with a woman in her building who also had a baby and nobody else to depend on. But inevitably there were schedule clashes, and after missing a few too many shifts, Danielle had lost her job.

Which was when she had gotten her first warning from Child Services.

Well, she had a job now.

And, apparently, a full nursery.

Joshua was refreshingly nowhere to be seen, which made dealing with her new circumstances much easier. Without him looming over her, being in his house felt a lot like being in the world's fanciest vacation rental. At least, the fanciest vacation rental she could imagine.

She had a baby monitor in her pocket, one that would

allow her to hear when Riley woke up. A baby monitor that provided her with more freedom than she'd had since Riley had been born. But, she supposed, in her old apartment a monitor would have been a moot point considering there wasn't anywhere she could go and not hear the baby cry.

But in this massive house, having Riley take his nap in the bedroom—in the new crib, his first crib—would have meant she couldn't have also run down to the kitchen to grab snacks. But she had the baby monitor. A baby monitor that vibrated. Which meant she could also listen to music.

She had the same ancient MP3 player her mother had given her for her sixteenth birthday years ago, but Danielle had learned early to hold on to everything she had, because she didn't know when something else would come along. And in the case of frills like her MP3 player, nothing else had ever come along.

Of course, that meant her music was as old as her technology. But really, music hadn't been as good since she was sixteen anyway.

She shook her hips slightly, walking through the kitchen, singing about how what didn't kill her would only make her stronger. Digging through cabinets, she came up with a package of Pop-Tarts. *Pop-Tarts!*

Her mother had never bought those. They were too expensive. And while Danielle had definitely indulged herself when she had moved out, that hadn't lasted. Because they were too expensive.

Joshua had strawberry. And some kind of mixed berry with bright blue frosting. She decided she would eat one of each to ascertain which was best.

Then she decided to eat one more of each. She hadn't

realized how hungry she was. She had a feeling the hunger wasn't a new development. She had a feeling she had been hungry for days. Weeks even.

Suddenly, sitting on the plush couch in his living area, shoving toaster pastries into her mouth, she felt a whole lot like crying in relief. Because she and Riley were warm; they were safe. And there was hope. Finally, an end point in sight to the long, slow grind of poverty she had existed in for her entire life.

It seemed too good to be true, really. That she had managed to jump ahead in her life like this. That she was really managing to get herself out of that hole without prostituting herself.

Okay, so some people might argue this agreement with Joshua *was* prostituting herself, a little bit. But it wasn't like she was going to have sex with him.

She nearly choked on her Pop-Tart at the thought. And she lingered a little too long on what it might be like to get close to a man like Joshua. To any man, really. The way her mother had behaved all of her life had put Danielle off men. Or, more specifically, she supposed it was the way men had behaved toward Danielle's mother that had put her off.

As far as Danielle could tell, relationships were a whole lot of exposing yourself to pain, deciding you were going to depend on somebody and then having that person leave you high and dry.

No, thank you.

But she supposed she could see how somebody might lose their mind enough to take that risk. Especially when the person responsible for the mind loss had eyes that were blue like Joshua's. She leaned back against the couch, her hand falling slack, the Pop-Tart dangling from her fingertips.

Yesterday there had been the faint shadow of golden stubble across that strong face and jaw, his eyes glittering with irritation. Which she supposed shouldn't be a bonus, shouldn't be appealing. Except his irritation made her want to rise to the unspoken challenge. To try to turn that spark into something else. Turn that irritation into something more...

"Are you eating my Pop-Tarts?"

The voice cut through the music and she jumped, flinging the toaster pastry into the air. She ripped her headphones out of her ears and turned around to see Joshua, his arms crossed over his broad chest, his eyebrows flat on his forehead, his expression unreadable.

"You said whatever was in your house was mine to use," she squeaked. "And a warning would've been good. You just about made me jump out of my skin. Which was maybe your plan all along. If you wanted to make me into a skin suit."

"That's ridiculous. I would not fit into your skin."

She swallowed hard, her throat dry. "Well, it's a figure of speech, isn't it?"

"Is it?" he asked.

"Yes. Everybody knows what that means. It means that I think you might be a serial killer."

"You don't really think I'm a serial killer, or you wouldn't be here."

"I am pretty desperate." She lifted her hand and licked off a remnant of jam. "I mean, obviously."

"There are no Pop-Tarts left," he said, his tone filled with annoyance.

"You said I could have whatever I wanted. I wanted Pop-Tarts."

"You ate all of them."

"Why do you even have Pop-Tarts?" She stood up, crossing her arms, mimicking his stance. "You don't look like a man who eats Pop-Tarts."

"I like them. I like to eat them after I work outside."

"You work outside?"

"Yes," he said. "I have horses."

Suddenly, all of her annoyance fell away. Like it had been melted by magic. *Equine* magic. "You have horses?" She tried to keep the awe out of her voice, but it was nearly impossible.

"Yes," he said.

"Can I... Can I see them?"

"If you want to."

She had checked the range on the baby monitor, so depending on how far away from the house the horses were, she could go while Riley was napping.

"Could we see the house from the barn? Or wherever you keep them?"

"Yeah," he said, "it's just right across the driveway."

"Can I see them *now*?"

"I don't know. You ate my Pop-Tarts. Actually, more egregious than eating my Pop-Tarts, you threw the last half of one on the ground."

"Sorry about your Pop-Tarts. But I'm sure that a man who can have an entire nursery outfitted in less than twenty-four hours can certainly acquire Pop-Tarts at a moment's notice."

"Or I could just go to the store."

She had a hard time picturing a man like Joshua Grayson walking through the grocery store. In fact, the image almost made her laugh. He was way too commanding to do something as mundane as pick up a head of lettuce and try to figure out how fresh it was. Far too…masculine to go around squeezing avocados.

"What?" he asked, his eyebrows drawing together.

"I just can't imagine you going to the grocery store. That's all."

"Well, I do. Because I like food. Food like Pop-Tarts."

"My mom would never buy those for me," she said. "They were too expensive."

He huffed out a laugh. "My mom would never buy them for me."

"This is why being an adult is cool, even when it sucks."

"Pop-Tarts whenever you want?"

She nodded. "Yep."

"That seems like a low bar."

She lifted a shoulder. "Maybe it is, but it's a tasty one."

He nodded. "Fair enough. Now, why don't we go look at the horses."

Joshua didn't know what to expect by taking Danielle outside to see the horses. He had been irritated that she had eaten his preferred afternoon snack, and then, perversely, even more irritated that she had questioned the fact that it was his preferred afternoon snack. Irritated that he was put in the position of explaining to someone what he did with his time and what he put into his body.

He didn't like explaining himself.

But then she saw the horses. And all his irritation faded as he took in the look on her face. She was filled with…wonder. Absolute wonder over this thing he took for granted.

The fact that he owned horses at all, that he had felt

compelled to acquire some once he had moved into this place, was a source of consternation. He had hated doing farm chores when he was a kid. Hadn't been able to get away from home and to the city fast enough. But in recent years, those feelings had started to change. And he'd found himself seeking out roots. Seeking out home.

For better or worse, this was home. Not just the misty Oregon coast, not just the town of Copper Ridge. But a ranch. Horses. A morning spent riding until the sun rose over the mountains, washing everything in a pale gold.

Yeah, that was home.

He could tell this ranch he loved was something beyond a temporary home for Danielle, who was looking at the horses and the barn like they were magical things.

She wasn't wearing her beanie today. Her dark brown hair hung limply around her face. She was pale, her chin pointed, her nose slightly pointed, as well. She was elfin, and he wasn't tempted to call her beautiful, but there was something captivating about her. Something fascinating. Watching her with the large animals was somehow just as entertaining as watching football and he couldn't quite figure out why.

"You didn't grow up around horses?"

"No," she said, taking a timid step toward the paddock. "I grew up in Portland."

He nodded. "Right."

"Always in apartments," she said. Then she frowned. "I think one time we had a house. I can't really remember it. We moved a lot. But sometimes when we lived with my mom's boyfriends, we had nicer places. It had its perks."

"What did?"

"My mom being a codependent hussy," she said, her

voice toneless so it was impossible to say whether or not she was teasing.

"Right." He had grown up in one house. His family had never moved. His parents were still in that same farmhouse, the one his family had owned for a couple of generations. He had moved away to go to college and then to start the business, but that was different. He had always known he could come back here. He'd always had roots.

"Will you go back to Portland when you're finished here?" he asked.

"I don't know," she said, blinking rapidly. "I've never really had a choice before. Of where I wanted to live."

It struck him then that she was awfully young. And that he didn't know quite *how* young. "You're twenty-two?"

"Yes," she said, sounding almost defensive. "So I haven't really had a chance to think about what all I want to do and, like, be. When I grow up and stuff."

"Right," he said.

He'd been aimless for a while, but before he'd graduated high school, he'd decided he couldn't deal with a life of ranching in Copper Ridge. He had decided to get out of town. He had wanted more. He had wanted bigger. He'd gone to school for marketing because he was good at selling ideas. Products. He wasn't necessarily the one who created them, or the one who dreamed them up, but he was the one who made sure a consumer would see them and realize that product was what their life had been missing up until that point.

He was the one who took the straw and made it into gold.

He had always enjoyed his job, but it would have been especially satisfying if he'd been able to start his career by building a business with his brother and sister. To be able to market Faith's extraordinary talent to the world, as he did now. But he wasn't sure that he'd started out with a passion for what he did so much as a passion for wealth and success, and that had meant leaving behind his sister and brother too, at first. But his career had certainly grown into a passion. And he'd learned that he was the practical piece. The part that everybody needed.

A lot of people had ideas, but less than half of them had the follow-through to complete what they started. And less than half of *those* people knew how to get to the consumer. That was where he came in.

He'd had his first corporate internship at the age of twenty. He couldn't imagine being aimless at twenty-two.

But then, Danielle had a baby and he couldn't imagine having a baby at that age either.

A hollow pang struck him in the chest.

He didn't like thinking of babies at all.

"You're judging me," she said, taking a step back from the paddock.

"No, I'm not. Also, you can get closer. You can pet them."

Her head whipped around to look at the horses, then back to him, her eyes round and almost comically hopeful. "I can?"

"Of course you can. They don't bite. Well, they *might* bite, just don't stick your fingers in their mouths."

"I don't know," she said, stuffing her hands in her pockets. Except he could tell she really wanted to. She was just afraid.

"Danielle," he said, earning himself a shocked look when he used her name. "Pet the horses."

She tugged her hand out of her pocket again, then took a tentative step forward, reaching out, then drawing her hand back just as quickly.

He couldn't stand it. Between her not knowing what she wanted to be when she grew up and watching her struggle with touching a horse, he just couldn't deal with it. He stepped forward, wrapped his fingers around her wrist and drew her closer to the paddock. "It's fine," he said.

A moment after he said the words, his body registered what he had done. More than that, it registered the fact that she was very warm. That her skin was smooth.

And that she was way, way too thin.

A strange combination of feelings tightened his whole body. Compassion tightened his heart; lust tightened his groin.

He gritted his teeth. "Come on," he said.

He noticed the color rise in her face, and he wondered if she was angry, or if she was feeling the same flash of awareness rocking through him. He supposed it didn't matter either way. "Come on," he said, drawing her hand closer to the opening of the paddock. "There you go, hold your hand flat like that."

She complied, and he released his hold on her, taking a step back. He did his best to ignore the fact that he could still feel the impression of her skin against his palm.

One of his horses—a gray mare named Blue—walked up to the bars and pressed her nose against Danielle's outstretched hand. Danielle made a sharp, shocked sound, drew her hand back, then giggled. "Her whiskers are soft."

"Yeah," he said, a smile tugging at his lips. "And she is about as gentle as they come, so you don't have to be afraid of her."

"I'm not afraid of anything," Danielle said, sticking her hand back in, letting the horse sniff her.

He didn't believe that she wasn't afraid of anything. She was definitely tough. But she was brittle. Like one of those people who might withstand a beating, but if something ever hit a fragile spot, she would shatter entirely.

"Would you like to go riding sometime?" he asked.

She drew her hand back again, her expression… Well, he couldn't quite read it. There was a softness to it, but also an edge of fear and suspicion.

"I don't know. Why?"

"You seem to like the horses."

"I do. But I don't know how to ride."

"I can teach you."

"I don't know. I have to watch Riley." She began to withdraw, both from him and from the paddock.

"I'm going to hire somebody to help watch Riley," he said, making that decision right as the words exited his mouth.

There was that look again. Suspicion. "Why?"

"In case I need you for something that isn't baby friendly. Which will probably happen. We have over a month ahead of us with you living with me, and one never knows what kinds of situations we might run into. I wasn't expecting you to come with a baby, and while I agree that it will definitely help make the case that you're not suitable for me, I also think we'll need to be able to go out without him."

She looked very hesitant about that idea. And he could understand why. She clung to that baby like he was a life preserver. Like if she let go of him, she might sink and be in over her head completely.

"And I would get to ride the horses?" she asked, her eyes narrowed, full of suspicion still.

"I said so."

"Sure. But that doesn't mean a lot to me, Mr. Grayson," she said. "I don't accept people at their word. I like legal documents."

"Well, I'm not going to draw up a legal document about giving you horse-riding lessons. So you're going to have to trust me."

"You want me to trust the sketchy rich dude who put an ad in the paper looking for a fake wife?"

"He's the devil you made the deal with, Ms. Kelly. I would say it's in your best interest to trust him."

"We shake on it at least."

She stuck her hand out, and he could see she was completely sincere. So he stuck his out in kind, wrapping his fingers around hers, marveling at her delicate bone structure. Feeling guilty now about getting angry over her eating his Pop-Tarts. The woman needed him to hire a gourmet chef too. Needed him to make sure she was getting three meals a day. He wondered how long it had been since she'd eaten regularly. She certainly didn't have the look of a woman who had recently given birth. There was no extra weight on her to speak of. He wondered how she had survived something so taxing as labor and delivery. But those were questions he was not going to ask. They weren't his business.

And he shouldn't even be curious about them.

"All right," she said. "You can hire somebody. And I'll learn to ride horses."

"You're a tough negotiator," he said, releasing his hold on her hand.

"Maybe I should go into business."

He tried to imagine this fragile, spiky creature in a boardroom, and it nearly made him laugh. "If you want to," he said, instead of laughing. Because he had a feeling she might attack him if he made fun of her. And another feeling that if Danielle attacked, she would likely go straight for the eyes. Or the balls.

He was attached to both of those things, and he liked them attached to him.

"I should go back to the house. Riley might wake up soon. Plus, I'm not entirely sure if I trust the new baby monitor. I mean, it's probably fine. But I'm going to have to get used to it before I really depend on it."

"I understand," he said, even though he didn't.

He turned and walked with her back toward the house. He kept his eyes on her small, determined frame. On the way, she stuffed her hands in her pockets and hunched her shoulders forward. As though she were trying to look intimidating. Trying to keep from looking at her surroundings in case her surroundings looked back.

And then he reminded himself that none of this mattered. She was just a means to an end, even if she was a slightly more multifaceted means than he had thought she might be.

It didn't matter how many facets she had. Danielle Kelly needed to fulfill only one objective. She had to be introduced to his parents and be found completely wanting.

He looked back at her, at her determined walk and her posture that seemed to radiate with *I'll cut you*.

Yeah. He had a feeling she would fulfill that objective just fine.

Chapter 4

Danielle was still feeling wobbly after her interaction with Joshua down at the barn. She had touched a horse. And she had touched *him*. She hadn't counted on doing either of those things today. And he had told her they were going to have dinner together tonight and he was going to give her a crash course on the Grayson family. She wasn't entirely sure she felt ready for that either.

She had gone through all her clothes, looking for something suitable for having dinner with a billionaire. She didn't have anything. Obviously.

She snorted, feeling like an idiot for thinking she could find something relatively appropriate in that bag of hers. A bag he thought had scabies.

She turned her snort into a growl.

Then, rebelliously, she pulled out the same pair of faded pants she had been wearing yesterday.

He had probably never dealt with a woman who wore

the same thing twice. Let alone the same thing two days in a row. Perversely, she kind of enjoyed that. Hey, she was here to be unsuitable. Might as well start now.

She looked in the mirror, grabbed one stringy end of her hair and blew out a disgusted breath. She shouldn't care how her hair looked.

But he was just so good-looking. It made her feel like a small, brown mouse standing next to him. It wasn't fair, really. That he had the resources to buy himself nice clothes and that he just naturally looked great.

She sighed, picking Riley up from his crib and sticking him in the little carrier she would put him in for dinner. He was awake and looking around, so she wanted to be in his vicinity, rather than leaving him upstairs alone. He wasn't a fussy baby. Really, he hardly ever cried.

But considering how often his mother had left him alone in those early days of his life, before Danielle had realized she couldn't count on her mother to take good care of him, she was reluctant to leave him by himself unless he was sleeping.

Then she paused, going back over to her bag to get the little red, dog-eared dictionary inside. She bent down, still holding on to Riley, and retrieved it. Then she quickly looked up scabies.

"I knew it," she said derisively, throwing the dictionary back into her bag.

She walked down the stairs and into the dining room, setting Riley in his seat on the chair next to hers. Joshua was already sitting at the table, looking as though he had been waiting for them. Which, she had a feeling, he was doing just to be annoying and superior.

"My bag can't have scabies," she said by way of greeting.

"Oh really?"

"Yes. I looked it up. Scabies are mites that burrow into your skin. Not into a duffel bag."

"They have to come from somewhere."

"Well, they're not coming from my bag. They're more likely to come from your horses, or something."

"You like my horses," he said, his tone dry. "Anyway, we're about to have dinner. So maybe we shouldn't be discussing skin mites?"

"You're the one who brought up scabies. The first time."

"I had pretty much dropped the subject."

"Easy enough for you to do, since it wasn't your hygiene being maligned."

"Sure." He stood up from his position at the table. "I'm just going to go get dinner, since you're here. I had it warming."

"Did you cook?"

He left the room without answering and returned a moment later holding two plates full of hot food. Her stomach growled intensely. She didn't even care what was on the plates. As far as she was concerned, it was gourmet. It was warm and obviously not from a can or a frozen pizza box. Plus, she was sitting at a real dining table and not on a patio set that had been shoved into her tiny living room.

The meal looked surprisingly healthy, considering she had discovered his affinity for Pop-Tarts earlier. And it was accompanied by a particularly nice-looking rice. "What is this?"

"Chicken and risotto," he said.

"What's risotto?"

"Creamy rice," he said. "At least, that's the simple explanation."

Thankfully, he wasn't looking at her like she was an alien for not knowing about risotto. But then she remembered he had spoken of having simple roots. So maybe he was used to dealing with people who didn't have as sophisticated a palate as he had.

She wrinkled her nose, then picked up her fork and took a tentative bite. It was good. So good. And before she knew it, she had cleared out her portion. Her cheeks heated when she realized he had barely taken two bites.

"There's plenty more in the kitchen," he said. Then he took her plate from in front of her and went back into the kitchen. She was stunned, and all she could do was sit there and wait until he returned a moment later with the entire pot of risotto, another portion already on her plate.

"Eat as much as you want," he said, setting everything in front of her.

Well, she wasn't going to argue with that suggestion. She polished off the chicken, then went back for thirds of the risotto. Eventually, she got around to eating the salad.

"I thought we were going to talk about my responsibilities for being your fiancée and stuff," she said after she realized he had been sitting there staring at her for the past ten minutes.

"I thought you should have a chance to eat a meal first."

"Well," she said, taking another bite, "that's unexpectedly kind of you."

"You seem…hungry."

That was the most loaded statement of the century. She was so hungry. For so many things. Food was kind of the least of it. "It's just been a really crazy few months."

"How old is the baby? Riley. How old is Riley?"

For the first time, because of that correction, she became aware of the fact that he seemed reluctant to call Riley by name. Actually, Joshua seemed pretty reluctant to deal with Riley in general.

Riley was unperturbed. Sitting in that reclined seat, his muddy blue eyes staring up at the ceiling. He lifted his fist, putting it in his mouth and gumming it idly.

That was one good thing she could say about their whole situation. Riley was so young that he was largely unperturbed by all of it. He had gone along more or less unaffected by their mother's mistakes. At least, Danielle hoped so. She really did.

"He's almost four months old," she said. She felt a soft smile touch her lips. Yes, taking care of her half brother was hard. None of it was easy. But he had given her a new kind of purpose. Had given her a kind of the drive she'd been missing before.

Before Riley, she had been somewhat content to just enjoy living life on her own terms. To enjoy not cleaning up her mother's messes. Instead, working at the grocery store, going out with friends after work for coffee or burritos at the twenty-four-hour Mexican restaurant.

Her life had been simple, and it had been carefree. Something she hadn't been afforded all the years she'd lived with her mother, dealing with her mother's various heartbreaks, schemes to try to better their circumstances and intense emotional lows.

So many years when Danielle should have been a child but instead was expected to be the parent. If her mother passed out in the bathroom after having too much to drink, it was up to Danielle to take care of her. To put a pillow underneath her mother's head, then make herself a piece of toast for dinner and get her homework done.

In contrast, taking care of only herself had seemed simple. And in truth, she had resented Riley at first, resented the idea that she would have to take care of another person again. But taking care of a baby was different. He wasn't a victim of his own bad choices. No, he was a victim of circumstances. He hadn't had a chance to make a single choice for himself yet.

To Danielle, Riley was the child she'd once been.

Except she hadn't had anyone to step in and take care of her when her mother failed. But Riley did. That realization had filled Danielle with passion. Drive.

And along with that dedication came a fierce, unexpected love like she had never felt before toward another human being. She would do anything for him. Give anything for him.

"And you've been alone with him all this time?"

She didn't know why she was so reluctant to let Joshua know that Riley wasn't her son. She supposed it was partly because, for all intents and purposes, he was her son. She intended to adopt him officially as soon as she had the means to do so. As soon as everything in her life was in order enough that Child Services would respond to her favorably.

The other part was that as long as people thought Riley was hers, they would be less likely to suggest she make a different decision about his welfare. Joshua Grayson had a coldness to him. He seemed to have a family who loved and supported him, but instead of finding it endearing, he got angry about it. He was using her to get back at his dad for doing something that, in her opinion, seemed mostly innocuous. And yes, she was benefiting from his pettiness, so she couldn't exactly judge.

Still, she had a feeling that if he knew Riley wasn't her son, he would suggest she do the "responsible" thing and allow him to be raised by a two-parent family, or whatever. She just didn't even want to have that discussion with him. Or with anybody. She had too many things against her already.

She didn't want to fight about this too.

"Mostly," she said carefully, treading the line between the truth and a lie. "Since he was about three weeks old. And I thought... I thought I could do it. I'd been self-sufficient for a long time. But then I realized there are a lot of logistical problems when you can't just leave your apartment whenever you want. It's harder to get to work. And I couldn't afford childcare. There wasn't any space at the places that had subsidized rates. So I was trading childcare with a neighbor, but sometimes our schedules conflicted. Anyway, it was just difficult. You can imagine why responding to your ad seemed like the best possible solution."

"I already told you, I'm not judging you for taking me up on an offer I made."

"I guess I'm just explaining that under other circumstances I probably wouldn't have sought you out. But things have been hard. I lost my job because I wasn't flexible enough and I had missed too many shifts because babysitting for Riley fell through."

"Well," he said, a strange expression crossing his face, "your problems should be minimized soon. You should be independently wealthy enough to at least afford childcare."

Not only that, she would actually be able to make decisions about her life. About what she wanted. When Joshua had asked her earlier today about whether or not she would go back to Portland, it had been the first time she had truly realized she could make decisions about where she wanted to live, rather than just parking herself somewhere because she happened to be there already.

It would be the first time in her life she could make proactive decisions rather than just reacting to her situation.

"Right. So I guess we should talk about your family," she said, determined to move the conversation back in the right direction. She didn't need to talk about herself. They didn't need to get to know each other. She just needed to do this thing, to trick his family, lie…whatever he needed her to do. So she and Riley could start their new life.

"I already told you my younger sister is an architectural genius. My older brother Isaiah is the financial brain. And I do the public relations and marketing. We have another brother named Devlin, and he runs a small ranching operation in town. He's married, no kids. Then there are my parents."

"The reason we find ourselves in this situation," she said, folding her hands and leaning forward. Then she cast a glance at the pot of risotto and decided to grab the spoon and serve herself another helping while they were talking.

"Yes. Well, not my mother so much. Sure, she wrings her hands and looks at me sadly and says she wishes I would get married. My father is the one who…actively meddles."

"That surprises me. I mean, given what I know about fathers. Which is entirely based on TV. I don't have one."

He lifted a brow.

"Well," she continued, "sure, I guess I do. But I never met him. I mean, I don't even know his name."

She realized that her history was shockingly close to the story she had given about Riley. Which was a true one. It just wasn't about Danielle. It was about her mother. And the fact that her mother repeated the same cycle over and over again. The fact that she never seemed to change. And never would.

"That must've been hard," he said. "I'm sorry."

"Don't apologize. I bet he was a jerk. I mean, circumstances would lead you to believe that he must be, right?"

"Yeah, it's probably a pretty safe assumption."

"Well, anyway, this isn't about my lack of a paternal figure. This is about the overbearing presence of yours."

He laughed. "My mother is old-fashioned—so is my father. My brother Devlin is a little bit too, but he's also something of a rebel. He has tattoos and things. He's a likely ally for you, especially since he got married a few months ago and is feeling soft about love and all of that. My brother Isaiah isn't going to like you. My sister, Faith, will try. Basically, if you cuss, chew with your mouth open, put your elbows on the table and in general act like a feral cat, my family will likely find you unsuitable. Also, if you could maybe repeatedly bring up the fact that you're really looking forward to spending my money, and that you had another man's baby four months ago, that would be great."

She squinted. "I think the fact that I have a four-month-old baby in tow will be reminder enough."

The idea of going into his family's farmhouse and behaving like a nightmare didn't sit as well with her as it had when the plan had been fully abstract. But now he had given names to the family members. Now she had been here for a while. And now it was all starting to feel a little bit real.

"It won't hurt. Though, he's pretty quiet. It might help if he screamed."

She laughed. "Oh, I don't know about that. I have a feeling your mom and sister might just want to hold him. That will be the real problem. Not having everyone hate me. That'll be easy enough. It'll be keeping everyone from loving him."

That comment struck her square in the chest, made her realize just what they were playing at here. She was going to be lying to these people. And yes, the idea was to alienate them, but they were going to think she might be their daughter-in-law, sister-in-law...that Riley would be their grandson or nephew.

But it would be a lie.

That's the point, you moron. And who cares? They're strangers. Riley is your life. He's your responsibility. And you'll never see these people again.

"We won't let them hold the baby," he said, his expression hard, as if he'd suddenly realized she wasn't completely wrong about his mother and sister and it bothered him.

She wished she could understand why he felt so strongly about putting a stop to his father playing matchmaker. As someone whose parents were ambivalent about her existence, his disregard for his family's well wishes was hard to comprehend.

"Okay," she said. "Fine by me. And you just want me to...be my charming self?"

"Obviously we'll have to come up with a story about our relationship. We don't have to make up how we met. We can say we met through the ad."

"The ad your father placed, not the ad you placed."

"Naturally."

She looked at Joshua then, at the broad expanse of table between them. Two people who looked less like a couple probably didn't exist on the face of the planet. Honestly, two strangers standing across the street from each other probably looked more like a happily engaged unit than they did.

She frowned. "This is very unconvincing."

"What is? Be specific."

She rolled her eyes at his impatience. "Us."

She stood up and walked toward him, sitting down in the chair right next to him. She looked at him for a moment, at the sharp curve of his jaw, the enticing shape of his lips. He was an attractive man. That was an understatement. He was also so uptight she was pretty sure he had a stick up his behind.

"Look, you want your family to think you've lost your mind, to think you have hooked up with a totally unsuitable woman, right?"

"That is the game."

"Then you have to look like you've lost your mind over me. Unfortunately, Joshua, you look very much in your right mind. In fact, a man of sounder mind may not exist. You are...responsible. You literally look like The Man."

"Which man?"

"Like, The Man. Like, fight the power. *You're* the power. Nobody's going to believe you're with me. At least, not if you don't seem a little bit...looser."

A slight smile tipped up those lips she had been thinking about only a moment before. His blue eyes warmed, and she felt an answering warmth spread low in her belly. "So what you're saying is we need to look like we have more of a connection?"

Her throat went dry. "It's just a suggestion."

He leaned forward, his gaze intent on hers. "An essential one, I think." Then he reached up and she jerked backward, nearly toppling off the side of her chair. "It looks like I'm not the only one who's wound a bit tight."

"I'm not," she said, taking a deep breath, trying to get her jittery body to calm itself down.

She wasn't used to men. She wasn't used to men touching her. Yes, intermittently she and her mother had lived with some of her mother's boyfriends, but none of them had ever been inappropriate with her. And she had never been close enough to even give any of them hugs.

And she really, really wasn't used to men who were so beautiful it was almost physically painful to look directly at them.

"You're right. We have to do a better job of looking like a couple. And that would include you not scampering under the furniture when I get close to you."

She sat up straight and folded her hands in her lap. "I did not scamper," she muttered.

"You were perilously close to a scamper."

"Was not," she grumbled, and then her breath caught in her throat as his warm palm made contact with her cheek.

He slid his thumb down the curve of her face to that dent just beneath her lips, his eyes never leaving hers. She felt…stunned and warm. No, hot. So very hot. Like there was a furnace inside that had been turned up the moment his hand touched her bare skin.

She supposed she was meant to be flirtatious. To play the part of the moneygrubbing tart with loose morals he needed her to be, that his family would expect her to be. But right now, she was shocked into immobility.

She took a deep breath, fighting for composure. But his thumb migrated from the somewhat reasonable point just below her mouth to her lip and her composure dissolved completely. His touch felt…shockingly intimate and filthy somehow. Not in a bad way, just in a way she'd never experienced before.

For some reason she would never be able to articulate—not even to herself—she darted her tongue out and touched the tip to his thumb. She tasted salt, skin and a promise that arrowed downward to the most private part of her body, leaving her feeling breathless. Leaving her feeling new somehow.

As if a wholly unexpected and previously unknown part of herself had been uncovered, awoken. She wanted to do exactly what he had accused her of doing earlier. She wanted to turn away. Wanted to scurry beneath the furniture or off into the night. Somewhere safe. Somewhere less confrontational.

But he was still looking at her. And those blue eyes were like chains, lashing her to the seat, holding her in place. And his thumb, pressed against her lip, felt heavy. Much too heavy for her to push against. For her to fight.

And when it came right down to it, she didn't even want to.

Something expanded in her chest, spreading low, opening up a yawning chasm in her stomach. Deepening her need, her want. Her desire for things she hadn't known she could desire until now.

Until he had made a promise with his touch that she hadn't known she wanted fulfilled.

She was just about to come back to herself, to pull away. And then he closed the distance between them.

His lips were warm and firm. The kiss was nothing like she had imagined it might be. She had always thought a kiss must reach inside and steal your brain. Transform you. She had always imagined a kiss to be powerful, considering the way her mother acted.

When her mother was under the influence of love—at least, that was what her mother had called it; Danielle had always known it was lust—she acted like someone entirely apart from herself.

Yes, Danielle had always known a kiss could be powerful. But what she hadn't counted on was that she might feel wholly like *herself* when a man fused his lips to hers. That she would be so perfectly aware of where she was, of what she was doing.

Of the pressure of his lips against hers, the warmth of his hand as he cradled her face, the hard, tightening knot of desire in her stomach that told her how insufficient the kiss was.

The desire that told her just how much more she wanted. Just how much more there could be.

He was kissing her well, this near stranger, and she never wanted it to end.

Instinctively, she angled her head slightly, parting her lips, allowing him to slide his tongue against hers. It was unexpectedly slick, unexpectedly arousing. Unexpectedly everything she wanted.

That was the other thing that surprised her. Because not only had she imagined a woman might lose herself entirely when a man kissed her, she had also imagined she would be immune. Because she knew better. She knew the cost. But she was sitting here, allowing him to kiss her and kiss her and kiss her. She was Danielle Kelly, and she was submitting herself to this sensual assault with almost shocking abandon.

Her hands were still folded in her lap, almost primly, but her mouth was parted wide, gratefully receiving every stroke of his tongue, slow and languorous against her own. Sexy. Deliciously affecting.

He moved his hands then, sliding them around the back of her neck, down between her shoulder blades, along the line of her spine until his hands spanned her waist. She arched, wishing she could press her body against his. Wishing she could do something to close the distance between them. Because he was still sitting in his chair and she in hers.

He pulled away, and she followed him, leaning into him with an almost humiliating desperation, wanting to taste him again. To be kissed again. By Joshua Grayson, the man she was committing an insane kind of fraud with. The man who had hired her to play the part of his pretend fiancée.

"That will do," he said, lifting his hand and squeezing her chin gently, those blue eyes glinting with a sharpness that cut straight to her soul. "Yes, Ms. Kelly, that will do quite nicely."

Then he released his hold on her completely, settling back in his seat, his attention returning to his dinner plate.

A slash of heat bled across Danielle's cheekbones. He hadn't felt anything at all. He had been proving a point. Just practicing the ruse they would be performing for his family tomorrow night. The kiss hadn't changed anything for him at all. Hadn't been more than the simple meeting of mouths.

It had been her first kiss. It had been everything.

And right then she got her first taste of just how badly a man could make a woman feel. Of how—when wounded—feminine pride could be a treacherous and testy thing.

She rose from her seat and rounded to stand behind his. Then, without fully pausing to think about what she might be doing, she placed her hands on his shoulders, leaned forward and slid her hands beneath the collar of his shirt and down his chest.

Her palms made contact with his hot skin, with hard muscle, and she had to bite her lip to keep from groaning out loud. She had to plant her feet firmly on the wood floor to keep herself from running away, from jerking her hands back like a child burned on a hot oven.

She'd never touched a man like this before. It was shocking just how arousing she found it, this little form of revenge, this little rebellion against his blasé response to the earthquake he had caused in her body.

She leaned her head forward, nearly pressing her lips against his ear. Then her teeth scraped his earlobe.

"Yes," she whispered. "I think it's quite convincing."

She straightened again, slowly running her fingernails over his skin as she did. She didn't know where this confidence had come from. Where the know-how and seemingly deep, feminine instinct had come from that allowed her to toy with him. But there it was.

She was officially playing the part of a saucy minx. Considering that was what he had hired her for, her flirtation was a good thing. But her heart thundered harder than a drum as she walked back to Riley, picked up his carrier and flipped her hair as she turned to face Joshua.

"I think I'm going to bed. I had best prepare myself to meet your family."

"You'll be wearing something different tomorrow," he said, his tone firm.

"Why?" She looked down at her ragged sweatshirt and skinny jeans. "That doesn't make any sense. You wanted me to look unsuitable. I might as well go in this."

"No, you brought up a very good point. You have to look unsuitable, but this situation also has to be believable. Plus, I think a gold digger would demand a new wardrobe, don't you?" One corner of his lips quirked upward, and she had a feeling he was punishing her for her little display a moment ago.

If only she could work out quite where the trap was.

"I don't know," she said, her voice stiff.

"But, Ms. Kelly, you told me yourself that you *are* a gold digger. That's why you're here, after all. For my gold."

"I suppose so," she said, keeping her words deliberately hard. "But I want actual gold, not clothes. So this is another thing that's going to be on you."

Those blue eyes glinted, and right then she got an idea of just how dangerous he was to her. "Consider it done."

And if there was one thing she had learned so far about Joshua Grayson, it was that if he said something would be done, it would be.

Chapter 5

Joshua wasn't going to try to turn Danielle into a sophisticate overnight. He was also avoiding thinking about the way it had felt to kiss her soft lips. Was avoiding remembering the way her hands had felt sliding down his chest.

He needed to make sure the two of them looked like a couple, that much was true. But he wouldn't allow himself to be distracted by her. There were a million reasons not to touch Danielle Kelly—unless they were playing a couple. Yes, there would have to be some touching, but he was not going to take advantage of her.

First of all, she was at his financial mercy. Second of all, she was the kind of woman who came with entanglements. And he didn't want any entanglements.

He wasn't the type to have trouble with self-control. If it wasn't a good time to seek out a physical relationship, he didn't. It wasn't a good time now, which meant he would defer any kind of sexual gratification until the end of his association with Danielle.

That should be fine.

He should be able to consider any number of women who he had on-again, off-again associations with, choose one and get in touch with her after Danielle left. His mind and body should be set on that.

Sadly, all he could think of was last night's kiss and the shocking heat that had come with it.

And then Danielle came down the stairs wearing the simple black dress he'd had delivered for her.

His thoughts about not transforming her into a sophisticated woman overnight held true. Her long, straight brown hair still hung limp down to her waist, and she had no makeup on to speak of except pale pink gloss on her lips.

But the simple cut of the dress suited her slender figure and displayed small, perky breasts that had been hidden beneath her baggy, threadbare sweaters.

She was holding on to the handle of the baby's car seat with both hands, lugging it down the stairs. For one moment, he was afraid she might topple over. He moved forward quickly, grabbing the handle and taking the seat from her.

When he looked down at the sleeping child, a strange tightness invaded his chest. "It wouldn't be good for you or for Riley if you fell and broke your neck trying to carry something that's too heavy for you," he said, his tone harder than he'd intended it to be.

Danielle scowled. "Well, offer assistance earlier next time. I had to get down the stairs somehow. Anyway, I've been navigating stairs like this with the baby since he was born. I lived in an apartment. On the third floor."

"I imagine he's heavier now than he used to be."

"An expert on child development?" She arched one dark brow as she posed the question.

He gritted his teeth. "Hardly."

She stepped away from the stairs, and the two of them walked toward the door. Just because he wanted to make it clear that he was in charge of the evening, he placed his hand low on her back, right at the dip where her spine curved, right above what the dress revealed to be a magnificent backside.

He had touched her there to get to her, but he had not anticipated the touch getting to him.

He ushered her out quickly, then handed the car seat to her, allowing her to snap it into the base—the one he'd had installed in his car when all of the nursery accoutrements had been delivered—then sat waiting for her to get in.

As they started to pull out of the driveway, she wrapped her arms around herself, rubbing her hands over her bare skin. "Do you think you could turn the heater on?"

He frowned. "Why didn't you bring a jacket?"

"I don't have one? All I have are my sweaters. And I don't think either of them would go with the dress. Would kind of ruin the effect."

He put the brakes on, slipped out of his own jacket and handed it to her. She just looked at him like he was offering her a live gopher. "Take it," he said.

She frowned but reached out, taking the jacket and slipping it on. "Thank you," she said, her voice sounding hollow.

They drove to his parents' house in silence, the only sounds coming from the baby sitting in the back seat. A sobering reminder of the evening that was about to unfold. He was going to present a surprise fiancée and a surprise baby to his parents, and suddenly, he didn't look at this plan in quite the same way as he had before.

He was throwing Danielle into the deep end. Throwing Riley into the deep end.

Joshua gritted his teeth, tightening his hold on the steering wheel. Finally, the interminable drive through town was over. He turned left off a winding road and onto a dirt drive that led back to the familiar, humble farmhouse his parents still called home.

That some part of his heart still called home too.

He looked over at Danielle, who had gone pale. "It's fine," he said.

Danielle looked down at the ring on her finger, then back up at him. "I guess it's showtime."

Danielle felt warm all over, no longer in need of Joshua's jacket, and conflicted down to the brand-new shoes Joshua had ordered for her.

But it wasn't the dress, or the shoes, that had her feeling warm. It was the jacket. Well, obviously a jacket was supposed to make her warm, but this was different. Joshua had realized she was cold. And it had mattered to him.

He had given her his own jacket so she could keep warm.

It was too big, the sleeves went well past the edges of her fingertips, and it smelled like him. From the moment she had slipped it on, she had been fighting the urge to bury her nose in the fabric and lose herself in the sharp, masculine smell that reminded her of his skin. Skin she had tasted last night.

Standing on the front step of this modest farmhouse that she could hardly believe Joshua had ever lived in, wearing his coat, with him holding Riley's car seat, it was too easy to believe this actually was some kind of "meet the parents" date.

In effect, she supposed it was. She was even wearing his jacket. His jacket that was still warm from his body and smelled—

Danielle was still ruminating about the scent of Joshua's jacket when the door opened. A blonde woman with graying hair and blue eyes that looked remarkably like her son's gave them a warm smile.

"Joshua," she said, glancing sideways at Danielle and clearly doing her best not to look completely shocked, "I didn't expect you so early. And I didn't know you were bringing a guest." Her eyes fell to the carrier in Joshua's hand. "Two guests."

"I thought it would be a good surprise."

"What would be?"

A man who could only be Joshua's father came to the door behind the woman. He was tall, with dark hair and eyes. He looked nice too. They both did. There was a warmth to them, a kindness, that didn't seem to be present in their son.

But then Danielle felt the warmth of the jacket again, and she had to revise that thought. Joshua might not exude kindness, but it was definitely there, buried. And for the life of her, she couldn't figure out why he hid it.

She was prickly and difficult, but at least she had an excuse. Her family was the worst. As far as she could tell, his family was guilty of caring too much. And she just couldn't feel that sorry for a rich dude whose parents loved him and were involved in his life more than he wanted them to be.

"Who is this?" Joshua's father asked.

"Danielle, this is my mom and dad, Todd and Nancy

Grayson. Mom, Dad, this is Danielle Kelly," Joshua said smoothly. "And I have you to thank for meeting her, Dad."

His father's eyebrows shot upward. "Do you?"

"Yes," Joshua said. "She responded to your ad. Mom, Dad, Danielle is my fiancée."

They were ushered into the house quickly after that announcement, and there were a lot of exclamations. The house was already full. A young woman sat in the corner holding hands with a large, tattooed man who was built like a brick house and was clearly related to Joshua somehow. There was another man, as tall as Joshua, with slightly darker hair and the same blue eyes but who didn't carry himself quite as stiffly. His build was somewhere in between Joshua and the tattooed man, muscular but not a beast.

"My brother Devlin," Joshua said, indicating the tattooed man before putting his arm around Danielle's waist as they moved deeper into the room, "and his wife, Mia. And this is my brother Isaiah. I'm surprised his capable assistant, Poppy, isn't somewhere nearby."

"Isaiah, did you want a beer or whiskey?" A petite woman appeared from the kitchen area, her curly, dark hair swept back into a bun, a few stray pieces bouncing around her pretty face. She was impeccable. From that elegant updo down to the soles of her tiny, high-heeled feet. She was wearing a high-waisted skirt that flared out at the hips and fell down past her knees, along with a plain, fitted top.

"Is that his...girlfriend?" Danielle asked.

Poppy laughed. "Absolutely not," she said, her tone clipped. "I'm his assistant."

Danielle thought it strange that an assistant would be at a family gathering but didn't say anything.

"She's more than an assistant," Nancy Grayson said. "She's part of the family. She's been with them since they started the business."

Danielle had not been filled in on the details of his family's relationships because she only needed to know how to alienate them, not how to endear herself to them.

The front door opened again and this time it was a younger blonde woman whose eyes also matched Joshua's who walked in. "Sorry I'm late," she said, "I got caught up working on a project."

This had to be his sister, Faith. The architect he talked about with such pride and fondness. A woman who was Danielle's age and yet so much more successful they might be completely different species.

"This is Joshua's fiancée," Todd Grayson said. "He's engaged."

"Shut the front door," Faith said. "Are you really?"

"Yes," Joshua said, the lie rolling easily off his tongue.

Danielle bit back a comment about his PR skills. She was supposed to be hard to deal with, but they weren't supposed to call attention to the fact this was a ruse.

"That's great?" Faith took a step forward and hugged her brother, then leaned in to grab hold of Danielle, as well.

"Is nobody going to ask about the baby?" Isaiah asked.

"Obviously *you* are," Devlin said.

"Well, it's kind of the eight-hundred-pound gorilla in the room. Or the ten-pound infant."

"It's my baby," Danielle said, feeling color mount in her cheeks.

She noticed a slight shift in Joshua's father's expression. Which was the general idea. To make him suspicious of her. To make him think he had gone and caught his son a gold digger.

"Well, that's…" She could see Joshua's mother searching for words. "It's definitely unexpected." She looked apologetically at Danielle the moment the words left her mouth. "It's just that Joshua hasn't shown much interest in marriage or family."

Danielle had a feeling that was an understatement. If Joshua was willing to go to such lengths to get his father out of his business, then he must be about as anti-marriage as you could get.

"Well," Joshua said, "Danielle and I met because of Dad."

His mother's blue gaze sharpened. "How?"

His father looked guilty. "Well, I thought he could use a little help," he said finally.

"What kind of help?"

"It's not good for a man to be alone, especially not our boys," he said insistently.

"Some of us like to be alone," Isaiah pointed out.

"You wouldn't feel that way if you didn't have a woman who cooked for you and ran your errands," his father responded, looking pointedly at Poppy.

"She's an employee," Isaiah said.

Poppy looked more irritated and distressed by Isaiah's comment than she did by the Grayson family patriarch's statement. But she didn't say anything.

"You were right," Joshua said. "I just needed to find the right woman. You placed that ad, listing all of my assets, and the right woman responded."

This was so ridiculous. Danielle felt her face heating. The assets Joshua's father had listed were his bank account, and there was no way in the world that wasn't exactly what everyone in his family was thinking.

She knew this was her chance to confirm her gold-digging motives. But right then, Riley started to cry.

"Oh," she said, feeling flustered. "Just let me… I need to…"

She fumbled around with the new diaper bag, digging around for a bottle, and then went over to the car seat, taking the baby out of it.

"Let me help," Joshua's mother said.

She was being so kind. Danielle felt terrible.

But before Danielle could protest, the other woman was taking Riley from her arms. Riley wiggled and fussed, but then she efficiently plucked the bottle from Danielle's hand and stuck it right in his mouth. He quieted immediately.

"What a good baby," she said. "Does he usually go to strangers?"

Danielle honestly didn't know. "Other than a neighbor whose known him since he was born, I'm the only one who takes care of him," she said.

"Don't you have any family?"

Danielle shook her head, feeling every inch the curiosity she undoubtedly was. Every single eye in the room was trained on her, and she knew they were all waiting for her to make a mistake. She was *supposed* to make a mistake, dammit. That was what Joshua was paying her to do.

"I don't have any family," she said decisively. "It's just been me and Riley from the beginning."

"It must be nice to have some help now," Faith said, not unkindly, but definitely probing.

"It is," Danielle said. "I mean, it's really hard taking care of a baby by yourself. And I didn't make enough money to…well, anything. So meeting Joshua has been great. Because he's so…helpful."

A timer went off in the other room and Joshua's mother blinked. "Oh, I have to get dinner." She turned to her son. "Since you're so helpful, Joshua." And before Danielle could protest, before Joshua could protest, Nancy dumped Riley right into his arms.

He looked like he'd been handed a bomb. And frankly, Danielle felt a little bit like a bomb might detonate at any moment. It had not escaped her notice that Joshua had never touched Riley. Yes, he had carried his car seat, but he had never voluntarily touched the baby. Which, now that she thought about it, must have been purposeful. But then, not everybody liked babies. She had never been particularly drawn to them before Riley. Maybe Joshua felt the same way.

She could tell by his awkward posture, and the way Riley's small frame was engulfed by Joshua's large, muscular one, that any contact with babies was not something he was used to.

She imagined Joshua's reaction would go a long way in proving how unsuitable she was. Maybe not in the way he had hoped, but it definitely made his point.

He took a seat on the couch, still holding on to Riley, still clearly committed to the farce.

"So you met through an ad," Isaiah said, his voice full of disbelief. "An ad that Dad put in the paper."

Everyone's head swiveled, and they looked at Todd. "I did what any concerned father would do for his son."

Devlin snorted. "Thank God I found a wife on my own."

"You found a wife by pilfering from my friendship pool," Faith said, her tone disapproving. "Isaiah and

Joshua have too much class to go picking out women that young."

"Actually," Danielle said, deciding this was the perfect opportunity to highlight another of the many ways in which she was unsuitable, "I'm only twenty-two."

Joshua's father looked at him, his gaze sharp. "Really?"

"Really," Danielle said.

"That's unexpected," Todd said to his son.

"That's what's so great about how we met," Joshua said. "Had I looked for a life partner on my own, I probably would have chosen somebody with a completely different set of circumstances. Had you asked me only a few short weeks ago, I would have said I didn't want children. And now look at me."

Everybody *was* looking at him, and it was clear he was extremely uncomfortable. Danielle wasn't entirely sure he was making the point he hoped to make, but he did make a pretty amusing picture. "I also would have chosen somebody closer to my age. But the great thing about Danielle is that she is so mature. I think it's because she's a mother. And yes, it happened for her in non-ideal circumstances, but her ability to rise above her situation and solve her problems—namely by responding to the ad—is one of the many things I find attractive about her."

She wanted to kick him in the shin. He was being a complete jerk, and he was making her sound like a total flake... But that was the whole idea. And, honestly, given the information Joshua had about her life...he undoubtedly thought she *was* a flake. It was stupid, and it wasn't fair. One of the many things she had learned about people since becoming the sole caregiver for Riley was that even though everyone had sex, a woman was an immediate pariah the minute she bore the evidence of that sex.

All that mattered to the hypocrites was that Danielle appeared to be a scarlet woman, therefore she was one.

Never mind that in reality she was a virgin.

Which was not a word she needed to be thinking while sitting in the Grayson family living room.

Her cheeks felt hot, like they were being stung by bees.

"Fate is a funny thing," Danielle said, edging closer to Joshua. She took Riley out of his arms, and from the way Joshua surrendered the baby, she could tell he was more than ready to hand him over.

The rest of the evening passed in a blur of awkward moments and stilted conversation. It was clear to her that his family was wonderful and warm, but that they were also seriously questioning Joshua's decision making. Todd Grayson looked as if he was going to be physically assaulted by his wife.

Basically, everything was going according to Joshua's plan.

But Danielle couldn't feel happy about it. She couldn't feel triumphant. It just felt awful.

Finally, it was time to go, and Danielle was ready to scurry out the door and keep on scurrying away from the entire Grayson family—Joshua included.

She was gathering her things, and Joshua was talking to one of his brothers, when Faith approached.

"We haven't gotten a chance to talk yet," she said.

"I guess not," Danielle said, feeling instantly wary. She had a feeling that being approached by Joshua's younger sister like this wouldn't end well.

"I'm sure he's told you all about me," Faith said, and Danielle had a feeling that statement was a test.

"Of course he has." She sounded defensive, even though

there was no reason for her to feel defensive, except that she kind of did anyway.

"Great. So here's the thing. I don't know exactly what's going on here, but my brother is not a 'marriage and babies' kind of guy. My brother dates a seemingly endless stream of models, all of whom are about half a foot taller than you without their ridiculous high heels on. Also, he likes blondes."

Danielle felt her face heating again as the other woman appraised her and found her lacking. "Right. Well. Maybe I'm a really great conversationalist. Although, it could be the fact that I don't have a gag reflex."

She watched the other woman's cheeks turn bright pink and felt somewhat satisfied. Unsophisticated, virginal Danielle had made the clearly much more sophisticated Faith Grayson blush.

"Right. Well, if you're leading him around by his... *you know*...so you can get into his wallet, I'm not going to allow that. There's a reason he's avoided commitment all this time. And I'm not going to let you hurt him. He's been hurt enough," she said.

Danielle could only wonder what that meant, because Joshua seemed bulletproof.

"I'm not going to break up with him," Danielle said. "Why would I do that? I'd rather stay in his house than in a homeless shelter."

She wanted to punch her own face. And she was warring with the fact that Faith had rightly guessed that she was using Joshua for his money—though not in the way his sister assumed. And Danielle needed Faith to think the worst. But it also hurt to have her assume something so negative based on Danielle's circumstances. Based on her appearance.

People had been looking at Danielle and judging her as low-class white trash for so long—not exactly incorrectly—that it was a sore spot.

"We're a close family," Faith said. "And we look out for each other. Just remember that."

"Well, your brother loves me."

"If that's true," Faith said, "then I hope you're very happy together. I actually do hope it's true. But the problem is, I'm not sure I believe it."

"Why?" Danielle was bristling, and there was no reason on earth why she should be. She shouldn't be upset about this. She shouldn't be taking it personally. But she was.

Faith Grayson had taken one look at Danielle and judged her. Pegged her for exactly the kind of person she was, really—a low-class nobody who needed the kind of money and security a man like Joshua could provide. Danielle had burned her pride to the ground to take part in this charade. Poking at the embers of that pride was stupid. But she felt compelled to do it anyway.

"Is it because I'm some kind of skank he would never normally sully himself with?"

"Mostly, it's because I know my brother. And I know he never intended to be in any kind of serious relationship again."

Again.

That word rattled around inside of Danielle. It implied he had been in a serious relationship before. He hadn't mentioned that. He'd just said he didn't want his father meddling. Didn't want marriage. He hadn't said it was because he'd tried before.

She blinked.

Faith took that momentary hesitation and ran with it.

"So you don't know that much about him. You don't actually know anything about him, do you? You just know he's rich."

"And he's hot," Danielle said.

She wasn't going to back down. Not now. But she would have a few very grumpy words with Joshua once they left.

He hadn't prepared her for this. She looked like an idiot. As she gathered her things, she realized looking like an idiot was his objective. She could look bad in a great many ways, after all. The fact that they might be an unsuitable couple because she didn't know anything about him would be one way to accomplish that.

When she and Joshua finally stepped outside, heading back to the car amid a thunderous farewell from the family, Danielle felt like she could breathe for the first time in at least two hours. She hadn't realized it, but being inside that house—all warm and cozy and filled with the kind of love she had only ever seen in movies—had made her throat and lungs and chest, and even her fingers, feel tight.

They got into the car, and Danielle folded her arms tightly, leaning her head against the cold passenger-side window, her breath fanning out across the glass, leaving mist behind. She didn't bother fighting the urge to trace a heart in it.

"Feeling that in character?" Joshua asked, his tone dry, as he put the car in Reverse and began to pull out of the driveway.

She stuck her tongue out and scribbled over the heart. "Not particularly. I don't understand. Now that I've met them, I understand even less. Your sister grilled me the minute she got a chance to talk to me alone. Your father is worried about the situation. Your mother is trying to be supportive in spite of the fact that we are clearly the worst couple of all time. And you're doing this why, Joshua? I don't understand."

She hadn't meant to call him out in quite that way. After all, what did she care about his motivations? He was paying her. The fact that he was a rich, eccentric idiot kind of worked in her favor. But tonight had felt wrong. And while she was more into survival than into the nuances of right and wrong, the ruse was getting to her.

"I explained to you already," he said, his tone so hard it elicited a small, plaintive cry from Riley in the back.

"Don't wake up the baby," she snapped.

"We really are a convincing couple," he responded.

"Not to your sister. Who told me we didn't make any sense together because you had never shown any interest in falling in love *again*."

It was dark in the car, so she felt rather than saw the tension creep up his spine. It was in the way he shifted in his seat, how his fists rolled forward as he twisted his hands on the steering wheel.

"Well," he said, "that's the thing. They all know. Because family like mine doesn't leave well enough alone. They want to know about all your injuries, all your scars, and then they obsess over the idea that they might be able to heal them. And they don't listen when you tell them healing is not necessary."

"Right," she said, blowing out an exasperated breath. "Here's the thing. I'm just a dumb bimbo you picked up through a newspaper ad who needed your money. So I don't understand all this coded nonsense. Just tell me what's going on. Especially if I'm going to spend more nights trying to alienate your family—who are basically a childhood sitcom fantasy of what a family should be."

"I've done it before, Danielle. Love. It's not worth it. Not considering how badly it hurts when it ends. But even more, it's not worth it when you consider how badly you can hurt the other person."

His words fell flat in the car, and she didn't know how to respond to them. "I don't…"

"Details aren't important. You've been hurt before, haven't you?"

He turned the car off the main road and headed up the long drive to his house. She took a deep breath. "Yes."

"By Riley's father?"

She shifted uncomfortably. "Not exactly."

"You didn't love him?"

"No," she said. "I didn't love him. But my mother kind of did a number on me. I do understand that love hurts. I also understand that a supportive family is not necessarily guaranteed."

"Yeah," Joshua said, "supportive family is great." He put the car in Park and killed the engine before getting out and stalking toward the house.

Danielle frowned, then unbuckled quickly, getting out of the car and pushing the sleeves of Joshua's jacket back so she could get Riley's car seat out of the base. Then she headed up the stairs and into the house after him.

"And yet you are trying to hurt yours. So excuse me if I'm not making all the connections."

"I'm not trying to hurt my family," he said, turning around, pushing his hand through his blond hair. His blue eyes glittered, his jaw suddenly looking sharper, his cheekbones more hollow. "What I want is for them to leave well enough alone. My father doesn't understand. He thinks all I need is to find somebody to love again and I'm going to be fixed. But there is no fixing this. There's no fixing me. I don't want it. And yeah, maybe this scheme is over the top, but don't you think putting an ad in the paper looking for a wife for your son is over the top too? I'm not giving him back anything he didn't dish out."

"Maybe you could talk to him."

"You think I haven't talked to him? You think this was my first resort? You're wrong about that. I tried reasonable discourse, but you can't reason with an unreasonable man."

"Yeah," Danielle said, picking at the edge of her thumbnail. "He seemed like a real monster. What with the clear devotion to your mother, the fact that he raised all of you, that he supported you well enough that you could live in that house all your life and then go off to become more successful than he was."

She set the car seat down on the couch and unbuckled it, lifting Riley into her arms and heading toward the stairs.

"We didn't have anything when I was growing up," he said, his tone flat and strange.

Danielle swallowed hard, lifting her hand to cradle Riley's soft head. "I'm sorry. But unless you were homeless or were left alone while one of your parents went to work all day—and I mean *alone*, not with siblings—then we might have different definitions of nothing."

"Fine," he said. "We weren't that poor. But we didn't have anything extra, and there was definitely nothing to do around here but get into trouble when you didn't have money."

She blinked. "What kind of trouble?"

"The usual kind. Go out to the woods, get messed up, have sex."

"Last I checked, condoms and drugs cost money." She

held on to Riley a little bit tighter. "Pretty sure you could have bought a movie ticket."

He lifted his shoulder. "Look, we pooled our money. We did what we did. Didn't worry about the future, didn't worry about anything."

"What changed?" Because obviously something had. He hadn't stayed here. He hadn't stayed aimless.

"One day I looked up and realized this was all I would ever have unless I changed something. Let me tell you, that's pretty sobering. A future of farming, barely making it, barely scraping by? That's what my dad had. And I hated it. I drank in the woods every night with my friends to avoid that reality. I didn't want to have my dad's life. So I made some changes. Not really soon enough to improve my grades or get myself a full scholarship, but I ended up moving to Seattle and getting myself an entry-level job with a PR firm."

"You just moved? You didn't know anybody?"

"No. I didn't know anyone. But I met people. And, it turned out, I was good at meeting people. Which was interesting because you don't meet very many new people in a small town that you've lived in your entire life. But in Seattle, no one knew me. No one knew who my father was, and no one had expectations for me. I was judged entirely on my own merit, and I could completely rewrite who I was. Not just some small-town deadbeat, but a young, bright kid who had a future in front of him."

The way he told that story, the very idea of it, was tantalizing to Danielle. The idea of starting over. Having a clean slate. Of course, with a baby in tow, a change like that would be much more difficult. But her association with Joshua would allow her to make it happen.

It was…shocking to realize he'd had to start over once.

Incredibly encouraging, even though she was feeling annoyed with him at the moment.

She leaned forward and absently pressed a kiss to Riley's head. "That must've been incredible. And scary."

"The only scary thing was the idea of going back to where I came from without changing anything. So I didn't allow that to happen. I worked harder than everybody else. I set goals and I met them. And then I met Shannon."

Something ugly twisted inside of Danielle's stomach the moment he said the other woman's name. For the life of her she couldn't figure out why. She felt...curious. But in a desperate way. Like she needed to know everything about this other person. This person who had once shared Joshua's life. This person who had undoubtedly made him the man standing in front of her. If she didn't know about this woman, then she would never understand him.

"What, then? Who was Shannon?" Her desperation was evident in her words, and she didn't bother hiding it.

"She was my girlfriend. For four years, while I was getting established in Seattle. We lived together. I was going to ask her to marry me."

He looked away from her then, something in his blue eyes turning distant. "Then she found out she was pregnant, and I figured I could skip the elaborate proposal and move straight to the wedding."

She knew him well enough to know this story wasn't headed toward a happy ending. He didn't have a wife. He didn't have a child. In fact, she was willing to bet he'd never had a child. Based on the way he interacted with Riley. Or rather, the very practiced way he avoided interacting with Riley.

"That didn't happen," she said, because she didn't know what else to say, and part of her wanted to spare him having to tell the rest of the story. But, also, part of her needed to know.

"She wanted to plan the wedding. She wanted to wait until after the baby was born. You know, wedding dress sizes and stuff like that. So I agreed. She miscarried late, Danielle. Almost five months. It was…the most physically harrowing thing I've ever watched anyone go through. But the recovery was worse. And I didn't know what to do. So I went back to work. We had a nice apartment, we had a view of the city, and if I worked, she didn't have to. I could support her, I could buy her things. I could do my best to make her happy, keep her focused on the wedding."

He had moved so quickly through the devastating, painful revelation of his lost baby that she barely had time to process it. But she also realized he had to tell the story this way. There was no point lingering on the details. It was simple fact. He had been with a woman he loved very much. He had intended to marry her, had been expecting a child with her. And they had lost the baby.

She held on a little bit more tightly to Riley.

"She kept getting worse. Emotionally. She moved into a different bedroom, then she didn't get out of bed. She had a lot of pain. At first, I didn't question it, because it seemed reasonable that she'd need pain medication after what she went through. But then she kept taking it. And I wondered if that was okay. We had a fight about it. She said it wasn't right for me to question her pain—physical or otherwise—when all I did was work. And you know… I thought she was probably right. So I let it go. For a year, I let it go. And then I found out the situation with the prescription drugs was worse than I realized. But when I confronted Shannon, she just got angry."

It was so strange for Danielle to imagine what he was

telling her. This whole other life he'd had. In a city where he had lived with a woman and loved her. Where he had dreamed of having a family. Of having a child. Where he had buried himself in work to avoid dealing with the pain of loss, while the woman he loved lost herself in a different way.

The tale seemed so far removed from the man he was now. From this place, from that hard set to his jaw, that sharp glitter in his eye, the way he held his shoulders straight. She couldn't imagine this man feeling at a loss. Feeling helpless.

"She got involved with another man, someone I worked with. Maybe it started before she left me, but I'm not entirely sure. All I know is she wasn't sleeping with me at the time, so even if she was with him before she moved out, it hardly felt like cheating. And anyway, the affair wasn't really the important part. That guy was into recreational drug use. It's how he functioned. And he made it all available to her."

"That's...that's awful, Joshua. I know how bad that stuff can be. I've seen it."

He shook his head. "Do you have any idea what it's like? To have somebody come into your life who's beautiful, happy, and to watch her leave your life as something else entirely. Broken, an addict. I ruined her."

Danielle took a step back, feeling as though she had been struck by the impact of his words. "No, you didn't. It was drugs. It was..."

"I wasn't there for her. I didn't know how to be. I didn't like hard things, Danielle. I never did. I didn't want to stay in Copper Ridge and work the land—I didn't want to deal with a lifetime of scraping by, because it was too hard."

"Right. You're so lazy that you moved to Seattle and

started from scratch and worked your way to the highest ranks of the company? I don't buy that."

"There's reward in that kind of work, though. And you don't have to deal with your life when it gets bad. You just go work more. And you can tell yourself it's fine because you're making more money. Because you're making your life easier, life for the other person easier, even while you let them sit on the couch slowly dying, waiting for you to help them. I convinced myself that what I was doing was important. It was the worst kind of narcissism, Danielle, and I'm not going to excuse it."

"But that was… It was a unique circumstance. And you're different. And…it's not like every future relationship…"

"And here's the problem. You don't know me. You don't even like me and yet you're trying to fix this. You're trying to convince me I should give relationships another try. It's your first instinct, and you don't even actually care. My father can't stop any more than you could stop yourself just now. So I did this." He gestured between the two of them. "I did this because he escalated it all the way to putting an ad in the paper. Because he won't listen to me. Because he knows my ex is a junkie somewhere living on the damned street, and that I feel responsible for that, and still he wants me to live his life. This life here, where he's never made a single mistake or let anyone down."

Danielle had no idea what to say to that. She imagined that his dad had made mistakes. But what did she know? She only knew about absentee fathers and mothers who treated their children like afterthoughts.

Her arms were starting to ache. Her chest ached too. All of her ached.

"I'm going to take Riley up to bed," she said, turning and heading up the stairs.

She didn't look back, but she could hear the heavy footfalls behind her, and she knew he was following her. Even if she didn't quite understand why.

She walked into her bedroom, and she left the door open. She crossed the space and set Riley down in the crib. He shifted for a moment, stretching his arms up above his head and kicking his feet out. But he didn't wake up. She was sweaty from having his warm little body pressed against her chest, but she was grateful for that feeling now. Thinking about Joshua and his loss made her feel especially grateful.

Joshua was standing in the doorway, looking at her. "Did you still want to argue with me?"

She shook her head. "I never wanted to argue with you."

She went to walk past him, but his big body blocked her path. She took a step toward him, and he refused to move, his blue eyes looking straight into hers.

"You seemed like you wanted to argue," he responded.

"No," she said, reaching up to press her hand against him, to push him out of the way. "I just wanted an explanation."

The moment her hand made contact with his shoulder, something raced through her. Something electric. Thrilling. Something that reached back to that feeling, that tightening low in her stomach when he'd first mentioned Shannon.

The two feelings were connected.

Jealousy. That was what she felt. Attraction. That was what this was.

She looked up, his chin in her line of sight. She saw a

dusting of golden whiskers, and they looked prickly. His chin looked strong. The two things in combination—the strength and the prickliness—made her want to reach out and touch him, to test both of those hypotheses and see if either was true.

Touching him was craziness. She knew it was. So she curled her fingers into a fist and lowered her hand back down to her side.

"Tell me," he said, his voice rough. "After going through what you did, being pregnant. Being abandoned… You don't want to jump right back into relationships, do you?"

He didn't know the situation. And he didn't know it because she had purposefully kept it from him. Still, because of the circumstances surrounding Riley's birth, because of the way her mother had always conducted relationships with men, because of the way they had always ended, Danielle wanted to avoid romantic entanglements.

So she could find an honest answer in there somewhere.

"I don't want to jump into anything," she said, keeping her voice even. "But there's a difference between being cautious and saying never."

"Is there?"

He had dipped his head slightly, and he seemed to loom over her, to fill her vision, to fill her senses. When she breathed in, the air was scented with him. When she felt warm, the warmth was from his body.

Her lips suddenly felt dry, and she licked them. Then became more aware of them than she'd ever been in her entire life. They felt…obvious. Needy.

She was afraid she knew exactly what they were needy for.

His mouth. His kiss.

The taste of him. The feel of him.

She wondered if he was thinking of their kiss too. Of course, for him, a kiss was probably a commonplace event.

For her, it had been singular.

"You can't honestly say you want to spend the rest of your life alone?"

"I'm only alone when I want to be," he said, his voice husky. "There's a big difference between wanting to share your life with somebody and wanting to share your bed sometimes." He tilted his head to the side. "Tell me. Have you shared your bed with anyone since you were with him?"

She shook her head, words, explanations, getting stuck in her throat. But before she knew it, she couldn't speak anyway, because he had closed the distance between them and claimed her mouth with his.

Chapter 6

He was hell bound, that much was certain. After everything that had happened tonight with his family, after Shannon, his fate had been set in stone. But if it hadn't been, then this kiss would have sealed that fate, padlocked it and flung it right down into the fire.

Danielle was young, she was vulnerable and contractually she was at his mercy to a certain degree. Kissing her, wanting to do more with her, was taking being jackass to extremes.

Right now, he didn't care.

If this was hell, he was happy to hang out for a while. If only he could keep kissing her, if only he could keep tasting her.

She held still against his body for a moment before angling her head, wrapping her arms around his neck, sliding her fingers through his hair and cupping the back of his head as if she was intent on holding him against her mouth.

As if she was concerned he might break the kiss. As if he was capable of that.

Sanity and reasonable decision making had exited the building the moment he had closed the distance between them. It wasn't coming back anytime soon. Not as long as she continued to make those sweet, kittenish noises. Not as long as she continued to stroke her tongue against his— tentatively at first and then with much more boldness.

He gripped the edge of the doorjamb, backing her against the frame, pressing his body against hers. He was hard, and he knew she would feel just how much he wanted her.

He slipped his hands around her waist, then down her behind to the hem of her dress. He shoved it upward, completely void of any sort of finesse. Void of anything beyond the need and desperation screaming inside of him to be inside her. To be buried so deep he wouldn't remember anything.

Not why he knew her. Why she was here. Not what had happened at his parents' house tonight. Not the horrific, unending sadness that had happened in his beautiful high-rise apartment overlooking the city he'd thought of as his. The penthouse that should have kept him above the struggle and insulated him from hardship.

Yeah, he didn't want to think about any of it.

He didn't want to think of anything but the way Danielle tasted. How soft her skin was to the touch.

Why the hell some skinny, bedraggled urchin had suddenly managed to light a fire inside of him was beyond him.

He didn't really care about the rationale right now. No. He just wanted to be burned.

He moved his hands around, then dipped one between her legs, rubbing his thumb against the silken fabric of her panties. She gasped, arching against him, wrenching her mouth away from his and letting her head fall back against the door frame.

That was an invitation to go further. He shifted his stance, drawing his hand upward and then down beneath the waistband of her underwear. He made contact with slick, damp skin that spoke of her desire for him. He had to clench his teeth to keep from embarrassing himself then and there.

He couldn't remember the last time a woman had affected him like this, if ever. When a simple touch, the promise of release, had pushed him so close to the edge.

When so little had felt like so much.

He stroked her, centering his attention on her most sensitive place. Her eyes flew open wide as if he had discovered something completely new. As if she was discovering something completely new. And that did things to him. Things it shouldn't do. Mattered in ways it shouldn't.

Because this shouldn't matter and neither should she.

He pressed his thumb against her chin, leaned forward and captured her open mouth with his.

"I have to have you," he said, the words rough, unpracticed, definitely not the way he usually propositioned a woman.

His words seemed to shock her. Like she had made contact with a naked wire. She went stiff in his arms, and then she pulled away, her eyes wide. "What are we doing?"

She was being utterly sincere, the words unsteady, her expression one of complete surprise and even...fear.

"I'm pretty sure we were about to make love," he said, using a more gentle terminology than he normally would have because of that strange vulnerability lurking in her eyes.

She shook her head, wiggling out of his hold and moving away from the door, backing toward the crib. "We can't do that. We can't." She pressed her hand against her cheek, and she looked so much like a stereotypical distressed female from some 1950s comic that he would have laughed if she hadn't successfully made him feel like he would be the villain in that piece. "It would be... It would be wrong."

"Why exactly?"

"Because. You're paying me to be here. You're paying me to play the part of your fiancée, and if things get physical between us, then I don't understand exactly what separates me from a prostitute."

"I'm not paying you for sex," he said. "I'm paying you to pretend to be my fiancée. I want you. And that's entirely separate from what we're doing here."

She shook her head, her eyes glistening. "Not to me. I already feel horrible. Like the worst person ever, after what I did to your family. After the way we tricked them tonight. After the way we will continue to trick them. I can't add sex to this situation. I have to walk away from this, Joshua. I have to walk away and not feel like I lost myself. I can't face the idea that I might finally sort out the money, where I'm going to live, how I'll survive...and lose the only thing I've always had. Myself. I just can't."

He had never begged a woman in his life, but he realized right then that he was on the verge of begging her to agree that it would feel good enough for whatever consequences to be damned. But as he looked behind her at the crib—the crib with the woman's baby in it, for heaven's sake—he realized the argument wasn't going to work with her.

She had been badly used, and though she had never

really given him details, the evidence was obvious. She was alone. She had been abandoned at her most vulnerable. For her, the deepest consequences of sex were not hypothetical.

Though, they weren't for him either. And he was a stickler for safe sex, so there was that. Still, he couldn't blame her for not trusting him. And he should want nothing more than to find a woman who was less complicated. One who didn't have all the baggage that Danielle carried.

Still, he wanted to beg.

But he didn't.

"Sex isn't that big of a deal for me," he said. "If you're not into it, that's fine."

She nodded, the gesture jerky. "Good. That's probably another reason we shouldn't."

"I'm going to start interviewing nannies tomorrow," he said, abruptly changing the subject, because if he didn't, he would haul her back into his arms and finish what he had started.

"Okay," she said, looking shell-shocked.

"You'll have a little bit more freedom then. And we can go out riding."

She blinked. "Why? I just turned you down. Why do you want to do anything for me?"

"I already told you. None of this is a trade for sex. You turning me down doesn't change my intentions."

She frowned. "I don't understand." She looked down, picking at her thumbnail. "Everything has a price. There's no reason for you to do something for me when you're not looking for something in return."

"Not everything in life is a transaction, Danielle."

"I suppose it's not when you care about somebody."

She tilted her head to the side. "But nobody's ever really cared about me."

If he hadn't already felt like a jerk, then her words would have done it. Because his family did care about him. His life had been filled with people doing things for him just because they wanted to give him something. They'd had no expectation of receiving anything in return.

But after Shannon, something had changed inside of him. He wanted to hold everybody at arm's length. Explaining himself felt impossible.

He hadn't wanted to give to anyone, connect with anyone, in a long time. But for some reason, he wanted to connect with Danielle. Wanted to give to that fragile, sweet girl.

It wasn't altruistic. Not really. She had so little that it was easy to step in and do something life altering. She didn't understand the smallest gesture of kindness, which meant the smallest gesture was enough.

"Tomorrow the interview process starts. I assume you want input?"

"Do I want input over who is going to be watching my baby? Yeah. That would be good."

She reached up, absently touching her lips, then lowered her hand quickly, wiggling her fingers slightly. "Good night," she said, the words coming out in a rush.

"Good night," he said, his voice hard. He turned, closing the door resolutely behind him, because if he didn't, he couldn't be responsible for what he might do.

He was going to leave her alone. He was going to do something nice for her. As if that would do something for his tarnished soul.

Well, maybe it wouldn't. But maybe it would do something for her. And for some reason, that mattered.

Maybe that meant he wasn't too far gone, after all.

* * *

Danielle had never interviewed anyone who was going to work for her. She had interviewed for several jobs herself, but she had never been on the reverse side. It was strange and infused her with an inordinate sense of power.

Which was nice, considering she rarely felt powerful.

Certainly not the other night when Joshua had kissed her. Then she had felt weak as a kitten. Ready to lie down and give him whatever he wanted.

Except she hadn't. She had said no. She was proud of herself for that, even while she mourned the loss of whatever pleasure she might have found with him.

It wasn't about pleasure. It was about pride.

Pride and self-preservation. What she had said to him had been true. If she walked away from this situation completely broken, unable to extricate herself from him, from his life, because she had allowed herself to get tangled up in ways she hadn't anticipated, then she would never forgive herself. If she had finally made her life easier in all the ways she'd always dreamed of, only to snare herself in a trap she knew would end in pain...

She would judge herself harshly for that.

Whatever she wanted to tell herself about Joshua—he was a tool, he didn't deserve the wonderful family he had—she was starting to feel things for him. Things she really couldn't afford to feel.

That story about his girlfriend had hit her hard and deep. Hit her in a place she normally kept well protected.

Dammit.

She took a deep breath and looked over at the new nanny, Janine, who had just started today, and who was going to watch Riley while Joshua and Danielle went for a ride.

She was nervous. Unsteady about leaving Riley for

the first time in a while. Necessity had meant she'd had to leave him when she was working at the grocery store. Still, this felt different. Because it wasn't necessary. It made her feel guilty. Because she was leaving him to do something for herself.

She shook her head. Her reaction was ridiculous. But she supposed it was preferable to how her mother had operated. Which was to never think about her children at all. Her neglect of Danielle hadn't come close to her disinterest in her youngest child. Danielle supposed that by the time Riley was born, her mother had been fully burned-out. Had exhausted whatever maternal instinct she'd possessed.

Danielle shook her head. Then took a deep breath and turned to face Janine. "He should nap most of the time we're gone. And even if he wakes up, he's usually really happy."

Janine smiled. "He's just a baby. I've watched a lot of babies. Not that he isn't special," she said, as though she were trying to cover up some faux pas. "I just mean, I'm confident that I can handle him."

Danielle took a deep breath and nodded. Then Joshua came into the room and the breath she had just drawn into her lungs rushed out.

He was wearing a dark blue button-down shirt and jeans, paired with a white cowboy hat that made him look like the hero in an old Western movie.

Do not get that stupid. He might be a hero, but he's not your hero.

No. Girls like her didn't get heroes. They had to be their own heroes. And that was fine. Honestly, it was.

If only she could tell her heart that. Her stupid heart, which was beating out of control.

It was far too easy to remember what it had been like to kiss him. To remember what it had felt like when his stubble-covered cheek scraped against hers. How sexy it had felt. How intoxicating it had been to touch a man like that. To experience the differences between men and women for the first time.

It was dangerous, was what it was. She had opened a door she had never intended to open, and now it was hard to close.

She shook her hands out, then balled them into fists, trying to banish the jitters that were racing through her veins.

"Are you ready?" he asked.

His eyes met hers and all she could think was how incredible it was that his eyes matched his shirt. They were a deep, perfect shade of navy.

There was something wrong with her. She had never been this stupid around a man before.

"Yes," she said, the answer coming out more as a squeak than an actual word. "I'm ready."

The corner of his mouth lifted into a lopsided grin. "You don't have to be nervous. I'll be gentle with you."

She nearly choked. "Good to know. But I'm more worried about the horse being gentle with me."

"She will be. Promise. I've never taught a girl how to ride before, but I'm pretty confident I can teach you."

His words ricocheted around inside of her, reaching the level of double entendre. Which wasn't fair. That wasn't how he'd meant it.

Or maybe it was.

He hadn't been shy about letting her know exactly what he wanted from her that night. He had put his hand between her legs. Touched her where no other man ever had. He'd made her see stars, tracked sparks over her skin.

It was understandable for her to be affected by the experience. But like he'd said, sex didn't really matter to him. It wasn't a big deal. So why he would be thinking of it now was beyond her. He had probably forgotten already. Probably that kiss had become an indistinct blur in his mind, mixed with all his other sexual encounters.

There were no other encounters for her. So there he was in her mind, and in front of her, far too sharp and far too clear.

"I'm ready," she said, the words rushed. "Totally ready."

"Great," he said. "Let's go."

Taking Danielle out riding was submitting himself to a particular kind of torture, that was for sure. But he was kind of into punishing himself...so he figured it fit his MO.

He hadn't stopped thinking about her since they had kissed—and more—in her bedroom the other night. He had done his best to throw himself into work, to avoid her, but still, he kept waking up with sweat slicked over his skin, his body hard and dreams of...her lips, her tongue, her scent...lingering in his thoughts.

Normally, the outdoors cleared his mind. Riding his horse along the length of the property was his therapy. Maneuvering her over the rolling hills, along the ridge line of the mountain, the evergreen trees rising behind them in a stately backdrop that left him feeling small within the greater context of the world. Which was something a man like him found refreshing some days.

But not today.

Today, he was obsessing. He was watching Danielle's

behind as she rode her horse in front of him, the motion of the horse's gait making him think of what it would look like if the woman was riding him instead of his mare.

He couldn't understand this. Couldn't understand this obsession with her.

She wasn't the kind of sophisticated woman he tended to favor. In a lot of ways, she reminded him of the kind of girl he used to go for here in town, back when he had been a good-for-nothing teenager spending his free time drinking and getting laid out in the woods.

Back then he had liked hometown girls who wanted the same things he did. A few hours to escape, a little bit of fun.

The problem was, he already knew Danielle didn't want that. She didn't find casual hookups fun. And he didn't have anything to offer beyond a casual hookup.

The other problem was that the feelings he had for her were not casual. If they were, then he wouldn't be obsessing. But he was.

In the couple of weeks since she had come to live with him, she had started to fill out a bit. He could get a sense of her figure, of how she would look if she were thriving rather than simply surviving. She was naturally thin, but there was something elegant about her curves.

But even more appealing than the baser things, like the perky curve of her high breasts and the subtle slope of her hips, was the stubborn set of her jaw. The straight, brittle weight of her shoulders spoke of both strength and fragility.

While there was something unbreakable about her, he worried that if a man ever were to find her weakness, she would do more than just break. She would shatter.

He shook his head. And then he forced himself to look

away from her, forced himself to look at the scenery. At the mountain spread out before them, and the ocean gray and fierce behind it.

"Am I doing okay?"

Danielle's question made it impossible to ignore her, and he found himself looking at her ass again. "You haven't fallen off yet," he said, perhaps a bit unkindly.

She snorted, then looked over her shoulder, a challenging light glittering in her brown eyes. "Yet? I'm not going to fall off, Joshua Grayson. It would take a hell of a lot to unseat me."

"Says the woman who was shaking when I helped her mount up earlier."

She surprised him by releasing her hold on the reins with one hand and waving it in the air. "Well, I'm getting the hang of it."

"You're a regular cowgirl," he said.

Suddenly, he wanted that to be true. It was the strangest thing. He wanted her to have this outlet, this freedom. Something more than a small apartment. Something more than struggle.

You're giving her that. That's what this entire bargain is for. Like she said, she's a gold digger, and you're giving her your gold.

Yes, but he wanted to give her more than that.

Just like he had told her the other day, what he wanted to give her wasn't about an exchange. He wanted her to have something for herself. Something for Riley.

Maybe it was a misguided attempt to atone for what he hadn't managed to give Shannon. What he hadn't ever been able to give the child he lost.

He swallowed hard, taking in a deep breath of the sharp pine and salt air, trying to ease the pressure in his chest.

She looked at him again, this time a dazzling smile on her lips. It took all that pressure in his chest and punched a hole right through it. He felt his lungs expand, all of him begin to expand.

He clenched his teeth, grinding them together so hard he was pretty sure his jaw was going to break. "Are you about ready to head back?"

"No. But I'm not sure I'm ever going to be ready to head back. This was… Thank you." She didn't look at him this time. But he had a feeling it was because she was a lot less comfortable with sincere connection than she was with sarcasm.

Well, that made two of them.

"You're welcome," he said, fixing his gaze on the line of trees beside them.

He maneuvered his horse around in front of hers so he could lead the way back down to the barn. They rode on in silence, but he could feel her staring holes into his back.

"Are you looking at my butt, Danielle?"

He heard a sputtering noise behind him. "No."

They rode up to the front of the barn and he dismounted, then walked over to her horse. "Liar. Do you need help?"

She frowned, her brows lowering. "Not from you. You called me a liar."

"Because you were looking at my butt and we both know it." He raised his hand up, extending it to her. "Now let me help you so you don't fall on your pretty face."

"Bah," she said, reaching out to him, her fingers brushing against his, sending an electrical current arcing between them. He chose to ignore it. Because there was no way in the whole damn world that the brush of a woman's fingertips against his should get him hot and bothered.

He grabbed hold of her and helped get her down from the horse, drawing her against him when her feet connected with the ground. And then it was over.

Pretending that this wasn't a long prelude to him kissing her again. Pretending that the last few days hadn't been foreplay. Pretending that every time either of them had thought about the kiss hadn't been easing them closer and closer to the inevitable.

She wanted him, he knew that. It was clear in the way she responded to him. She might have reservations about acting on it, and he had his own. But need was bigger than any of that right now, building between them, impossible to ignore.

He was a breath away from claiming her mouth with his when she shocked him by curving her fingers around his neck and stretching up on her toes.

Her kiss was soft, tentative. A question where his kiss would have been a command. But that made it all the sweeter. The fact that she had come to him. The fact that even though she was still conflicted about all of it, she couldn't resist any longer.

He cupped her cheek, calling on all his restraint—what little there was—to allow her to lead this, to allow her to guide the exploration. There was something so unpracticed about that pretty mouth of hers, something untutored about the way her lips skimmed over his. About the almost sweet, soft way her tongue tested his.

What he wanted to do was take it deep. Take it hard. What he wanted to do was grab hold of her hips and press her back against the barn. Push her jeans down her thighs and get his hand back between her gorgeous legs so he could feel all that soft, slick flesh.

What he wanted was to press himself against her and

slide in slowly, savoring the feel of her desire as it washed over him.

But he didn't.

And it was the damned hardest thing he had ever done. To wait. To let her lead. To let her believe she had the control here. Whatever she needed to do so she wouldn't get scared again. If he had to be patient, if he had to take it slow, he could. He would.

If it meant having her.

He had to have her. Had to exorcise the intense demon that had taken residence inside of him, that demanded he take her. Demanded he make her his own.

His horse snickered behind them, shifting her bulk, drawing Danielle's focus back to the present and away from him. Dammit all.

"Let me get them put away," he said.

He was going to do it quickly. And then he was going to get right back to tasting her. He half expected her to run to the house as he removed the tack from the animals and got them brushed down, but she didn't. Instead, she just stood there watching him, her eyes large, her expression one of absolute indecision.

Because she knew.

She knew that if she stayed down here, he wasn't going to leave it at a kiss. He wasn't going to leave it at all.

But he went about his tasks, slowing his movements, forcing himself not to rush. Forcing himself to draw it out. For her torture as well as his. He wanted her to need it, the way that he did.

And yes, he could see she wanted to run. He could also tell she wanted him, she wanted this. She was unbearably curious, even if she was also afraid.

And he was counting on that curiosity to win out.

Finally, she cleared her throat, shifting impatiently. "Are you going to take all day to do that?"

"You have to take good care of your horses, Danielle. I know a city girl like you doesn't understand how that works."

She squinted, then took a step forward, pulling his hat off his head and depositing it on her own. "Bull. You're playing with me."

He couldn't hold back the smile. "Not yet. But I plan to."

After that, he hurried a bit. He put the horses back in their paddock, then took hold of Danielle's hand, leading her deeper into the barn, to a ladder that went up to the loft.

"Can I show you something?"

She bit her lip, hesitating. "Why do I have a feeling that it isn't the loft you're going to show me?"

"I'm going to show you the loft. It's just not all I'm going to show you."

She took a step back, worrying her lip with her teeth. He reached out, cupping the back of her head and bringing his mouth down on hers, kissing her the way he had wanted to when she initiated the kiss outside. He didn't have patience anymore. And he wasn't going to let her lead. Not now.

He cupped her face, stroking her cheeks with his thumbs. "This has nothing to do with our agreement. It has nothing to do with the contract. Nothing to do with the ad or my father or anything other than the fact that I want you. Do you understand?"

She nodded slowly. "Yes," she said, the word coming out a whisper.

Adrenaline shot through him, a strange kind of triumph

that came with a kick to the gut right behind it. He wanted her. He knew he didn't deserve her. But he wasn't going to stop himself from having her in spite of that.

Then he took her hand and led her up the ladder.

Chapter 7

Danielle's heart was pounding in her ears. It was all she could hear. The sound of her own heart beating as she climbed the rungs that led up to the loft.

It was different than she had imagined. It was clean. There was a haystack in one corner, but beyond that the floor was immaculate, every item stored and organized with precision. Which, knowing Joshua like she now did, wasn't too much of a surprise.

That made her smile, just a little. She did know him. In some ways, she felt like she knew him better than she knew anyone.

She wasn't sure what that said about her other relationships. For a while, she'd had friends, but they'd disappeared when she'd become consumed with caring for her pregnant mother and working as much as possible at the grocery store. And then no one had come back when Danielle ended up with full care of Riley.

In some ways, she didn't blame them. Life was hard enough without dealing with a friend who was juggling all of that. But just because she understood didn't mean she wasn't lonely.

She looked at Joshua, their eyes connecting. He had shared his past with her. But she was keeping something big from him. Even while she was prepared to give him her body, she was holding back secrets.

She took a breath, opening her mouth to speak, but something in his blue gaze stopped the words before they could form. Something sharp, predatory. Something that made her feel like she was the center of the world, or at least the center of his world.

It was intoxicating. She'd never experienced it before.

She wanted more, all of it. Wherever it would lead.

And that was scary. Scarier than agreeing to do something she had never done before. Because she finally understood. Understood why her mother had traded her sanity, and her self-worth, for that moment when a man looked at you like you were his everything.

Danielle had spent so long being nothing to anyone. Nothing but a burden. Now, feeling like the solution rather than the problem was powerful, heady. She knew she couldn't turn back now no matter what.

Even if sanity tried to prevail, she would shove it aside. Because she needed this. Needed this balm for all the wounds that ran so deep inside of her.

Joshua walked across the immaculate space and opened up a cabinet. There were blankets inside, thick, woolen ones with geometric designs on them. He pulled out two and spread one on the ground.

She bit her lip, fighting a rising tide of hysteria, fighting a giggle that was climbing its way up her throat.

"I know this isn't exactly a fancy hotel suite."

She forced a smile. "It works for me."

He set the other blanket down on the end of the first one, still folded, then he reached out and took her hand, drawing her to him. He curved his fingers around her wrist, lifting her arm up, then shifted his hold, lacing his fingers through hers and dipping his head, pressing his lips to her own.

Her heart was still pounding that same, steady beat, and she was certain he must be able to hear it. Must be aware of just how he was affecting her.

There were all sorts of things she should tell him. About Riley's mother. About this being her first time.

But she didn't have the words.

She had her heartbeat. The way her limbs trembled. She could let him see that her eyes were filling with tears, and no matter how fiercely she blinked, they never quite went away.

She was good at manipulating conversation. At giving answers that walked the line between fact and fiction.

Her body could only tell the truth.

She hoped he could see it. That he understood. Later, they would talk. Later, there would be honesty between them. Because he would have questions. God knew. But for now, she would let the way her fingertips trailed down his back—uncertain and tentative—the way she peppered kisses along his jaw—clumsy and broken—say everything she couldn't.

"It doesn't need to be fancy," she said, her voice sounding thick even to her own ears.

"Maybe it should be," he said, his voice rough. "But if I was going to take you back to my bedroom, I expect I would have to wait until tonight. And I don't want to wait."

She shook her head. "It doesn't have to be fancy. It just has to be now. And it has to be you."

He drew his head back, inhaling sharply. And then he cupped her cheek and consumed her. His kiss was heat and fire, sparking against the dry, neglected things inside her and raging out of control.

She slid her hands up his arms, hanging on to his strong shoulders, using his steadiness to hold her fast even as her legs turned weak.

He lifted her up against him, then swept his arm beneath her legs, cradling her against his chest like she was a child. Then he set her down gently on the blanket, continuing to kiss her as he did so.

She was overwhelmed. Overwhelmed by the intensity of his gaze, by his focus. Overwhelmed by his closeness, his scent.

He was everywhere. His hands on her body, his face filling her vision.

She had spent the past few months caring for her half brother, pouring everything she had onto one little person she loved more than anything in the entire world. But in doing so, she had left herself empty. She had been giving continually, opening a vein and bleeding whenever necessary, and taking nothing in to refill herself.

But this… This was more than she had ever had. More than she'd ever thought she could have. Being the focus of a man's attention. Of his need.

This was a different kind of need than that of a child. Because it wasn't entirely selfish. Joshua's need gave her something in return; it compelled him to be close. Compelled him to kiss her, to skim his hands over her body, teasing and tormenting her with the promise of a pleasure she had never experienced.

Before she could think her actions through, she was pushing her fingertips beneath the hem of his shirt, his hard, flat stomach hot to the touch. And then it didn't matter what she had done before or what she hadn't done. Didn't matter that she was a virgin and this was an entirely new experience.

Need replaced everything except being skin to skin with him. Having nothing between them.

Suddenly, the years of feeling isolated, alone, cold and separate were simply too much. She needed his body over hers, his body inside hers. Whatever happened after that, whatever happened in the end, right now she couldn't care.

Because her desire outweighed the consequences. A wild, desperate thing starving to be fed. With his touch. With his possession.

She pushed his shirt up, and he helped her shrug it over his head. Her throat dried, her mouth opening slightly as she looked at him. His shoulders were broad, his chest well-defined and muscular, pale hair spreading over those glorious muscles, down his ridged abdomen, disappearing in a thin trail beneath the waistband of his low-slung jeans.

She had never seen a man who looked like him before, not in person. And she had never been this close to a man ever. She pressed her palm against his chest, relishing his heat and his hardness beneath her touch. His heart raging out of control, matching the beat of her own.

She parted her thighs and he settled between them. She could feel the hard ridge of his arousal pressing against that place where she was wet and needy for him. She was shocked at how hard he was, even through layers of clothing.

And she lost herself in his kiss, in the way he rocked his hips against hers. This moment, this experience was like everything she had missed growing up. Misspent teenage years when she should have been making out with boys in barns and hoping she didn't get caught. In reality, her mother wouldn't have cared.

This was a reclamation. More than that, it was something completely new. Something she had never even known she could want.

Joshua was something she had never known she could want.

It shouldn't make sense, the two of them. This brilliant businessman in his thirties who owned a ranch and seemed to shun most emotional connections. And her. Poor. In her twenties. Desperately clinging to any connection she could forge because each one was so rare and special.

But somehow they seemed to make sense. Kissing each other. Touching each other. For some reason, he was the only man that made sense.

Maybe it was because he had taught her to ride a horse. Maybe it was because he was giving her and Riley a ticket out of poverty. Maybe it was because he was handsome. She had a feeling this connection transcended all those things.

As his tongue traced a trail down her neck to the collar of her T-shirt, she was okay with not knowing. She didn't need to give this connection a name. She didn't even want to.

Her breath caught as he pushed her shirt up and over her head, then quickly dispensed with her bra using a skill not even she possessed. Her nipples tightened, and she was painfully aware of them and of the fact that she was a little lackluster in size.

If Joshua noticed, he didn't seem to mind.

Instead, he dipped his head, sucking one tightened bud between his lips. The move was so sudden, so shocking and so damned unexpected that she couldn't stop herself from arching into him, a cry on her lips.

He looked up, the smile on his face so damned cocky she should probably have been irritated. But she wasn't. She just allowed herself to get lost. In his heat. In the fire that flared between them. In the way he used his lips, his teeth and his tongue to draw a map of pleasure over her skin. All the way down to the waistband of her pants. He licked her. Just above the snap on her jeans. Another sensation so deliciously shocking she couldn't hold back the sound of pleasure on her lips.

She pressed her fist against her mouth, trying to keep herself from getting too vocal. From embarrassing herself. From revealing just how inexperienced she was. The noises she was making definitely announced the fact that these sensations were revelatory to her. And that made her feel a touch too vulnerable.

She was so used to holding people at a distance. So used to benign neglect and general apathy creating a shield around her feelings. Her secrets.

But there was no distance here.

And certainly none as he undid the button of her jeans and drew the zipper down slowly. As he pushed the rough denim down her legs, taking her panties with them.

If she had felt vulnerable a moment before, that was nothing compared to now. She felt so fragile. So exposed. And then he reached up, pressing his hand against her leg at the inside of her knee, spreading her wide so he could look his fill.

She wanted to snap her legs together. Wanted to cover up. But she was immobilized. Completely captive to whatever might happen next. She was so desperate to find out, and at the same time desperate to escape it.

Rough fingertips drifted down the tender skin on her inner thigh, brushing perilously close to her damp, needy flesh. And then he was there. His touch in no way gentle or tentative as he pressed his hand against her, the heel of his palm putting firm pressure on her most sensitive place before he pressed his fingers down and spread her wide.

He made his intentions clear as he lowered his head, tasting her deeply. She lifted her hips, a sharp sound on her lips, one she didn't even bother to hold back. He shifted his hold, gripping her hips, holding her just wide enough for his broad shoulders to fit right there, his sensual assault merciless.

Tension knotted her stomach like a fist, tighter and tighter with each pass of his tongue. Then he pressed his thumb against her at the same time as he flicked his tongue in the same spot. She grabbed hold of him, her fingernails digging into his back.

He drew his thumb down her crease, teasing the entrance of her body. She rocked her hips with the motion, desperate for something. Feeling suddenly empty and achy and needy in ways she never had before.

He rotated his hand, pressing his middle finger deep inside of her, and she gasped at the foreign invasion. But any discomfort passed quickly as her body grew wetter beneath the ministrations of his tongue. By the time he added a second finger, it slipped in easily.

He quickened his pace, and it felt like there was an earthquake starting inside her. A low, slow pull at her core that spread outward, her limbs trembling as the pressure at her center continued to mount.

His thumb joined with his tongue as he continued to

pump his fingers inside her, and it was that added pressure that finally broke her. She was shaken. Rattled completely. The magnitude of measurable aftershocks rocking her long after the primary force had passed.

He moved into a sitting position, undoing his belt and the button on his jeans. Then he stood for a moment, drawing the zipper down slowly and pushing the denim down his muscular thighs.

She had never seen a naked man in person before, and the stark, thick evidence of his arousal standing out from his body was a clear reminder that they weren't finished, no matter how wrung out and replete she felt.

Except, even though she felt satisfied, limp from the intensity of her release, she did want more. Because there was more to have. Because she wanted to be close to him. Because she wanted to give him even an ounce of the satisfaction that she had just experienced.

He knelt back down, pulling his jeans closer and taking his wallet out of his back pocket. He produced a condom packet and she gave thanks for his presence of mind. She knew better than to have unprotected sex with someone. For myriad reasons. But still, she wondered if she would have remembered if he had not.

Thank God one of them was thinking. She was too overwhelmed. Too swamped by the release that had overtaken her, and by the enormity of what was about to happen. When he positioned himself at the entrance of her body and pressed against her, she gasped in shock.

It *hurt*. Dear God it hurt. His fingers hadn't prepared her for the rest of him.

He noticed her hesitation and slowed his movements, pressing inside her inch by excruciating inch. She held on to his shoulders, closing her eyes and burying her face in his neck as he jerked his hips forward, fully seating himself inside her.

She did her best to breathe through it. But she was in a daze. Joshua was inside her, and she wasn't a virgin anymore. It felt… Well, it didn't feel like losing anything. It felt like gaining something. Gaining a whole lot.

The pain began to recede and she looked up, at his face, at the extreme concentration there, at the set of his jaw, the veins in his neck standing out.

"Are you okay?" he asked, his voice strangled.

She nodded wordlessly, then flexed her hips experimentally.

He groaned, lowering his head, pressing his forehead against hers, before kissing her. Then he began to move.

Soon, that same sweet tension began to build again in her stomach, need replacing the bone-deep satisfaction that she had only just experienced. She didn't know how it was possible to be back in that needy place only moments after feeling fulfilled.

But she was. And then she was lost in the rhythm, lost in the feeling of his thick length stroking in and out of her, all of the pain gone now, only pleasure remaining. It was so foreign, so singular and unlike anything she had ever experienced. And she loved it. Reveled in it.

But even more than her own pleasure, she reveled in watching his unraveling.

Because he had pulled her apart in a million astounding ways, and she didn't know if she could ever be reassembled. So it was only fair that he lost himself too. Only fair that she be his undoing in some way.

Sweat beaded on his brow, trickled down his back. She reveled in the feel of it beneath her fingertips. In the obvious evidence of what this did to him.

His breathing became more labored, his muscles shaking as each thrust became less gentle. As he began to pound into her. And just as he needed to go harder, go faster, so did she.

Her own pleasure wound around his, inextricably linked.

On a harsh growl he buried his face in her neck, his arms shaking as he thrust into her one last time, slamming into her, breaking a wave of pleasure over her body as he found his own release.

He tried to pull away, but she wrapped her arms around him, holding him close. Because the sooner he separated from her body, the sooner they would have to talk. And she wasn't exactly sure she wanted to talk.

But when he lifted his head, his blue eyes glinting in the dim light, she could tell that whether or not she wanted to talk, they were going to.

He rolled away from her, pushing into a sitting position. "Are you going to explain all of this to me? Or are you going to make me guess?"

"What?" She sounded overly innocent, her eyes wider than necessary.

"Danielle, I'm going to ask you a question, and I need you to answer me honestly. Were you a virgin?"

Joshua's blood was still running hot through his veins, arousal still burning beneath the surface of his skin. And he knew the question he had just asked her was probably insane. He could explain her discomfort as pain because she hadn't taken a man to her bed since she'd given birth.

But that wasn't it. It wasn't.

The more credence he gave to his virgin theory, the more everything about her started to make sense. The way she responded to his kiss, the way she acted when he touched her.

Her reaction had been about more than simple attraction, more than pleasure. There had been wonder there. A sense of discovery.

But that meant Riley wasn't her son. And it meant she had been lying to him.

"Well, Joshua, given that this is not a New Testament kind of situation…"

He reached out, grabbing hold of her wrist and tugging her upward, drawing her toward him. "Don't lie to me."

"Why would you think that?" she asked, her words small. Admission enough as far as he was concerned.

"A lot of reasons. But I have had sex with a virgin before. More accurately, Sadie Miller and I took each other's virginity in the woods some eighteen years ago. You don't forget that. And, I grant you, there could be other reasons for the fact that it hurt you, for the fact that you were tight." A flush spread over her skin, her cheeks turning beet red. "But I don't think any of those reasons are the truth. So what's going on? Who is Riley's mother?"

A tear slid down her cheek, her expression mutinous and angry. "I am," she said, her voice trembling. "At least, I might as well be. I should be."

"You didn't give birth to Riley."

She sniffed loudly, another tear sliding down her cheek. "No. I didn't."

"Are you running from somebody? Is there something I need to know?"

"It's not like that. I'm not hiding. I didn't steal him. I have legal custody of Riley. But my situation was problematic. At least, as far as Child Services was concerned.

I lost my job because of the babysitting situation and I needed money."

She suddenly looked so incredibly young, so vulnerable... And he felt like the biggest jerk on planet Earth.

She had lied to him. She had most definitely led him to believe she was in an entirely different circumstance than she was, and still, he was mostly angry at himself.

Because the picture she was painting was even more desperate than the one he had been led to believe. Because she had been a virgin and he had just roughly dispensed with that.

She had been desperate. Utterly desperate. And had taken this post with him because she hadn't seen another option. Whatever he'd thought of her before, he was forced to revise it, and there was no way that revision didn't include recasting himself as the villain.

"Whose baby is he?"

She swallowed hard, drawing her knees up to her chest, covering her nudity. "Riley is my half brother. My mother showed up at my place about a year ago pregnant and desperate. She needed someone to help her out. When she came to me, she sounded pretty determined to take care of him. She even named him. She told me she would do better for him than she had for me, because she was done with men now and all of that. But she broke her promises. She had the baby, she met somebody else. I didn't know it at first. I didn't realize she was leaving Riley in the apartment alone sometimes while I was at work."

She took a deep, shuddering breath, then continued. "I didn't mess around when I found out. I didn't wait for her to decide to abandon him. I called Child Services. And I got temporary guardianship. My mother left. But then things started to fall apart with the work, and I didn't know how I was going to pay for the apartment... Then I saw your ad."

He swore. "You should have told me."

"Maybe. But I needed the money, Joshua. And I didn't want to do anything to jeopardize your offer. I could tell you were uncomfortable that I brought a baby with me, and now I know why. But, regardless, at the time, I didn't want to do anything that might compromise our arrangement."

He felt like the jackass he undoubtedly was. The worst part was, it shone a light on all the BS he'd put her through. Regardless of Riley's parentage, she'd been desperate and he'd taken advantage of that. Less so when he'd been keeping his hands to himself. At least then it had been feasible to pretend it was an even exchange.

But now?

Now he'd slept with her and it was impossible to keep pretending.

And frankly, he didn't want to.

He'd been wrestling with this feeling from the moment they'd gone out riding today, or maybe since they'd left his parents' house last week.

But today...when he'd looked at her, seen her smile... noticed the way she'd gained weight after being in a place where she felt secure...

He'd wanted to give her more of that.

He'd wanted to do more good than harm. Had wanted to fix something instead of break it.

It was too late for Shannon. But he could help Danielle. He could make sure she always felt safe. That she and Riley were always protected.

The realization would have made him want to laugh if it didn't all feel too damned grim. Somehow his father's ad had brought him to this place when he'd been determined to teach the old man a lesson.

But Joshua hadn't counted on Danielle.

Hadn't counted on how she would make him feel. That she'd wake something inside him he'd thought had been asleep for good.

It wasn't just chemistry. Wasn't just sex. It was the desire to make her happy. To give her things.

To fix what was broken.

He knew the solution wouldn't come from him personally, but his money could sure as hell fix her problems. And they did have chemistry. The kind that wasn't common. It sure as hell went beyond anything he'd ever experienced before.

"The truth doesn't change anything," she said, lowering her face into her arms, her words muffled. "It doesn't."

He reached out, taking her chin between his thumb and forefinger, tilting her face back up. "It does. Even if it shouldn't. Though, maybe it's not Riley that changes it. Maybe it's just the two of us."

She shook her head. "It doesn't have to change anything."

"Danielle… I can't…"

She lurched forward, grabbing his arm, her eyes wide, her expression wild. "Joshua, please. I need this money. I can't go back to where we were. I'm being held to a harsher standard than his biological mother would be and I can't lose him."

He grabbed her chin again, steadying her face, looking into those glistening brown eyes. "Danielle, I would never let you lose him. I want to protect you. Both of you."

She tilted her head to the side, her expression growing suspicious. "You…do?"

"I've been thinking. I was thinking this earlier when we were riding, but now, knowing your whole story... I want you and Riley to stay with me."

She blinked. "What?"

"Danielle, I want you to marry me."

Chapter 8

Danielle couldn't process any of this.

She had expected him to be angry. Had expected him to get mad because she'd lied to him.

She hadn't expected a marriage proposal.

At least, she was pretty sure that was what had just happened. "You want to…marry me? For real marry me?"

"Yes," he said, his tone hard, decisive. "You don't feel good about fooling my family—neither do I. You need money and security and, hell, I have both. We have chemistry. I want… I don't want to send you back into the world alone. You don't even know where you're going."

He wasn't wrong. And dammit his offer was tempting. They were both naked, and he was so beautiful, and she wanted to kiss him again. Touch him again. But more than that, she wanted him to hold her in his arms again.

She wanted to be close to him. Bonded to him.

She wanted—so desperately—to not be alone.

But there had to be a catch.

There was always a catch. He could say whatever he wanted about how all of this wasn't a transaction, how he had taken her riding just to take her riding. But then they'd had sex. And he'd had a condom in his wallet.

So he'd been prepared.

That made her stomach sour.

"Did you plan this?" she asked. "The horse-riding seduction?"

"No, I didn't plan it. I carry a condom because I like to be prepared to have sex. You never know. You can get mad at me for that if you want, but then, we did need one, so it seems a little hypocritical."

"Are you tricking me?" she asked, feeling desperate and panicky. "Is this a trick? Because I don't understand how it benefits you to marry me. To keep Riley and me here. You don't even like Riley, Joshua. You can't stand to be in the same room with him."

"I broke Shannon," he said, his voice hard. "I ruined her. I did that. But I won't break you. I want to fix this."

"You can't slap duct tape and a wedding band on me and call it done," she said, her voice trembling. "I'm not a leaky faucet."

"I didn't say you were. But you need something I have and I... Danielle, I need you." His voice was rough, intense. "I'm not offering you love, but I can be faithful. I was ready to be a husband years ago, that part doesn't faze me. I can take care of you. I can keep you safe. And if I send you out into the world with nothing more than money and something happens to you or Riley, I won't forgive myself. So stay with me. Marry me."

It was crazy. He was crazy.

And she was crazy for sitting there fully considering everything he was offering.

But she was imagining a life here. For her, for Riley. On Joshua's ranch, in his beautiful house.

And she knew—she absolutely knew—that what she had felt physically with him, what had just happened, was a huge reason why they were having this conversation at all.

More than the pleasure, the closeness drew her in. Actually, that was the most dangerous part of his offer. The idea that she could go through life with somebody by her side. To raise Riley with this strong man backing her up.

Something clenched tight in her chest, working its way down to her stomach. Riley. He could have a father figure. She didn't know exactly what function Joshua would play in his life. Joshua had trouble with the baby right now. But she knew Joshua was a good man, and that he would never freeze Riley out intentionally. Not when he was offering them a life together.

"What about Riley?" she asked, her throat dry. She swallowed hard. She had to know what he was thinking.

"What about him?"

"This offer extends to him too. And I mean…not just protection and support. But would you… Would you teach him things? Would your father be a grandfather to him? Would your brothers be uncles and your sister be an aunt? I understand that having a child around might be hard for you, after you lost your chance at being a father. And I understand you want to fix me, my situation. And it's tempting, Joshua, it's very tempting. But I need to know if that support, if all of that, extends to Riley."

Joshua's face looked as though it had been cast in stone. "I'm not sure if I would be a good father, Danielle. I was going to be a father, and so I was going to figure it out—how to do that, how to be that. I suppose I can apply that same intent here. I can't guarantee that I'll be the best, but I'll try. And you're right. I have my family to back me up. And he has you."

That was it.

That was the reason she couldn't say no. Because if she walked away from Joshua now, Riley would have her. Only her. She loved him, but she was just one person. If she stayed here with Joshua, Riley would have grandparents. Aunts and uncles. Family. People who knew how to be a family. She was doing the very best she could, but her idea of family was somewhere between cold neglectful nightmare and a TV sitcom.

The Grayson family knew—Joshua knew—what it meant to be a family. If she said yes, she could give that to Riley.

She swallowed again, trying to alleviate the scratchy feeling in her throat.

"I guess… I guess I can't really say no to that." She straightened, still naked, and not even a little bit embarrassed. There were bigger things going on here than the fact that he could see her breasts. "Okay, Joshua. I'll marry you."

Chapter 9

The biggest problem with this sudden change in plan was the fact that Joshua had deliberately set out to make his family dislike Danielle. And now he was marrying her for real.

Of course, the flaw in his original plan was that Danielle *hadn't* been roundly hated by his family. They'd distrusted the whole situation, certainly, but his family was simply too fair, too nice to hate her.

Still, guilt clutched at him, and he knew he was going to have to do something to fix this. Which was why he found himself down at the Gray Bear Construction office rather than working from home. Because he knew Faith and Isaiah would be in, and he needed to have a talk with his siblings.

The office was a newly constructed building fashioned to look like a log cabin. It was down at the edge of town, by where Rona's diner used to be, a former greasy spoon that had been transformed into a series of smaller, hipper shops that were more in line with the interests of Copper Ridge's tourists.

It was a great office space with a prime view of the ocean, but still, Joshua typically preferred to work in the privacy of his own home, secluded in the mountains.

Isaiah did too, which was why it was notable that his brother was in the office today, but he'd had a meeting of some kind, so he'd put on a decent shirt and a pair of nice jeans and gotten himself out of his hermitage.

Faith, being the bright, sharp creature she was, always came into the office, always dressed in some variation of her personal uniform. Black pants and a black top—a sweater today because of the chilly weather.

"What are you doing here?" Faith asked, her expression scrutinizing.

"I came here to talk to you," he said.

"I'll make coffee." Joshua turned and saw Poppy standing there. Strange, he hadn't noticed. But then, Poppy usually stayed in the background. He couldn't remember running the business without her, but like useful office supplies, you really only noticed them when they didn't work. And Poppy always worked.

"Thanks, Poppy," Faith said.

Isaiah folded his arms over his chest and leaned back in his chair. "What's up?"

"I'm getting married in two weeks."

Faith made a scoffing sound. "To that child you're dating?"

"She's your age," he said. "And yes. Just like I said I was."

"Which begs the question," Isaiah said. "Why are you telling us again?"

"Because. The first time I was lying. Dad put that ad

in the paper trying to find a wife for me, and I selected Danielle in order to teach him a lesson. The joke's on me it turns out." Damn was it ever.

"Good God, Joshua. You're such a jerk," Faith said, leaning against the wall, her arms folded, mirroring Isaiah's stance. "I knew something was up, but of all the things I suspected, you tricking our mother and father was not one of them."

"What did you suspect?"

"That you were thinking with your... Well. And now I'm back to that conclusion. Because why are you marrying her?"

"I care about her. And believe me when I say she's had it rough."

"You've slept with her?" This question came from Isaiah, and there was absolutely no tact in it. But then, Isaiah himself possessed absolutely no tact. Which was why he handled money and not people.

"Yes," Joshua said.

"She must be good. But I'm not sure that's going to convince either of us you're thinking with your big brain." His brother stood up, not unfolding his arms.

"Well, you're obnoxious," Joshua returned. "The sex has nothing to do with it. I can get sex whenever I want."

Faith made a hissing sound. He tossed his younger sister a glance. "You can stop hissing and settle down," he said to her. "You were the one who brought sex into it, I'm just clarifying. You know what I went through with Shannon, what I put Shannon through. If I send Danielle and her baby back out into the world and something happens to them, I'll never forgive myself."

"Well, Joshua, that kind of implies you aren't already living in a perpetual state of self-flagellation," Faith said.

"Do you want to see if it can get worse?"

She shook her head. "No, but marrying some random woman you found through an ad seems like an extreme way to go about searching for atonement. Can't you do some Hail Marys or something?"

"If it were that simple, I would have done it a long time ago." He took a deep breath. "I'm not going to tell Mom and Dad the whole story. But I'm telling you because I need you to be nice about Danielle. However it looked when I brought her by to introduce her to the family... I threw her under the bus, and now I want to drag her back out from under it."

Isaiah shook his head. "You're a contrary son of a gun."

"Well, usually that's your function. I figured it was my turn."

The door to the office opened and in walked their business partner, Jonathan Bear, who ran the construction side of the firm. He looked around the room, clearly confused by the fact that they were all in residence. "Is there a meeting I didn't know about?"

"Joshua is getting married," Faith said, looking sullen.

"Congratulations," Jonathan said, smiling, which was unusual for the other man, who was typically pretty taciturn. "I can highly recommend it."

Jonathan had married the pastor's daughter, Hayley Thompson, in a small ceremony recently.

In the past, Jonathan had walked around like he had his own personal storm cloud overhead, and since meeting Hayley, he had most definitely changed. Maybe there was something to that whole marriage thing. Maybe Joshua's idea of atonement wasn't as outrageous as it might have initially seemed.

"There," Joshua said. "Jonathan recommends it. So you two can stop looking at me suspiciously."

Jonathan shrugged and walked through the main area and into the back, toward his office, leaving Joshua alone with his siblings.

Faith tucked her hair behind her ear. "Honestly, whatever you need, whatever you want, I'll help. But I don't want you to get hurt."

"And I appreciate that," he said. "But the thing is, you can only get hurt if there's love involved. I don't love her."

Faith looked wounded by that. "Then what's the point? I'm not trying to argue. I just don't understand."

"Love is not the be-all and end-all, Faith. Sometimes just committing to taking care of somebody else is enough. I loved Shannon, but I still didn't do the right thing for her. I'm older now. And I know what's important. I'm going to keep Danielle safe. I'm going to keep Riley safe. What's more important than that?" He shook his head. "I'm sure Shannon would have rather had that than any expression of love."

"Fine," she said. "I support you. I'm in."

"So you aren't going to be a persnickety brat?"

A small smile quirked her lips upward. "I didn't say that. I said I would support you. But as a younger sister, I feel the need to remind you that being a persnickety brat is sometimes part of my support."

He shot Isaiah a baleful look. "I suppose you're still going to be obnoxious?"

"Obviously."

Joshua smiled then. Because that was the best he was going to get from his siblings. But it was a step toward making sure Danielle felt like she had a place in the family, rather than feeling like an outsider.

And if he wanted that with an intensity that wasn't strictly normal or healthy, he would ignore that. He had never pretended to be normal or healthy. He wasn't going to start now.

Danielle was getting fluttery waiting for Joshua to come home. The anticipation was a strange feeling. It had been a long time since she'd looked forward to some-one coming home. She remembered being young, when it was hard to be alone. But she hadn't exactly wished for her mother to come home, because she knew that when her mother arrived, she would be drunk. And Danielle would be tasked with managing her in some way.

That was the story of her life. Not being alone meant taking care of somebody. Being alone meant isolation, but at least she had time to herself.

But Joshua wasn't like that. Being with him didn't mean she had to manage him.

She thought of their time together in the barn, and the memory made her shiver. She had gone to bed in her own room last night, and he hadn't made any move toward her since his proposal. She had a feeling his hesitation had something to do with her inexperience.

But she was ready for him again. Ready for more.

She shook her hands out, feeling jittery. And a little scared.

It was so easy to want him. To dream about him com-ing home, how she would embrace him, kiss him. And maybe even learn to cook, so she could make him dinner. Learn to do something other than warm up Pop-Tarts.

Although, he liked Pop-Tarts, and so did she.

Maybe they should have Pop-Tarts at their wedding.

That was the kind of thing couples did. Incorporate the cute foundations of their relationships into their wedding ceremonies.

She made a small sound that was halfway between a whimper and a growl. She was getting loopy about him. About a guy. Which she had promised herself she would never do. But it was hard *not* to get loopy. He had offered her support, a family for Riley, a house to live in. He had become her lover, and then he had asked to become her husband.

And in those few short moments, her entire vision for the rest of her life had changed. It had become something so much warmer, so much more secure than she had ever imagined it could be. She just wasn't strong enough to reject that vision.

Honestly, she didn't know a woman who would be strong enough. Joshua was hot. And he was nice. Well, sometimes he was kind of a jerk, but mostly, at his core, he was nice and he had wonderful taste in breakfast food.

That seemed like as good a foundation for a marriage as any.

She heard the front door open and shut, and as it slammed, her heart lurched against her breastbone.

Joshua walked in looking so intensely handsome in a light blue button-up shirt, the sleeves pushed up his arms, that she wanted to swoon for the first time in her entire life.

"Do you think they can make a wedding cake out of Pop-Tarts?" She didn't know why that was the first thing that came out of her mouth. Probably, it would have been better if she had said something about how she couldn't wait to tear his clothes off.

But no. She had led with toaster pastry.

"I don't know. But we're getting married in two weeks,

so if you can stack Pop-Tarts and call them a cake, I suppose it might save time and money."

"I could probably do that. I promise that's not all I thought about today, but for some reason it's what came out of my mouth."

"How about I keep your mouth busy for a while," he said, his blue gaze getting sharp. He crossed the space between them, wrapping his arm around her waist and drawing her against him. And then he kissed her.

It was so deep, so warm, and she felt so…sheltered. Enveloped completely in his arms, in his strength. Who cared if she was lost in a fantasy right now? It would be the first time. She had never had the luxury of dreaming about men like him, or passion this intense.

It seemed right, only fair, that she have the fantasy. If only for a while. To have a moment where she actually dreamed about a wedding with cake. Where she fantasized about a man walking in the door and kissing her like this, wanting her like this.

"Is Janine here?" he asked, breaking the kiss just long enough to pose the question.

"No," she said, barely managing to answer before he slammed his lips back down on hers.

Then she found herself being lifted and carried from the entryway into the living room, deposited on the couch. And somehow, as he set her down, he managed to raise her shirt up over her head.

She stared at him, dazed, while he divested himself of his own shirt. "You're very good at this," she said. "I assume you've had a lot of practice?"

He lifted an eyebrow, his hands going to his belt buckle. "Is this a conversation you want to have?"

She felt…bemused rather than jealous. "I don't know. I'm just curious."

"I got into a lot of trouble when I was a teenager. I think I mentioned the incident with my virginity in the woods."

She nodded. "You did. And since I lost my virginity in a barn, I suppose I have to reserve judgment."

"Probably. Then I moved to Seattle. And I was even worse, because suddenly I was surrounded by women I hadn't known my whole life."

Danielle nodded gravely. "I can see how that would be an issue."

He smiled. Then finished undoing his belt, button and zipper before shoving his pants down to the floor. He stood in front of her naked, aroused and beautiful.

"Then I got myself into a long-term relationship, and it turns out I'm good at that. Well, at the being faithful part."

"That's a relief."

"In terms of promiscuity, though, my behavior has been somewhat appalling for the past five years. I have picked up a particular set of skills."

She wrinkled her nose. "I suppose that's something."

"You asked."

She straightened. "And I wanted to know."

He reached behind her back, undoing her bra, pulling it off and throwing it somewhere behind him. "Well, now you do." He pressed his hands against the back of the couch, bracketing her in. "You still want to marry me?"

"I had a very tempting proposal from the UPS man today. He asked me to sign for a package. So I guess you could say it's getting kind of serious."

"I don't think the UPS man makes you feel like this." He captured her mouth with his, and she found herself being pressed into the cushions, sliding to the side, until he'd maneuvered her so they were both lying flat on the couch.

He wrapped his fingers around her wrists, lifting them up over her head as he bent to kiss her neck, her collarbone, to draw one nipple inside his mouth.

She bucked against him, and he shifted, pushing his hand beneath her jeans, under the fabric of her panties, discovering just how wet and ready she was for him.

She rolled her hips upward, moving in time with the rhythm of his strokes, lights beginning to flash behind her eyelids, orgasm barreling down on her at an embarrassingly quick rate.

Danielle sucked in a deep breath, trying her best to hold her climax at bay. Because how embarrassing would it be to come from a kiss? A brief bit of attention to her breast and a quick stroke between the legs?

But then she opened her eyes and met his gaze. His lips curved into a wicked smile as he turned his wrist, sliding one finger deep inside as he flicked his thumb over her.

All she could do then was hold on tight and ride out the explosion. He never looked away from her, and as much as she wanted to, she couldn't look away from him.

It felt too intense, too raw and much too intimate.

But she was trapped in it, drowning in it, and there was nothing she could do to stop it. She just had to surrender.

While she was still recovering from her orgasm, Joshua made quick work of her jeans, flinging them in the same direction her bra had gone.

Then, still looking right at her, he stroked her, over the thin fabric of her panties, the tease against her overly sensitized skin almost too much to handle.

Then he traced the edge of the fabric at the crease

of her thigh, dipping one finger beneath her underwear, touching slick flesh.

He hooked his finger around the fabric, pulling her panties off and casting them aside. And here she was, just as she'd been the first time, completely open and vulnerable to him. At his mercy.

It wasn't as though she didn't want that. There was something wonderful about it. Something incredible about the way he lavished attention on her, about being his sole focus.

But she wanted more. She wanted to be... She wanted to be equal to him in some way.

He was practiced. And he had skill. He'd had a lot of lovers. Realistically, she imagined he didn't even know exactly how many.

She didn't have skill. She hadn't been tutored in the art of love by anyone. But she *wanted*.

If desire could equal skill, then she could rival any woman he'd ever been with. Because the depth of her need, the depth of her passion, reached places inside her she hadn't known existed.

She pressed her hands down on the couch cushions, launching herself into a sitting position. His eyes widened, and she reveled in the fact that she had surprised him. She reached out, resting one palm against his chest, luxuriating in the feel of all that heat, that muscle, that masculine hair that tickled her sensitive skin.

"Danielle," he said, his tone filled with warning.

She didn't care about his warnings.

She was going to marry this man. He was going to be her husband. That thought filled her with such a strange sense of elation.

He had all the power. He had the money. He had the beautiful house. What he was giving her…it bordered on charity. If she was ever going to feel like she belonged—like this place was really hers—they needed to be equals in some regard.

She had to give him something too.

And if it started here, then it started here.

She leaned in, cautiously tasting his neck, tracing a line down to his nipple. He jerked beneath her touch, his reaction satisfying her in a way that went well beyond the physical.

He was beautiful, and she reveled in the chance to explore him. To run her fingertips over each well-defined muscle. Over his abs and the hard cut inward just below his hip bone.

But she didn't stop there. No, she wasn't even remotely finished with him.

He had made her shake. He had made her tremble. He had made her lose her mind.

And she was going to return the favor.

She took a deep breath and kissed his stomach. Just one easy thing before she moved on to what she wanted, even though it scared her.

She lifted her head, meeting his gaze as she wrapped her fingers around him and squeezed. His eyes glittered like ice on fire, and he said nothing. He just sat there, his jaw held tight, his expression one of absolute concentration.

Then she looked away from his face, bringing her attention to that most masculine part of him. She was hungry for him. There was no other word for it.

She was starving for a taste.

And that hunger overtook everything else.

She flicked her tongue out and tasted him, his skin salty and hot. But the true eroticism was in his response. His head fell back, his breath hissing sharply through his teeth. And he reached out, pressing his hand to her back, spreading his fingers wide at the center of her shoulder blades.

Maybe she didn't have skill. Maybe she didn't know what she was doing. But he liked it. And that made her feel powerful. It made her feel needed.

She slid her hand down his shaft, gripping the base before taking him more deeply into her mouth. His groan sounded torn from him, wild and untamed, and she loved it.

Because Joshua was all about control. Had been from the moment she'd first met him.

That was what all this was, after all. From the ad in the paper to his marriage proposal—all of it was him trying to bend the situation to his will. To bend those around him to his will, to make them see he was right, that his way was the best way.

But right now he was losing control. He was at her mercy. Shaking. Because of her.

And even though she was the one pleasuring him, she felt an immense sense of satisfaction flood her as she continued to taste him. As she continued to make him tremble.

He needed her. He wanted her. After a lifetime of feeling like nobody wanted her at all, this was the most brilliant and beautiful thing she could ever imagine.

She'd heard her friends talk about giving guys blow jobs before. They laughed about it. Or said it was gross. Or said it was a great way to control their boyfriends.

They hadn't said what an incredible thing it was to

make a big, strong alpha male sweat and shake. They hadn't said it could make you feel so desired, so beloved. Or that giving someone else pleasure was even better—in some ways—than being on the receiving end of the attention.

She swallowed more of him, and his hand jerked up to her hair, tugging her head back. "Careful," he said, his tone hard and thin.

"Why?"

"You keep doing that and I'm going to come," he said, not bothering to sugarcoat it.

"So what? When you did it for me, that's what I did."

"Yes. But you're a woman. And you can have as many orgasms as I can give you without time off in between. I don't want it to end like this."

She was about to protest, but then he pulled her forward, kissing her hard and deep, stealing not just her ability to speak, but her ability to think of words.

He left her for a moment, retrieving his wallet and the protection in it, making quick work of putting the condom on before he laid her back down on the couch.

"Wait," she said, the word husky, rough. "I want… Can I be on top?"

He drew back, arching one brow. "Since you asked so nicely."

He gripped her hips, reversing their position, bringing her to sit astride him. He was hard beneath her, and she shifted back and forth experimentally, rubbing her slick folds over him before positioning him at the entrance of her body.

She bit her lip, lowering herself onto him, taking it slow, relishing that moment of him filling her so utterly and completely.

"I don't know what I'm doing," she whispered when he was buried fully inside of her.

He reached up, brushing his fingertips over her cheek before lowering his hand to grip both her hips tightly, lift her, then impale her on his hard length again.

"Just do what feels good," he ground out, the words strained.

She rocked her hips, then lifted herself slightly before taking him inside again. She repeated the motion. Again and again. Finding the speed and rhythm that made him gasp and made her moan. Finding just the right angle, just the right pressure, to please them both.

Pleasure began to ripple through her, the now somewhat familiar pressure of impending orgasm building inside her. She rolled her hips, making contact right where she needed it. He grabbed her chin, drawing her head down to kiss her. Deep, wet.

And that was it. She was done.

Pleasure burst behind her eyes, her internal muscles gripping him tight as her orgasm rocked her.

She found herself being rolled onto her back and Joshua began to pound into her, chasing his own release with a raw ferocity that made her whole body feel like it was on fire with passion.

He was undone. Completely. Because of her.

He growled, reaching beneath her to cup her behind, drawing her hard against him, forcing her to meet his every thrust. And that was when he proved himself right. She really could come as many times as he could make her.

She lost it then, shaking and shivering as her second orgasm overtook her already sensitized body.

He lowered his head, his teeth scraping against her collarbone as he froze against her, finding his own release.

He lay against her for a moment, his face buried in her neck, and she sifted her fingers through his hair, a small smile touching her lips as ripples of lingering pleasure continued to fan out through her body.

He looked at her, then brushed his lips gently over hers. She found herself being lifted up, cradled against his chest as he carried her from the couch to the stairs.

"Time for bed," he said, the words husky and rough.

She reached up and touched his face. "Okay."

He carried her to his room, laid her down on the expansive mattress, the blanket decadent and soft beneath her bare skin.

This would be their room. A room they would share.

For some reason, that thought made tears sting her eyes. She had spent so long being alone that the idea of so much closeness was almost overwhelming. But no matter what, she wanted it.

Wanted it so badly it was like a physical hunger.

Joshua joined her on the bed and she was overwhelmed by the urge to simply fold herself into his embrace. To enjoy the closeness.

But then he was naked. And so was she. So the desire for closeness fought with her desire to play with him a little more.

He pressed his hand against her lower back, then slid it down to her butt, squeezing tight. And he smiled.

Something intense and sharp filled her chest. It was almost painful.

Happiness, she realized. She was happy.

She knew in that moment that she never really had been happy before. At least, not without an equally weighty worry to balance it. To warn her that on the other side of the happiness could easily lie tragedy.

But she wasn't thinking of tragedy now. She couldn't.

Joshua filled her vision, and he filled her brain, and for now—just for now—everything in her world felt right.

For a while, she wanted that to be the whole story.

So she blocked out every other thought, every single what-if, and she kissed him again.

When Joshua woke up, the bedroom was dark. There was a woman wrapped around him. And he wasn't entirely sure what had pulled him out of his deep slumber.

Danielle was sleeping peacefully. Her dark hair was wrapped around her face like a spiderweb, and he reached down to push it back. She flinched, pursing her lips and shifting against him, tightening her arms around his waist.

She was exhausted. Probably because he was an animal who had taken her three, maybe four times before they'd finally both fallen asleep.

He looked at her, and the hunger was immediate. Visceral. And he wondered if he was fooling himself pretending, even for a moment, that any of this was for her.

That he had any kind of higher purpose.

He wondered if he had any purpose at all beyond trying to satisfy himself with her.

And then he realized what had woken him up.

He heard a high, keening cry that barely filtered through the open bedroom door. Riley.

He looked down at Danielle, who was still fast asleep, and who would no doubt be upset that they had forgotten to bring the baby monitor into the room. Joshua had barely been able to remember his own name, much less a baby monitor.

He extricated himself from her hold, scrubbing his hand over his face. Then he walked over to his closet, grabbing a pair of jeans and pulling them on with nothing underneath.

He had no idea what in the hell to do with the baby. But Danielle was exhausted, because of him, and he didn't want to wake her up.

The cries got louder as he made his way down the hall, and he walked into the room to see flailing movement coming from the crib. The baby was very unhappy, whatever the reason.

Joshua walked across the room and stood above the crib, looking down. If he was going to marry Danielle, then that meant Riley was his responsibility too.

Riley would be his son.

Something prickled at the back of his throat, making it tight. So much had happened after Shannon lost the baby that he didn't tend to think too much about what might have been. But it was impossible not to think about it right now.

His son would have been five.

He swallowed hard, trying to combat the rising tide of emotion in his chest. That emotion was why he avoided contact with Riley. Joshua wasn't so out of touch with his feelings that he didn't know that.

But his son wasn't here. He'd never had the chance to be born.

Riley was here.

And Joshua could be there for him.

He reached down, placing his hand on the baby's chest. His little body started, but he stopped crying.

Joshua didn't know the first thing about babies. He'd never had to learn. He'd never had the chance to hold his son. Never gone through a sleepless night because of crying.

He reached down, picking up the small boy from his crib, holding the baby close to his chest and supporting Riley's downy head.

There weren't very many situations in life that caused Joshua to doubt himself. Mostly because he took great care to ensure he was only ever in situations where he had the utmost control.

But holding this tiny creature in his arms made him feel at a loss. Made him feel like his strength might be a liability rather than an asset. Because at the moment, he felt like this little boy could be far too easily broken. Like he might crush the baby somehow.

Either with his hands or with his inadequacy.

Though, he supposed that was the good thing about babies. Right now, Riley didn't seem to need him to be perfect. He just needed Joshua to be there. Being there he could handle.

He made his way to the rocking chair in the corner and sat down, pressing Riley to his chest as he rocked back and forth.

"You might be hungry," Joshua said, keeping his voice soft. "I didn't ask."

Riley turned his head back and forth, leaving a small trail of drool behind on Joshua's skin. He had a feeling if his brother could see him now, he would mock him mercilessly. But then, he couldn't imagine Isaiah with a baby at all. Devlin, yes. But only since he had married Mia. She had changed Devlin completely. Made him more relaxed. Made him a better man.

Joshua thought of Danielle, sleeping soundly back in his room. Of just how insatiable he'd been for her earlier. Of how utterly trapped she was, and more or less at his mercy.

He had to wonder if there was any way she could make him a better man, all things considered.

Though, he supposed he'd kind of started to become a better man already. Since he had taken her on. And Riley.

He had to be the man who could take care of them, if he was so intent on fixing things.

Maybe they can fix you too.

Even though there was no one in the room but the baby, Joshua shook his head. That wasn't a fair thing to put on either of them.

"Joshua?"

He looked up and saw Danielle standing in the door-way. She was wearing one of his T-shirts, the hem falling to the top of her thighs. He couldn't see her expression in the darkened room.

"Over here."

"Are you holding Riley?" She moved deeper into the room and stopped in front of him, the moonlight streaming through the window shadowing one side of her face. With her long, dark hair hanging loose around her shoulders, and that silver light casting her in a glow, she looked ethereal. He wondered how he had ever thought she was pitiful. How he had ever imagined she wasn't beautiful.

"He was crying," he responded.

"I can take him."

He shook his head, for some reason reluctant to give him up. "That's okay."

A smile curved her lips. "Okay. I can make him a bottle."

He nodded, moving his hand up and down on the baby's back. "Okay."

Danielle rummaged around for a moment and then went across the room to the changing station, where he assumed she kept the bottle-making supplies. Warmers and filtered water and all of that. He didn't know much about it, only that he had arranged to have it all delivered to the house to make things easier for her.

She returned a moment later, bottle in hand. She tilted it upside down and tested it on the inside of her wrist. "It's all good. Do you want to give it to him?"

He nodded slowly and reached up. "Sure."

He shifted his hold on Riley, repositioning him in the crook of his arm so he could offer him the bottle.

"Do you have a lot of experience with babies?"

"None," he said.

"You could have fooled me. Although, I didn't really have any experience with babies until Riley was born. I didn't figure I would ever have experience with them."

"No?"

She shook her head. "No. I was never going to get married, Joshua. I knew all about men, you see. My mother got pregnant with me when she was fourteen. Needless to say, things didn't get off to the best start. I never knew my father. My upbringing was…unstable. My mother just wasn't ready to have a baby, and honestly, I don't know how she could have been. She didn't have a good home life, and she was so young. I think she wanted to keep me, wanted to do the right thing—it was just hard. She was always looking for something else. Looking for love."

"Not in the right places, I assume."

She bit her lip. "No. To say the least. She had a lot of boyfriends, and we lived with some of them. Sometimes that was better. Sometimes they were more established than us and had better homes. The older I got, the less like a mom my mom seemed. I started to really understand how young she was. When she would get her heart broken, I comforted her more like a friend than like a daughter. When she would go out and get drunk, I would put her to bed like I was the parent." Danielle took a deep breath. "I just didn't want that for myself. I didn't want to depend on anybody, or have anyone depend on me. I didn't want to pin my hopes on someone else. And I never saw a relationship that looked like anything else when I was growing up."

"But here you are," he said, his chest feeling tight. "And you're marrying me."

"I don't know if you can possibly understand what this is like," she said, laughing, a kind of shaky nervous sound. "Having this idea of what your life will be and just…changing that. I was so certain about what I would have, and what I wouldn't have. I would never get married. I would never have children. I would never have…a beautiful house or a yard." Her words got thick, her throat sounding tight. "Then there was Riley. And then there was your ad. And then there was you. And suddenly everything I want is different, everything I expect is different. I actually hope for things. It's kind of a miracle."

He wanted to tell her that he wasn't a miracle. That whatever she expected from him, he was sure to disappoint her in some way. But what she was describing was too close to his own truth.

He had written off having a wife. He had written off having children. That was the whole part of being human he'd decided wasn't for him. And yet here he was, feeding a baby at three in the morning staring at a woman who had just come from his bed. A woman who was wearing his ring.

The way Joshua needed it, the way he wanted to cling

to his new reality, to make sure that it was real and that it would last, shocked him with its ferocity.

A moment later, he heard a strange sucking sound and realized the bottle was empty.

"Am I supposed to burp him?"

Danielle laughed. "Yes. But I'll do that."

"I'm not helpless."

"He's probably going to spit up on your hot and sexy chest. Better to have him do it on your T-shirt." She reached out. "I got this."

She took Riley from him and he sat back and admired the expert way she handled the little boy. She rocked him over her shoulder, patting his back lightly until he made a sound that most definitely suggested he had spit up on the T-shirt she was wearing.

Joshua had found her to be such a strange creature when he had first seen her. Brittle and pointed. Fragile.

But she was made of iron. He could see that now.

No one had been there to raise her, not really. And then she had stepped in to make sure that her half brother was taken care of. Had upended every plan she'd made for her life and decided to become a mother at twenty-two.

"What?" she asked, and he realized he had been sitting there staring at her.

"You're an amazing woman, Danielle Kelly. And if no one's ever told you that, it's about time someone did."

She was so bright, so beautiful, so fearless.

All this time she had been a burning flame no one had taken the time to look at. But she had come to him, answered his ad and started a wildfire in his life.

It didn't seem fair, the way the world saw each of them. He was a celebrated businessman, and she... Well, hadn't he chosen her because he knew his family would simply see her as a poor, unwed mother?

She was worth ten of him.

She blinked rapidly and wasn't quite able to stop a tear from tracking down her cheek. "Why…why do you think that?"

"Not very many people would have done what you did. Taking your brother. Not after everything your mother already put you through. Not after spending your whole life taking care of the one person who should have been taking care of you. And then you came here and answered my ad."

"Some people might argue that the last part was taking the easy way out."

"Right. Except that I could have been a serial killer."

"Or made me dress like a teddy bear," she said, keeping her tone completely serious. "I actually feel like that last one is more likely."

"Do you?"

"There are more furries than there are serial killers, thank God."

"I guess, lucky for you, I'm neither one." He wasn't sure he was the great hope she seemed to think he was. But right now, he wanted to be.

"Very lucky for me," she said. "Oh… Joshua, imagine if someone were both."

"I'd rather not."

She went to the changing table and quickly set about getting Riley a new diaper before placing him back in the crib. Then she straightened and hesitated. "I guess I could… I can just stay in here. Or…"

"Get the baby monitor," he said. "You're coming back to my bed."

She smiled, and she did just that.

* * *

The next day there were wedding dresses in Danielle's room. Not just a couple of wedding dresses. At least ten, all in her size.

She turned in a circle, looking at all of the garment bags with heavy white satin, beads and chiffon showing through.

Joshua walked into the room behind her, his arms folded over his chest. She raised her eyebrows, gesturing wildly at the dresses. "What is this?"

"We are getting married in less than two weeks. You need a dress."

"A fancy dress to eat my Pop-Tart cake in," she said, moving to a joke because if she didn't she might cry. Because the man had ordered wedding dresses and brought them into the house.

And because if she were normal, she might have friends to share this occasion with her. Or her mother. Instead, she was standing in her bedroom, where her baby was napping, and her fiancé was the only potential spectator.

"You aren't supposed to see the dresses, though," she said.

"I promise you I cannot make any sense out of them based on how they look stuffed into those bags. I called the bridal store in town and described your figure and had her send dresses accordingly."

Her eyes flew wide, her mouth dropping open. "You described my figure?"

"To give her an idea of what would suit you."

"I'm going to need a play-by-play of this description. How did you describe my figure, Joshua? This is very important."

"Elfin," he said, surprising her because he didn't seem

to be joking. And that was a downright fanciful description coming from him.

"Elfin?"

A smile tipped his lips upward. "Yes. You're like an elf. Or a nymph."

"Nympho, maybe. And I blame you for that."

He reached out then, hooking his arm around her waist and drawing her toward him. "Danielle, I am serious."

She swallowed hard. "Okay," she said, because she didn't really know what else to say.

"You're beautiful."

Hearing him say that made her throat feel all dry and scratchy, made her eyes feel like they were burning. "You don't have to do that," she said.

"You think I'm lying? Why would I lie about that? Also, men can't fake this." He grabbed her hand and pressed it up against the front of his jeans, against the hardness there.

"You're asking me to believe your penis? Because penises are notoriously indiscriminate."

"You have a point. Plus, mine is pretty damn famously indiscriminate. By my own admission. But the one good thing about that is you can trust I know the difference between generalized lust and when a woman has reached down inside of me and grabbed hold of something I didn't even know was there. I told you, I like it easy. I told you… I don't deal with difficult situations or difficult people. That was my past failing. A huge failing, and I don't know if I'm ever going to forgive myself for it. But what we have here makes me feel like maybe I can make up for it."

There were a lot of nice words in there. A lot of beautiful sentiments tangled up in something that made her feel, well, kind of gross.

But he was looking at her with all that intensity, and there were wedding dresses hung up all around her, his ring glittering on her finger. And she just didn't want to examine the bad feelings. She was so tired of bad feelings.

Joshua—all of this—was like a fantasy. She wanted to live in the fantasy for as long as she could.

Was that wrong? After everything she had been through, she couldn't believe that it was.

"Well, get your penis out of here. The rest of you too. I'm going to try on dresses."

"I don't get to watch?"

"I grant you nothing about our relationship has been typical so far, but I would like to surprise you with my dress choice."

"That's fair. Why don't you let me take Riley for a while?"

"Janine is going to be here soon."

He shrugged. "I'll take him until then." He strode across the room and picked Riley up, and Riley flashed a small, gummy smile that might have been nothing more than a facial twitch but still made Danielle's heart do something fluttery and funny.

Joshua's confidence with Riley was increasing, and he made a massive effort to be proactive when it came to taking care of the baby.

Watching Joshua stand there with Riley banished any lingering gross feelings about being considered difficult, and when Joshua left the room and Danielle turned to face the array of gowns, she pushed every last one of her doubts to the side.

Maybe Joshua wasn't perfect. Maybe there were some issues. But all of this, with him, was a damn sight better than anything she'd had before.

And a girl like her couldn't afford to be too picky.

She took a deep breath and unzipped the first dress.

Chapter 10

The day of the wedding was drawing closer and Danielle was drawing closer to a potential nervous breakdown. She was happy, in a way. When Joshua kissed her, when he took her to bed, when he spent the whole night holding her in his strong arms, everything felt great.

It was the in-between hours. The quiet moments she spent with herself, rocking Riley in that gray time before dawn. That was when she pulled those bad feelings out and began to examine them.

She had two days until the wedding, and her dress had been professionally altered to fit her—a glorious, heavy satin gown with a deep V in the back and buttons that ran down the full skirt—and if for no other reason than that, she couldn't back out.

The thought of backing out sent a burst of pain blooming through her chest. Unfurling, spreading, expanding. No. She didn't want to leave Joshua. No matter the strange, imbalanced feelings between them, she wanted to be with him. She felt almost desperate to be with him.

She looked over at him now, sitting in the driver's seat of what was still the nicest car she had ever touched, much less ridden in, as they pulled up to the front of his parents' house.

Sometimes looking at him hurt. And sometimes looking away from him hurt. Sometimes everything hurt. The need to be near him, the need for distance.

Maybe she really had lost her mind.

It took her a moment to realize she was still sitting motionless in the passenger seat, and Joshua had already put the car in Park and retrieved Riley from the back seat. He didn't bother to bring the car seat inside this time. Instead, he wrapped the baby in a blanket and cradled him in his arms.

Oh, that hurt her in a whole different way.

Joshua was sexy. All the time. There was no question about that. But the way he was with Riley... Well, she was surprised that any woman who walked by him when he was holding Riley didn't fall immediately at his feet.

She nearly did. Every damned time.

She followed him to the front door, looking down to focus on the way the gravel crunched beneath her boots—new boots courtesy of Joshua that didn't have holes in them, and didn't need three pairs of socks to keep her toes from turning into icicles—because otherwise she was going to get swallowed up by the nerves that were riding through her.

His mother had insisted on making a prewedding dinner for them, and this was Danielle's second chance to make a first impression. Now it was real and she felt an immense amount of pressure to be better than she was, rather than simply sliding into the lowest expectation people like his family had of someone like her, as she'd done before.

She looked over at him when she realized he was staring at her. "You're going to be fine," he said.

Then he bent down and kissed her. She closed her eyes, her breath rushing from her lungs as she gave herself over to his kiss.

That, of course, was when the front door opened.

"You're here!"

Nancy Grayson actually looked happy to see them both, and even happier that she had caught them making out on the front porch.

Danielle tucked a stray lock of hair behind her ear. "Thank you for doing this," she said, jarred by the change in her role, but desperate to do a good job.

"Of course," the older woman said. "Now, let me hold my grandbaby."

Those words made Danielle pause, made her freeze up. Made her want to cry. Actually, she *was* crying. Tears were rolling down her cheeks without even giving her a chance to hold them back.

Joshua's mother frowned. "What's wrong, honey?"

Danielle swallowed hard. "I didn't ever expect that he would have grandparents. That he would have a family." She took a deep breath. "I mean like this. It means a lot to me."

Nancy took Riley from Joshua's arms. But then she reached out and put her hand on Danielle's shoulder. "He's not the only one who has a family. You do too."

Throughout the evening Danielle was stunned by the warm acceptance of Joshua's entire family. By the way his sister-in-law, Mia, made an effort to get to know her, and by the complete absence of antagonism coming from his younger sister, Faith.

But what really surprised her was when Joshua's father came and sat next to her on the couch during dessert. Joshua was engaged in conversation with his brothers across the room while Mia, Faith and Joshua's mother were busy playing with Riley.

"I knew you would be good for him," Mr. Grayson said.

Danielle looked up at the older man. "A wife, you mean," she said, her voice soft. She didn't know why she had challenged his assertion, why she'd done anything but blandly agree. Except she knew she wasn't the woman he would have chosen for his son, and she didn't want him to pretend otherwise.

He shook his head. "I'm not talking about the ad. I know what he did. I know that he placed another ad looking for somebody he could use to get back at me. But the minute I met you, I knew you were exactly what he needed. Somebody unexpected. Somebody who would push him out of his comfort zone. It's real now, isn't it?"

It's real now.

Those words echoed inside of her. What did real mean? They were really getting married, but was their relationship real?

He didn't love her. He wanted to fix her. And somehow, through fixing her, he believed he would fix himself.

Maybe that wasn't any less real than what most people had. Maybe it was just more honest.

"Yes," she said, her voice a whisper. "It's real."

"I know that my meddling upset him. I'm not stupid. And I know he felt like I wasn't listening to him. But he has been so lost in all that pain, and I knew... I knew he just needed to love somebody again. He thought everything I did, everything I said was because I don't understand a life that goes beyond what we have here." He gestured around the living room—small, cozy, essentially a stereotype of the happy, rural family. "But that's not it. Doesn't matter what a life looks like, a man needs love. And *that* man needs love more than most. He always was stubborn, difficult. Never could get him to talk about much of anything. He needs someone he can talk to. Someone who can see the good in him so he can start to see it too."

"Love," Danielle said softly, the word a revelation she had been trying to avoid.

That was why it hurt. When she looked at him. When she was with him. When she looked away from him. When he was gone.

That was the intense, building pressure inside her that felt almost too large for her body to contain.

It was every beautiful, hopeful feeling she'd had since meeting him.

She loved him.

And he didn't love her. That absence was the cause of the dark disquiet she'd felt sometimes. He wanted to use her as a substitute for his girlfriend, the one he thought he had failed.

"Every man needs love," Todd said. "Successful businessmen and humble farmers. Trust me. It's the thing that makes life run. The thing that keeps you going when crops don't grow and the weather doesn't cooperate. The thing that pulls you up from the dark pit when you can't find the light. I'm glad he found his light."

But he hadn't.

She had found hers.

For him, she was a Band-Aid he was trying to put

over a wound that would end up being fatal if he didn't do something to treat it. If he didn't do something more than simply cover it up.

She took a deep breath. "I don't…"

"Are you ready to go home?"

Danielle looked up and saw Joshua standing in front of her. And those words…

Him asking if she wanted to go home, meaning to his house, with him, like that house belonged to her. Like he belonged to her…

Well, his question allowed her to erase all the doubts that had just washed through her. Allowed her to put herself back in the fantasy she'd been living in since she'd agreed to his proposal.

"Sure," she said, pushing herself up from the couch.

She watched as he said goodbye to his family, as he collected Riley and slung the diaper bag over his shoulder. Yes. She loved him.

She was an absolute and total lost cause for him. In love. Something she had thought she could never be.

The only problem was, she was in love alone.

It was his wedding day.

Thankfully, only his family would be in attendance. A small wedding in Copper Ridge's Baptist church, which was already decorated for Christmas and so saved everyone time and hassle.

Which was a good thing, since he had already harassed local baker Alison Donnelly to the point where she was ready to assault him with a spatula over his demands related to a Pop-Tart cake.

It was the one thing Danielle had said she wanted, and

even if she had been joking, he wanted to make it happen for her.

He liked doing things for her. Whether it was teaching her how to ride horses, pleasuring her in the bedroom or fixing her nice meals, she always expressed a deep and sweet gratitude that transcended anything he had ever experienced before.

Her appreciation affected him. He couldn't pretend it didn't.

She affected him.

He walked into the empty church, looking up at the steeply pitched roof and the thick, curved beams of wood that ran the length of it, currently decked with actual boughs of holly.

Everything looked like it was set up and ready, all there was to do now was wait for the ceremony to start.

Suddenly, the doors that led to the fellowship hall opened wide and in burst Danielle. If he had thought she looked ethereal before, it was nothing compared to how she looked at this moment. Her dark hair was swept back in a loose bun, sprigs of baby's breath woven into it, some tendrils hanging around her face.

And the dress…

The bodice was fitted, showing off her slim figure, and the skirt billowed out around her, shimmering with each and every step. She was holding a bouquet of dark red roses, her lips painted a deep crimson to match.

"I didn't think I was supposed to see you until the wedding?" It was a stupid thing to say, but it was about the only thing he could think of.

"Yes. I know. I was here getting ready, and I was going to hide until everything started. Stay in the dressing room." She shook her head. "I need to talk to you, though. And I was already wearing this dress, and all of the layers of underwear that you have to wear underneath it to make it do this." She kicked her foot out, causing the skirt to flare.

"To make it do what?"

"You need a crinoline. Otherwise your skirt is like a wilted tulip. That's something I learned when the wedding store lady came this morning to help me get ready. But that's not what I wanted to talk to you about."

He wasn't sure if her clarification was a relief or not. He wasn't an expert on the subject of crinolines, but it seemed like an innocuous subject. Anything else that had drawn her out of hiding before the ceremony probably wasn't.

"Then talk."

She took a deep breath, wringing her hands around the stem of her bouquet. "Okay. I will talk. I'm going to. In just a second."

He shook his head. "Danielle Kelly, you stormed into my house with a baby and pretty much refused to leave until I agreed to give you what you wanted—don't act like you're afraid of me now."

"That was different. I wasn't afraid of losing you then." She looked up at him, her dark eyes liquid. "I'm afraid right now."

"You?" He couldn't imagine this brave, wonderfully strong woman being afraid of anything.

"I've never had anything that I wanted to keep. Or I guess, I never did before Riley. Once I had him, the thought of losing him was one of the things that scared me. It was the first time I'd ever felt anything like it. And now…it's the same with you. Do you know what you have in common with Riley?"

"The occasional tantrum?" His chest was tight. He

knew that was the wrong thing to say, knew it was wrong to make light of the situation when she was so obviously serious and trembling.

"Fair enough," she said. Then she took a deep breath. "I love you. That's what you have in common with Riley. That's why I'm afraid of losing you. Because you matter. Because you more than matter. You're…everything."

Her words were like a sucker punch straight to the gut. "Danielle…"

He was such a jerk. Of course she thought she was in love with him. He was her first lover, the first man to ever give her an orgasm. He had offered her a place to live and he was promising a certain amount of financial security, the kind she'd never had before.

Of course such a vulnerable, lonely woman would confuse those feelings of gratitude with love.

She frowned. "Don't use that tone with me. I know you're about to act like you're the older and wiser of the two of us. You're about to explain why I don't understand what I'm talking about. Remember when you told me about your penis?"

He looked over his shoulder, then back at Danielle. "Okay, I'm not usually a prude, but we are in a church."

She let out an exasperated sound. "Sorry. But the thing is, remember when you told me that because you had been indiscriminate you knew the difference between common, garden-variety sex—"

"Danielle, Pastor John is around here somewhere."

She straightened her arms at her sides, the flowers in her hand trembling with her unsuppressed irritation. "Who cares? This is our life. Anyway, what little I've read in the Bible was pretty honest about people. Everything I'm talking about—it's all part of being a person.

I'm not embarrassed about any of it." She tilted her chin up, looking defiant. "My point is, I don't need you telling me what you think I feel. I have spent so much time alone, so much time without love, that I've had a lot of time to think about what it might feel like. About what it might mean."

He lowered his voice and took a step toward her. "Danielle, feeling cared for isn't the same as love. Pleasure isn't the same as love."

"I know that!" Her words echoed in the empty sanctuary. "Trust me. If I thought being taken care of was the same thing as love, I probably would have repeated my mother's pattern for my entire life. But I didn't. I waited. I waited until I found a man who was worth being an idiot over. Here I am in a wedding dress yelling at the man I'm supposed to marry in an hour, wanting him to understand that I love him. You can't be much more of an idiot than that, Joshua."

"It's okay if you love me," he said, even though it made his stomach feel tight. Even though it wasn't okay at all. "But I don't know what you expect me to do with that."

She stamped her foot, the sound ricocheting around them. "Love me back, dammit."

He felt like someone had grabbed hold of his heart and squeezed it hard. "Danielle, I can't do that. I can't. And honestly, it's better if you don't feel that way about me. I think we can have a partnership. I'm good with those. I'm good with making agreements, shaking hands, holding up my end of the deal. But feelings, all that stuff in between... I would tell you to call Shannon and ask her about that, but I don't think she has a phone right now, because I'm pretty sure she's homeless."

"You can't take the blame for that. You can't take the

blame for her mistakes. I mean, I guess you can, you've been doing a great job of it for the past five years. And I get that. You lost a child. And then you lost your fiancée, the woman you loved. And you're holding on to that pain to try to insulate yourself from more."

He shook his head. "That's not it. It would be damned irresponsible of me not to pay attention to what I did to her. To what being with me can do to a woman." He cleared his throat. "She needed something that I couldn't give. I did love her—you're right. But it wasn't enough."

"You're wrong about that too," she said. "You loved her enough. But sometimes, Joshua, you can love somebody and love somebody, but unless they do something with that love it goes fallow. You can sow the seeds all you want, but if they don't water them, if they don't nurture them, you can't fix it for them."

"I didn't do enough," he said, tightening his jaw, hardening his heart.

"Maybe you were difficult. Maybe you did some wrong things. But at some point, she needed to reach out and tell you that. But she didn't. She shut down. Love can be everything, but it can't all be coming from one direction. The other person has to accept it. You can't love someone into being whole. They have to love themselves enough to want to be whole. And they have to love you enough to lay down their pain, to lay down their selfishness, and change—even when it's hard."

"I can't say she was selfish," he said, his voice rough. "I can't say she did anything wrong."

"What about my mother? God knows she had it hard, Joshua. I can't imagine having a baby at fourteen. It's hard enough having one at twenty-two. She has a lot of excuses. And they're valid. She went through hell, but the fact of the matter is she's choosing to go through it at this point. She has spent her whole life searching for the kind of love that either one of her children would have given her for nothing. I couldn't have loved her more. Riley is a baby, completely and totally dependent on whoever might take care of him. Could we have loved her more? Could we have made her stay?"

"That's different."

She stamped her foot again. "It is not!"

He didn't bother to yell at her about them being in a church again. "I understand that all of this is new to you," he said, fighting to keep his voice steady. "And honestly? It feels good, selfishly good, to know you see all this in me. It's tempting to lie to you, Danielle. But I can't do that. What I offered you is the beginning and end of what I have. Either you accept our partnership or you walk away."

She wouldn't.

She needed him too much. That was the part that made him a monster.

He knew he had all the power here, and he knew she would ultimately see things his way. She would have to.

And then what? Would she wither away living with him? Wanting something that he refused to give her?

The situation looked too familiar.

He tightened his jaw, steeling himself for her response.

What he didn't expect was to find a bouquet of flowers tossed at him. He caught them, and her petite shoulders lifted up, then lowered as she let out a shuddering breath. "I guess you're the next one to get married, then. Congratulations. You caught the flowers."

"Of course I damn well am," he said, tightening his

fist around the roses, ignoring the thorn that bit into his palm. "Our wedding is in an hour."

Her eyes filled with tears, and she shook her head. Then she turned and ran out of the room, pausing only to kick her shoes off and leave them lying on the floor like she was Cinderella.

And he just stood there, holding on to the flowers, a trickle of blood from the thorn dripping down his wrist as he watched the first ray of light, the first bit of hope he'd had in years, disappear from his life.

Of course, her exit didn't stop him from standing at the altar and waiting. Didn't stop him from acting like the wedding would continue without a hitch.

He knew she hadn't gone far, mostly because Janine was still at the church with Riley, and while Danielle's actions were painful and mystifying at the moment, he knew her well enough to know she wasn't going to leave without Riley.

But the music began to play and no bride materialized.

There he was, a fool in a suit, waiting for a woman who wasn't going to come.

His family looked at each other, trading expressions filled with a mix of pity and anger. But it was his father who spoke up. "What in hell did you do, boy?"

A damned good question.

Unfortunately, he knew the answer to it.

"Why are you blaming him?" Faith asked, his younger sister defending him to the bitter end, even when he didn't deserve it.

"Because that girl loves him," his father said, his tone full of confidence, "and she wouldn't have left him standing there if he hadn't done something."

Pastor John raised his hands, the gesture clearly meant

to placate. "If there are any doubts about a marriage, it's definitely best to stop and consider those doubts, as it is a union meant for life."

"And she was certain," Joshua's father said. "Which means he messed it up."

"When two people love each other…" The rest of Pastor John's words were swallowed up by Joshua's family, but those first six hit Joshua and pierced him right in the chest.

When two people love each other.

Two people. Loving each other.

Love going both ways. Giving and taking.

And he understood then. He really understood.

Why she couldn't submit to living in a relationship that she thought might be one-sided. Because she had already endured it once. Because she'd already lived it with her mother.

Danielle was willing to walk away from everything he'd offered her. From the house, from the money, from the security. Even from his family. Because for some reason his love meant that much to her.

That realization nearly brought him to his knees.

He had thought his love insufficient. Had thought it destructive. And as she had stood there, pleading with him to love her back, he had thought his love unimportant.

But to her, it was everything.

How dare he question her feelings for him? Love, to Danielle, was more than a ranch and good sex. And she had proved it, because she was clearly willing to sacrifice the ranch and the sex to have him return her love.

"It was my fault," he said, his voice sounding like a stranger's as it echoed through the room. "She said she loved me. And I told her I couldn't love her back."

"Well," Faith said, "not even I can defend you now."

His mother looked stricken, his father angry. His brothers seemed completely unsurprised.

"You do love her, though," his father said, his tone steady. "So why did you tell her you didn't?"

Of course, Joshua realized right then something else she'd been right about. He was afraid.

Afraid of wanting this life he really had always dreamed of but had written off because he messed up his first attempt so badly. Afraid because the first time had been so painful, had gone so horribly wrong.

"Because I'm a coward," he said. "But I'm not going to be one anymore."

He walked down off the stage and to the front pew, picking up the bouquet. "I'm going to go find her," he said. "I know she's not far, since Riley is here."

Suddenly, he knew exactly where she was.

"Do you have any other weddings today, Pastor?"

Pastor John shook his head. "No. This is the only thing I have on my schedule today. Not many people get married on a Thursday."

"Hopefully, if I don't mess this up, we'll need you."

Chapter 11

It was cold. And Danielle's bare feet were starting to ache. But there had been no way in hell she could run in those high heels. She would have broken her neck.

Of course, if she had broken her neck, she might have fully severed her spinal cord and then not been able to feel anything. A broken heart sadly didn't work that way. She felt everything. Pain, deep and unending. Pain that spread from her chest out to the tips of her fingers and toes.

She wiggled her toes. In fairness, they might just be frostbitten.

She knew she was being pathetic. Lying down on that Pendleton blanket in the loft. The place where Joshua had first made love to her. Hiding.

Facing everyone—facing Joshua again—was inevitable. She was going to have to get Riley. Pack up her things.

Figure out life without Joshua's money. Go back to

working a cash register at a grocery store somewhere. Wrestling with childcare problems.

She expected terror to clutch her at the thought. Expected to feel deep sadness about her impending poverty. But those feelings didn't come.

She really didn't care about any of that.

Well, she probably would care once she was neck deep in it again, but right now all she cared about was that she wouldn't have Joshua.

If he had no money, if he was struggling just like her, she would have wanted to struggle right along with him.

But money or no money, struggle or no struggle, she needed him to love her. Otherwise…

She closed her eyes and took in a breath of sharp, cold air.

She had been bound and determined to ignore all of the little warnings she'd felt in her soul when she'd thought about their relationship. But in the end, she couldn't.

She knew far too well what it was like to pour love out and never get it back. And for a while it had been easy to pretend. That his support, and the sex, was the same as getting something back.

But they were temporary.

The kinds of things that would fade over the years.

If none of his choices were rooted in love, if none of it was founded in love, then what they had couldn't last.

She was saving herself hideous heartbreak down the road by stabbing herself in the chest now.

She snorted. Right now, she kind of wondered what the point was.

Pride?

"Screw pride," she croaked.

She heard the barn door open, heard footsteps down

below, and she curled up into a ball, the crinoline under her dress scratching her legs. She buried her face in her arm, like a child. As if whoever had just walked into the barn wouldn't be able to see her as long as she couldn't see him.

Then she heard footsteps on the ladder rungs, the sound of calloused hands sliding over the metal. She knew who it was. Oh well. She had already embarrassed herself in front of him earlier. It was not like him seeing her sprawled in a tragic heap in a barn was any worse than her stamping her foot like a dramatic silent-film heroine.

"I thought I might find you here."

She didn't look up when she heard his voice. Instead, she curled into a tighter, even more resolute ball.

She felt him getting closer, which was ridiculous. She knew she couldn't actually feel the heat radiating from his body.

"I got you that Pop-Tart cake," he said. "I mean, I had Alison from Pie in the Sky make one. And I have to tell you, it looks disgusting. I mean, she did a great job, but I can't imagine that it's edible."

She uncurled as a sudden spout of rage flooded through her and she pushed herself into a sitting position. "Screw your Pop-Tart cake, Joshua."

"I thought we both liked Pop-Tarts."

"Yes. But I don't like lies. And your Pop-Tarts would taste like lies."

"Actually," he said slowly, "I think the Pop-Tart cake is closer to the truth than anything I said to you back in the church. You said a lot of things that were true. I'm a coward, Danielle. And guilt is a hell of a lot easier than grief."

"What the hell does that mean?" She drew her arm underneath her nose, wiping snot and tears away, tempted to ask him where his elfin princess was now. "Don't tease me. Don't talk in riddles. I'm ready to walk away from you if I need to, but I don't want to do it. So please, don't tempt me to hurt myself like that if you aren't…"

"I love you," he said, his voice rough. "And my saying so now isn't because I was afraid you were a gold digger and you proved you weren't by walking away. I realize what I'm about to say could be confused for that, but don't be confused. Because loving you has nothing to do with that. If you need my money… I've never blamed you for going after it. I've never blamed you for wanting to make your and Riley's lives easier. But the fact that you *were* willing to walk away from everything over three words… How can I pretend they aren't important? How can I pretend that I don't need your love when you demonstrated that you need my love more than financial security. More than sex. How can I doubt you and the strength of your feelings? How can I excuse my unwillingness to open myself up to you? My unwillingness to make myself bleed for you?"

He reached out, taking hold of her hands, down on his knees with her.

"You're going to get your suit dirty," she said inanely.

"Your dress is filthy," he returned.

She looked down at the dirt and smudges on the beautiful white satin. "Crap."

He took hold of her chin, tilting her face up to look at him. "I don't care. It doesn't matter. Because I would marry you in blue jeans, or I would marry you in this barn. I would sure as hell marry you in that dirty wedding dress. I… You are right about everything.

"It was easy to martyr myself over Shannon's pain. To blame myself so I didn't have to try again. So I didn't have to hurt again. Old pain is easier. The pain from that time in my life isn't gone, but it's dull. It throbs sometimes. It aches. When I look at Riley, he reminds me of my son, who never took a breath, and it hurts down deep. But I know that if I were to lose either of you now... That would be fresh pain. A fresh hell. And I have some idea of what that hell would be like because of what I've been through before.

"But it would be worse now. And... I was protecting myself from it. But now, I don't care about the pain, the fear. I want it all. I want you.

"I love you. Whatever might happen, whatever might come our way in the future... I love you. And I am going to do the hard yards for you, Danielle."

His expression was so fierce, his words so raw and real, all she could do was stare at him, listening as he said all the things she had never imagined she would hear.

"I was young and stupid the last time I tried love. Selfish. I made mistakes. I can't take credit for everything that went wrong. Some of it was fate. Some of it was her choices. But when things get hard this time, you have my word I won't pull away. I'm not going to let you shut me out. If you close the door on me, I'm going to kick it down. Because what we have is special. It's real. It's hope. And I will fight with everything I have to hold on to it."

She lurched forward, wrapping her arms around his neck, making them both fall backward. "I'll never shut you out." She squeezed her eyes closed, tears tracking down her cheeks. "Finding you has been the best thing that's ever happened to me. I don't feel alone, Joshua. Can you possibly understand what that means to me?"

He nodded gravely, kissing her lips. "I do understand," he said. "Because I've been alone in my own swamp for a long damned time. And you're the first person who made me feel like it was worth it to wade out."

"I love you," she said.

"I love you too. Do you still want to marry me?"

"Hell yeah."

"Good." He maneuvered them both so they were upright, taking her hand and leading her to the ladder. They climbed down, and she hopped from foot to foot on the cold cement floor. "Come on," he said, grabbing her hand and leading her through the open double doors.

She stopped when she saw that his whole family, Janine and Riley, and Pastor John were standing out there in the gravel.

Joshua's mother was holding the bouquet of roses, and she reached out, handing it back to Danielle. Then Joshua went to Janine and took Riley from her arms, holding the baby in the crook of his own. Then Joshua went back to Danielle, taking both of her hands with his free one.

"I look bedraggled," she said.

"You look perfect to me."

She smiled, gazing at everyone, at her new family. At this new life she was going to have.

And then she looked back at the man she loved with all her heart. "Well," she said, "okay, then. Marry me, cowboy."

Epilogue

December 5, 2017
FOUND A WIFE—

Local rancher Todd Grayson and his wife, Nancy, are pleased to announce the marriage of their son, a wealthy former bachelor, Joshua Grayson (no longer irritated with his father) to Danielle Kelly, formerly of Portland, now of Copper Ridge and the daughter of their hearts. Mr. Grayson knew his son would need a partner who was strong, determined and able to handle an extremely stubborn cuss, which she does beautifully. But best of all, she loves him with her whole heart, which is all his meddling parents ever wanted for him.

* * * * *

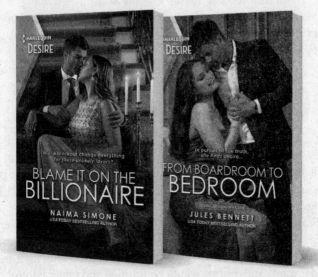

SPECIAL EXCERPT FROM

⬡ HARLEQUIN
DESIRE

Alaskan senator Jessup Outlaw needs an escape...
and he finds just what he needs on his Napa Valley vacation:
actress Paige Novak. What starts as a fling soon gets serious,
but a familiar face from Paige's past may ruin everything...

Read on for a sneak peek of
What Happens on Vacation...
by New York Times *bestselling author Brenda Jackson.*

"Hey, aren't you going to join me?" Paige asked, pushing wet hair back from her face and treading water in the center of the pool. "Swimming is on my list of fun things. We might as well kick things off with a bang."

Bang? Why had she said that? Lust immediately took over his senses. Desire beyond madness consumed him. He was determined that by the time they parted ways at the end of the month their sexual needs, wants and desires would be fulfilled and under control.

Quickly removing his shirt, Jess's hands went to his zipper, inched it down and slid the pants, along with his briefs, down his legs. He knew Paige was watching him and he was glad that he was the man she wanted.

"Come here, Paige."

She smiled and shook her head. "If you want me, Jess, you have to come and get me." She then swam to the far end of the pool, away from him.

Oh, so now she wanted to play hard to get? He had no problem going after her. Maybe now was a good time to tell her that not only had he been captain of his dog sled team, but he'd also been captain of his college swim team.

He glided through the water like an Olympic swimmer going after the gold, and it didn't take long to reach her. When she saw him getting close, she laughed and swam to the other side. Without missing a stroke or losing speed, he did a freestyle flip turn and reached out and caught her by the ankles. The capture was swift and the minute he touched her, more desire rammed through him to the point where water couldn't cool him down.

"I got you," he said, pulling her toward him and swimming with her in his arms to the edge of the pool.

When they reached the shallow end, he allowed her to stand, and the minute her feet touched the bottom she circled her arms around his neck. "No, Jess, I got you and I'm ready for you." Then she leaned in and took his mouth.

Don't miss what happens next in…
What Happens on Vacation…
by Brenda Jackson, the next book in her
Westmoreland Legacy: The Outlaws series!

Available March 2022 wherever
Harlequin Desire books and ebooks are sold.

Harlequin.com

"I remember. I remember it all, Bethany."

Jeez. He hadn't meant for his voice to turn so serious, so
reverent. But there was very little chance of hiding his real feelings
when she was around.

"Me, too," she said.

For a few moments they ate in silence.

"Thanks for helping me here," she said. "You've done a lot of
that since I've been back."

"Anytime. And I mean that."

"Ditto," she said.

He reached over and squeezed her hand but didn't let go.
And suddenly he was looking—with that seriousness, with that
reverence—into those green eyes that had also kept him up those
nights when he couldn't stop thinking about her. They both leaned
in at the same time, the kiss soft, tender, then with all the pent-up
passion they'd clearly both been feeling these last days.

She pulled slightly away. "Uh-oh."

He let out a rough exhale, trying to pull himself together. "Right? You're leaving in a couple weeks. Maybe three tops. And I'm solely focused on being the best father I can be. So that's two really good reasons why we shouldn't kiss again." Except he leaned in again.

And so did she. This time there was nothing soft or tender about the kiss. Instead, it was pure passion. His hand wound in her silky brown hair, her hands on his face.

A puppy started barking, then another, then yet another. The three cockapoos.

"They're saving us from getting into trouble," Bethany said, glancing at the time on her phone. "Time for their potty break. They'll be interrupting us all night, so that should keep us in line."

He smiled. "We can get into a lot of trouble in between, though."

Don't miss
Home is Where the Hound Is *by* Melissa Senate,
available March 2022 wherever
Harlequin Special Edition books and ebooks are sold.

Harlequin.com

Love Harlequin romance?

DISCOVER.

Be the first to find out about promotions, news and exclusive content!

f Facebook.com/HarlequinBooks

Twitter.com/HarlequinBooks

Instagram.com/HarlequinBooks

Pinterest.com/HarlequinBooks

YouTube YouTube.com/HarlequinBooks

ReaderService.com

EXPLORE.

Sign up for the Harlequin e-newsletter and download a free book from any series at **TryHarlequin.com**

CONNECT.

Join our Harlequin community to share your thoughts and connect with other romance readers!
Facebook.com/groups/HarlequinConnection